ALSO BY KRISTINE WINTERS
(CO-AUTHORED AS MAGGIE KNOX)

The Holiday Swap

All I Want for Christmas

The Christmas Cure

Kristine Winters

Published by Simon & Schuster

New York   Amsterdam/Antwerp   London
Toronto   Sydney/Melbourne   New Delhi

SIMON &
SCHUSTER
CANADA

A Division of Simon & Schuster, LLC
166 King Street East, Suite 300
Toronto, Ontario M5A 1J3

For more than 100 years, Simon & Schuster has championed authors and the stories they create. By respecting the copyright of an author's intellectual property, you enable Simon & Schuster and the author to continue publishing exceptional books for years to come. We thank you for supporting the author's copyright by purchasing an authorized edition of this book.

This book is a work of fiction. Any references to historical events, real people, or real places are used fictitiously. Other names, characters, places, and events are products of the author's imagination, and any resemblance to actual events or places or persons, living or dead, is entirely coincidental.

This Simon & Schuster Canada edition October 2025

SIMON & SCHUSTER CANADA and colophon are trademarks of Simon & Schuster, LLC

Simon & Schuster strongly believes in freedom of expression and stands against censorship in all its forms. For more information, visit BooksBelong.com.

For information about special discounts for bulk purchases, please contact Simon & Schuster Special Sales at 1-800-268-3216 or CustomerService@simonandschuster.ca.

Interior design by Ritika Karnik

Manufactured in the United States of America

10 9 8 7 6 5 4 3 2 1

Online Computer Library Center number: 1492483232

ISBN 978-1-6680-6959-2
ISBN 978-1-6680-6962-2 (ebook)

For Adam:
the cheese to my macaroni;
the meatloaf to my mashed potatoes;
the ornament to my Christmas tree;
the icing to my gingerbread house;
the marshmallow foam to my hot chocolate;
the love of my life

The Christmas Cure

1

December 16, Present Year

If I knew a potbellied pig named Mary Piggins would soon change my life forever, I would not have ordered extra bacon on my breakfast sandwich this morning. But I've yet to meet Miss Piggins, I'm starving, and I have only fifteen minutes before my break ends.

I'm an attending emergency physician and it's mid-December, which is one of the busiest months in any hospital. Not only does the season bring snow and ice to town (we take daily bets on the number of ankle fractures from slippery sidewalks), there's also the stress of the holiday rush. There are enough heart attacks this time of year to suggest Christmas may be an independent risk factor for sudden cardiac arrest.

It's nine in the morning, and I'm two hours into my ten-hour shift. My third to last before I start my holidays. The plan was a visit home for Christmas with my boyfriend of two years, Dr. Austin Whitmore, a plastic surgeon with ocean-blue eyes whose chiseled jaw is the envy of many of his clients. However, due to the fact that Austin is now my *ex*-boyfriend, said plan has been demolished like a tray of holiday shortbread cookies in the doctor's lounge. I'm not sure I have the stamina to go home carrying the three-month-old baggage of the breakup, along with my family's Christmas presents. Especially because everyone thought Austin wouldn't be my boyfriend this holiday season ... he would be my *fiancé*.

Unfortunately, after I texted the family group chat that I had "relationship-related news" (yes, by text ... sometimes my family can be, well, *a lot*), I was pulled into a mass casualty event and didn't get the second half of the message sent. When I checked my texts later, there were three responses—a heart-eyed emoji from Mom, a confetti cannon from Dad, and a ring emoji from Amelia, with three exclamation points.

I replied to that text thread with a cringing emoji and an "actually, we broke up ..." note, and before I could even turn off my phone, Amelia was calling. Then I had to somehow explain how a fight about toilet paper—"yes, Amelia, *toilet paper*"—ended my two-year relationship.

It began as a mostly teasing discussion about which direction the toilet paper is supposed to go onto the holder. Austin and I disagreed, both of us exceptionally confident in our choice. But the argument soon escalated, and epically. One moment we were fine, or as fine as a couple can be when faced with enormous work pressures and demanding schedules. The next moment, Austin was slamming the door to my apartment after I said, "I don't know if I can be with someone who believes toilet paper positioning doesn't matter!" to which he replied, "And I don't know if I can be with someone who treats toilet paper placement like it's a medical emergency!"

I thought it would be one of those arguments that went too far, but that we would come back from stronger than ever. With sheepish apologies and chuckles, agreeing that whoever changed the toilet paper roll would *obviously* decide. But a day of silence turned into two, then three, and when Austin texted, "Can I come over? Need to talk," I knew it wasn't going to be something we laughed about one day.

Our relationship may have ended with toilet paper, but our problems began long before that. Like when Austin told me—out of the blue, on vacation—that he wanted to move to L.A. Permanently. I did not want to move, and not only because I loved the hospital and my colleagues. I wanted to stay in Toronto, with its four seasons and vibrant cultures—it was home.

After the L.A. revelation, the microfractures in our relationship became easy to diagnose, though less easy to fix. I have always dreamt of doing a tour with Doctors Without Borders; Austin thought that was "noble and earnest," and while he said he loved that goal for me, he didn't share it. He isn't sure he wants kids, especially now that he is in his forties; I was pretty certain I wanted to become a mother, at least once. He is a vegetarian who doesn't touch sugar; I love bacon and anything sweet enough to make your teeth ache. Anyway, looking back now, it was clear we had some potentially insurmountable odds.

Breaking up over toilet paper, however, is ridiculous. When I finally recounted the story to Amelia, she replied, "You ended a two-year relationship . . . over two-ply?" It was four-ply (only the best for Austin), actually, but that hardly matters anymore.

No, I can't handle the fishbowl feel of Harmony Hills this Christmas. I need some R&R, especially before I start my new job in the new year. A job no one knows I've applied for yet, except my best friend, Helena, who is currently sitting across from me as we scarf down a quick breakfast.

"So Helly, any chance you want to take a trip to Mexico with me?" I ask.

"Yes," Helena immediately replies, before taking a bite of her breakfast sandwich. Helena "Helly" Perez, a physiotherapist, and I met a few years ago, shortly after I took the attending job. She was in line behind me at the cafeteria and ordered the exact same breakfast (double bacon and egg sandwich on a cheese biscuit, extra-large coffee with creamer and one sweetener) as me.

Despite being opposites in terms of appearance and upbringing—I'm tall, she's short, with about six inches separating us; my hair tends to go limp in high humidity, while hers turns into a glorious crown of shiny dark curls; I was raised in small-town Harmony Hills, which no one has ever heard of, and Helena in downtown Toronto—we have a lot in common, including the love of extra bacon, and soon we were inseparable. She's the first person I tell when something happens, and my last text every night.

"When are we taking this trip?" Helena asks, wiping her mouth with a napkin.

"I was thinking, like, for Christmas?" A smear of hot sauce transfers to my fingers, and I lick it off. Helena makes a face.

"What?" I ask, though I know what that face is about.

"You really are the opposite of a germaphobe," she says, shaking her head. Unlike me, Helena is always trying to avoid illness. With a toddler at home and her work at the hospital, she doesn't have any germ-free zones.

I shrug, ignoring the napkin she pushes my way. "It's good for my immune system."

"So you keep saying." Helena laughs. She's likely thinking about yesterday, when I complained that my stomach felt weird and was debating whether it was the dreaded norovirus, or because I hadn't eaten for a few hours. A blueberry muffin fixed the problem, which proved it was hunger and not germs.

Helena folds the square paper napkin into a triangle. "Okay, back to this girls' trip. If you're thinking *this* Christmas, obviously I'm out. Sorry, friend." She sighs in the way you do when you have a lot on your mind, folding and refolding the napkin a few times until the edges begin to rip.

"I knew it was a long shot, so don't even worry about it." I gently take the napkin from her and wipe my hands, flashing her an understanding smile as I do.

Unfortunately for both of us, I'm not the only one facing the combustion of my relationship. Helena and her partner, David, are going through a trial separation, but still live in the same condo and coparent. *Conscious uncoupling, like Gwynnie and Chris did*, Helena said, when she told me about her separation. But she and David have each agreed never to go more than forty-eight hours without seeing their three-year-old daughter, Adelaide, which makes a trip out of the country—especially at Christmas—impossible.

"I sure could use the break, though," Helena continues. "Dells is awesome—don't get me wrong. But she goes to bed at seven, and we don't like the same music or movies. 'Have a kid,' they said. 'It will be fun,' they said. Ha!"

I chuckle, knowing that, despite the quip, Adelaide is Helena's greatest joy. "I'll bring you back a bottle of tequila. The fancy sipping kind."

"I love you, and not just because of the promised tequila," Helena says, blowing on her hot coffee. "But you should definitely go. Of course, it won't be as much fun without me—obviously."

"Obviously," I say, for it's true.

"So do this for *us*." Helena grabs my hands in dramatic fashion. "Go drink margaritas at the swim-up bar and gorge on chips and guac. Make out with somebody, just because you can. I'll live vicariously through you while listening to Cocomelon for the gazillionth time."

"I'll do it. For us," I reply, and Helena nods solemnly, hand over her heart.

Like I said, Austin and I were supposed to be visiting my tiny blink-and-you'll-miss-it hometown for Christmas. But now that I'm single, well, Harmony Hills—a town that treats all holidays, but especially Christmas, with extreme reverence—is not the place to be when your mood leans "bah humbug."

Maybe only people who grow up in small towns will understand this, but Harmony Hills, while undeniably charming and picturesque, is a tough place to hide out. Your problems are everyone's business and are easily magnified in the petri dish of small-town life, where the gossip mill is well meaning but robust.

Helly's already back to work, but I have a few extra minutes so I get another coffee. Barb, the bubbly cashier who wears her silver-grey hair in an elaborate topknot and has a warm smile for everyone, scans my payment card.

"I like the hair, by the way," she says. "What made you decide to go shorter?"

I reach up and tug on the newly shorn ends. I've had long hair most of my life, but this past weekend I lopped off seven inches. It was supposed to be a trim, but I told the hairstylist to do what she wanted. *Just make me look like a different person*, I said, not understanding until later that looking different wouldn't make me *feel* different.

"Thanks. Time for a change," I reply to Barb, forcing my smile not to slip.

The truth of "why" is more nuanced, as the truth usually is. After the haircut, I welled up at the piles of chestnut-brown hair on the linoleum floor, reassuring the panicked stylist that my melancholy had nothing to do with the shaggy bob. "It's me, not you!" I said as I left the salon after tipping the poor woman double. That's precisely the problem—*I'm* the problem. Or maybe Austin and our old-news breakup is the problem . . . it's still a bit murky, if I'm being honest.

Four months ago, life was on track, and now I'm feeling lost about nearly everything. Well, except for loving the hospital's breakfast sandwich (with extra bacon), recognizing that Helly's my "person," and knowing that I'm great at my job. I regret a lot at the moment, including the impossible-to-style haircut, but when wearing scrubs and with a stethoscope hanging around my neck, I don't doubt myself.

Pausing at the cafeteria's exit, I reach up with my coffee-free hand—I'm tall like the rest of my family, about five nine in bare feet—and grab the dangling end of sparkling silver garland. It's grimy with age, like most of the hospital's decorations, reused year after year due to budget constraints. I press the sticky tack firmly into the corner of the doorframe. Eyeing the restrung garland, I'm pleased I fixed it, until the sticky tack gives way and the garland hangs limp again. I sigh. Check my watch. Break's over.

As I head back to the ER, I make two decisions.

One, I'm putting in my notice today. I haven't heard back about the attending job I interviewed for at a hospital across town, but a nurse friend who works there said I'll be a shoo-in. No point in pretending I won't be leaving here after the holidays—it's a big hospital, but not big enough for both Austin and me. Collateral damage of the breakup, but besides that, and like I told Barb, it's time for a change.

Two, I'm going to Mexico for Christmas. Even if I have to go solo, and will disappoint my family during the most-important-to-them holiday of the year. But it won't be the first time I've bailed for Christmas (in fact, I did it as recently as last year), so at least it won't be precedent-setting.

Running away from my problems—especially to a beach, and bottomless margaritas and sunshine for days—sounds exactly like the perfect antidote for my bah-humbug Christmastime woes.

2

December 17

The call that decimates daydreams of margaritas and beach time for the holidays comes the following day. I don't immediately answer, because I'm stitching a sliced hand that got between a cup of Christmas-cake walnuts and a sharp knife. The hand's owner, a midforties woman named Jennifer, has a bob similar to mine. Though hers is sleek, a polished curling under at the ends, while mine is staticky and limp from air-drying.

"I was rushing. You have to soak the cake in brandy for weeks, which obviously I'm weeks late for," Jennifer says, wincing as I place the third stitch—it will take five to close it. The phone in my scrubs' back pocket stops vibrating, the call sent to voicemail.

"Can you feel that?" I ask Jennifer, catching the wince.

"No. I feel nothing. Both literally, and figuratively," she says, then leans her head back and closes her eyes. "What is it about this season that can make you feel so empty?"

"Definitely not the cakes and cookies," I reply, and Jennifer lets out a short, mirthless laugh.

"You know, one of these years I'm going to spend Christmas under palm trees," she says, sighing. "No hustle and bustle.

Definitely not making my mother-in-law's cake recipe that *has* to be on the holiday table, because: 'tradition.'" She uses her good hand to signify the air quotes, eyes still closed.

"I'm thinking the same thing," I reply, tying off the fourth stitch. "In fact, I'm booking a last-minute trip south as soon as my shift is over."

Jennifer groans, cracking open one eye to look my way. "I am so jealous. Guessing you don't have a mother-in-law?"

I smile and shake my head, understanding this woman means nothing by it. But her comment lands like a punch to my centre. There's a pain in my chest that makes it hard to breathe. I tell myself it's heartburn from my earlier breakfast sandwich, which I ate too quickly.

"I don't. But I *do* have a mother." I then turn my attention back to the final stitch. "So how much brandy goes into this Christmas cake?"

With ten minutes left in my break, I have just enough time to eat the candy bar in my hand while I scroll through vacation deals. Also, I should probably check my messages. My sister, Amelia, has already left two voicemails, and I'm sure a third is coming if I don't get back to her soon. The moment I have this thought, my phone vibrates again, announcing an incoming call.

The Sister, I see on the screen. "You are very predictable, Sissy," I murmur, opening the candy bar wrapper. I suspect she's calling about Christmas—presents for our parents, holiday to-do-list items, which day I'm coming home. Then I take a big bite of the candy bar, watching my mailbox flag number increase by one.

Of course I should answer it—that's what a good sister would do. But I want to eat my candy bar without worrying about anything, including delivering the news that I will not be coming home for Christmas.

Almost immediately, a text message pings: "Call me back. It's an emergency."

I'm thrust back to this time last year, when I received a similar text from Amelia after ignoring her calls. Though that day I had not picked up the phone because it was Austin's birthday and we'd mostly spent it in bed, doing celebratory things.

If only we had the sort of chemistry in every other aspect of life that we did in the bedroom. For a moment I indulge *that* particular memory. Austin has the most amazing hands. The sort that can sculpt fine details into a person's face with flawless subtlety. They're creative, strong hands, and if there's one thing Austin was even better at than surgery, it was using those glorious hands on my skin, and body, and—

My phone pings another text from my sister, forcing me back to the present.

"THIS IS NOT A DRILL."

I'd laugh if I wasn't so worried now. Our parents often used that phrase when we were kids. "The leaves need to be raked before it snows this weekend, girls. *This is not a drill.*" ... "Breakfast, and out the door in five, or you'll be late for school. *This is not a drill.*" ... "Grandma is coming over for dinner, so time to clean up your rooms. *This is not a drill.*" Amelia and I still employ it when a situation requires immediate attention.

One of the best by-products of working in a busy Toronto emergency room is a relative immunity to panic, even though it takes some effort if the situation involves a loved one. I switch into doctor mode, relaxing my shoulders and taking a few deep breaths, before calling Amelia back. I use my shoulder to hold the phone in place against my ear so I have both hands free to peel back the candy bar wrapper.

"Finally!" Amelia says, picking up after one ring and right as I take another big bite.

"What's wrong?" I ask, my tone no-nonsense but also muffled because of the mouthful of chocolate and peanut nougat. "Is it Mom? Dad?"

Our parents—Monica and Stark Munro—run Harmony Hills' medical practice. Mom's the doctor, Dad the nurse, and they treat patients in a cedar-shingled Craftsman cottage near the town's square. The year prior, Mom, and the only doctor for miles, fell off a ladder while hanging twinkle lights on the clinic's roof and broke her ankle.

I raced home after receiving Amelia's panicked 911/this-is-not-a-drill! text and subsequent phone call, but stayed only a couple of days. Barely long enough to make a dent in the container of peppermint-mocha creamer my parents always made sure was in the fridge, knowing I like it in my morning coffee.

Austin and I were heading to L.A. for Christmas, a trip that he framed as an early Christmas present for me (and late birthday trip for him), but which ended up being neither. I had envisioned romantic beach walks and long dinners and late wake-ups in our gorgeous hotel with an ocean view. A stark contrast to Toronto in December, which is cold, grey, and often slushy. Instead, I spent much of the four days alone, as Austin charmed his way through early conversations about coveted positions at clinics serving celebrities' plastic surgery needs.

Like I said, up until that point I had no clue he wanted to leave Toronto, let alone live in L.A. "Eventually, Elizabeth—not tomorrow!" he said, chuckling at my shocked reaction to his casual mention of this as we sipped room-service coffee on our oceanfront balcony that first morning.

"We've talked about this, babe," he added, his tone mildly condescending. *Had we?* The coffee was suddenly bitter in my throat and hard to swallow. I had no recollection of this coming up, ever, despite our having dated for nearly a year. Austin was born in the United States—in Boston—and had dual citizenship, but there would be far more hoops for me to jump through if we moved to L.A. for work. When I reminded him of this fact, he merely said, "We'll figure it out," like it was a minor scheduling conflict rather than a major life change.

"Nothing's wrong. Everything and everyone's great, actually," my sister replies now to my question, her voice bright and cheery. That's Amelia: endlessly positive. An elementary-school teacher whose favourite saying is, "Let's turn that frown upside down!"

"But I knew you wouldn't call me back unless you *thought* something might be wrong," she adds. "Plus, your voicemail is full. *Again.*"

"*This is not a drill?*" I try to keep the irritation at Amelia's fake-out from bringing my shoulders up to my ears. I don't want to add a tension headache into the mix.

Amelia lets out a squeal of excitement, and I jerk my ear from the phone, causing it to fall. It clatters to the ground in a way that makes me wonder if my screen has cracked.

"Shoot," I mumble, then crouch quickly to grab the phone and put it back to my ear, just in time to hear Amelia say, ". . . in five days. December twenty-second! Can you believe it?"

"What's happening on December twenty-second?" I ask.

"You are a spectacular doctor, but you are a terrible listener, Libby," Amelia says.

"I know. But could you please repeat the first part? *In five days, on December twenty-second . . .*" I prompt, rolling my eyes at her admonishment while also acknowledging she's not wrong. I blame my work, which requires me to be a selective listener to seek out diagnostic clues. But my loved ones deserve my full attention. *New Year's Resolution Number One: Work on indiscriminate listening skills.*

"*Actually,* it's six, if you count today . . . but, I'm getting married, and you're my maid of honour!" Another squeal, but this time I press the phone firmly to my ear.

"You're what?" The words fly out of my mouth, along with a piece of candy bar, which lands on the nursing station I'm leaning against. The nurse behind the desk gives me a pointed look as she places a box of tissues in front of me.

"Sorry," I whisper, quickly wiping up the mess before crumpling the tissue in hand. Then I ask Amelia, "To who?"

At this she laughs, before letting out a sigh like she's a librarian who has had to ask students to be quiet for the tenth time in as many minutes. I resist the urge to remind her she is my baby sister, I practically raised her, and *so please don't treat me like I'm the immature one here when you've just announced you're getting married.* In five days.

"To *whom*," Amelia corrects, and my irritation flushes hotter. My shoulders rise to my ears. Here comes the headache. "And it's Beckett, obviously. What a question, Libby!"

Beckett is Amelia's girlfriend of nearly a year, so she's not wrong—it was a dumb question.

"But . . . so quick? When did this happen? How did this happen?" I sputter.

"We have almost a week before the wedding. Loads of time.

Besides, you're coming home for Christmas anyway. It saves you a trip!"

"A week is not *loads of time*," I reply. "It's a wedding, Mila, not a backyard barbecue."

There's quiet on the other end, and I squeeze my eyes shut. *Don't ruin this for her, Elizabeth.*

As if sensing my internal dialogue, Amelia says, "Don't be a Scrooge, okay? I'm happy, Libby. I know it seems spontaneous, but we've been talking about it for ages."

Ages? They've not even been dating for a full year. Austin and I were together for two, and we didn't even get close to an engagement, let alone a marriage. Of course, I assumed it would happen at some point, but we were too busy with work to think much beyond career ambitions. At least that's what I tell myself now, as I feel a hint of envy creeping in.

"Sorry, Mila—you caught me off guard. Busy morning," I say, walking to the trash bin and tossing in the tissue and partially eaten candy bar, my appetite gone. With a quiet grumble of acknowledgement that I'll need to cancel the bikini wax I booked earlier, I put a smile on my face and hope it translates to a more cheerful-sounding voice.

"Let me try that again. Congratulations! I am thrilled for you, and Beckett, too. I'd be honoured to be your maid of honour."

"Will you be bringing a plus-one?" Amelia asks, probing the way only a sibling can.

"Amelia . . ." I start, to which she quickly replies, "I'm only asking because Mom asked. She wants to make sure your bedroom is appropriately prepared, in quotes."

I groan lightly, closing my eyes. "As I've already explained, I have sworn off dating for at least a year . . . possibly forever . . ."

Amelia laughs. "So no, there will be no plus-one, but thank Mom for me for prying, okay?"

"You bet!" Amelia says brightly. "Better run, but I'll see you soon, Libby."

"Bye, Mila. Love you," I say, before hanging up. Then I click into my calendar, and delete the "Mexico" vacation banner. *Guess I'm going home for Christmas after all*, I think. *Well played, Universe. Well played.*

3

December 19

"No . . . no . . . this can't be happening!" I'm still driving the same VW Golf I left Harmony Hills in, when I was eighteen and off to university. The black car, which I named Pepper Munro, has been the most consistent thing in my life for the past decade and a half. It has never let me down. Until now.

The Check Engine light flashes, and the car is making concerning noises. I glance in my rearview mirror and pull over to the side of the otherwise empty road. The sign ten feet in front of me reads HARMONY HILLS 4 KILOMETRES. So close. Reaching into the glove box, I pull out the thick manual, flipping through the pages until I get to the Troubleshooting section.

"*The Check Engine indicator will stay solid or blink. Blinking Check Engine Lights mean the situation is serious, and you should slow down, find a safe place to stop, and contact a Volkswagen Service Centre,*" I read. Glancing at the dashboard, I see the blinking indicator and curse under my breath. The service centre is a one-hour tow away, and besides, I let my CAA membership lapse earlier in the year. Back when Austin drove us everywhere in his highly reliable and exceptionally more comfortable Range Rover.

Waking up my phone, I notice the lack of bars. Of course—this is a cell service dead zone, of which there are plenty out here in the middle of nowhere. Regardless, I try texting Amelia, but the message won't go through. I close my eyes and let out a long sigh.

"It's only four kilometres, Elizabeth," I tell myself, as I reach into my duffel bag for my running shoes. Tugging off my suede, knee-high boots—a feat in the cramped driver's seat—I manage to get my runners on and laced. I'm shoving my arms into my parka, only then realizing my gloves and hat didn't make it into my overnight bag, when there's a sharp rap against my window.

I scream, throwing my arms into the air. My phone goes flying, then skitters under the front seat. There's a guy at my window, with crossed arms and a tight look I interpret as annoyance. *What's he annoyed about?* He nearly gave me a heart attack, sneaking up on my car like that. He takes a half step back, clearly hearing my alarmed yelp, but his expression reads more irritation than apology. I crack the window an inch.

"Can I help you?" I ask, my tone confidently firm so he knows I can take care of myself.

The guy stuffs his hands in his coat's pockets and gives me a curious look. "Seems you're the one who needs help?"

I'm about to say, "All good here," but then we both notice the steam coming out from under the car's hood. I look at him and shrug, and he raises an eyebrow. First impression, aside from the evident grumpiness? He's gorgeous. Thick, dark, wavy hair and bright green eyes. Five-o'clock shadow that works *very well* on him. At least a handful of inches taller than my five-foot-nine height, probably over six feet. Broad shoulders under his corduroy jacket with a shearling collar, which nicely complements his perfectly faded jeans and rugged work boots. I'm not sure where he came from, but he looks like he just stepped off the cover of a romance novel.

Handsome, no question, but still a stranger. I muster a polite smile, roll my window all the way down so we don't have to speak through a one-inch crack. A chilly gust of wind bursts into the car, and I regret leaving my hat and gloves behind. "I'm . . . having car trouble."

He checks his watch, then his eyes drift again to the steam creeping out from under Pepper's hood. "I can see that."

I'm half considering telling him to *just move along, I've got this*, when he adds, "Do you need a ride into town?" Again, a hint of irritation in his tone. *Why did you even bother to stop?* I think. It's only four kilometres—I'd rather walk than get in the truck with Mr. Gorgeous-but-Grumpy.

"No, thanks," I reply, giving him a saccharin-sweet smile. "I haven't hit my ten thousand steps yet today."

He sighs, runs a hand through that wavy, dark hair. "Are you always this stubborn?" There's a twitch in his jaw, as though he's holding back a smile. But nothing else about his body language suggests this is someone with whom I want to spend a minute longer.

"Are you always this friendly?" I ask, matching his tone.

There's a brief pause, and then he lets out a booming laugh—a real one, and his entire demeanour changes. "Let's start over," he says, setting a hand to his chest. "I'm Liam, Liam Young, and I'm sorry for scaring you earlier. Also, for that terrible first impression—I'm usually much more charming," he adds, and I can't resist returning the smile. "But it's been one hell of *a day*."

His smile dims slightly, but he quickly recovers. "I promise you, I am neither a serial killer nor a jerk."

"Isn't that exactly what a jerky serial killer would say in a situation like this?" I raise an eyebrow, but my shoulders relax. I'm mesmerized by Liam's matching dimples, which have settled into his cheeks thanks to his mega-watt smile.

"I see your point. Okay, how's this . . ." Liam crouches, resting his crossed arms on my open window. He's only inches from me, and the scent of cloves and pine reaches my nose with another gust of wind. Up close, he's also somehow even more good-looking. "I live just outside Harmony Hills on a Christmas tree farm—true story—and I cry at life insurance commercials. Also, I have those bird-safety stickers up on every window in my house."

"A Christmas tree farm, huh?" I chuckle. "I would expect nothing less in Harmony Hills."

My small-town instincts kick my city-girl ones to the curb, and I decide I'm safe with this guy. "I will take you up on the ride," I say. "Otherwise, I'll be walking in the dark."

We both look up to the sky, which is quickly losing its light.

"Happy to give you a lift." He stands, checking his watch once more. "Again, sorry for my impatience earlier. I'm dealing with a starter emergency."

"That sounds . . . important," I say, before rolling up the window and opening the door. *Starter emergency?* I consider asking what that means but decide to mind my own business. "So, life insurance commercials? Really?"

"I've been told I'm too 'soft.'" He shrugs. "Can I take your bag for you . . . sorry, I didn't catch your name?"

"Um, sure. Thanks," I reply, handing him my duffel bag. "I'm Elizabeth. Nice to meet you, Liam." I grab my boots, lock the doors, and follow him to his truck, which is parked behind my car.

"Likewise," he says, opening the passenger door of his pickup. It's warm inside, and it smells like orange slices warming in cinnamon-laced apple cider. I inhale deeply. Then I immediately sneeze. And sneeze again.

"You don't happen to have a cat in here, do you?" My third sneeze is the most dramatic yet, embarrassingly so. I dig around in my crossbody purse for a tissue, feeling another sneeze building. My eyes are watering so much I can hardly see.

"Not today," he says. "But I did help a friend with a couple of cats the other day. May still be some fur arou—"

"AH-CHOO!"

Liam gives me a sympathetic look. "Guessing you're allergic to cats?"

"Good guess," I say, my tone nasally. I take the tissue he hands me. "Thanks."

"Fresh air might help," he says, powering our windows down a few inches. He also turns up the heat to counteract the cold air. "Do you have an antihistamine?"

I give him a wan smile, which he doesn't notice because he's pulling onto the road. As a doctor you might think I always have a mini medical kit handy—at the very least, some aspirin or a couple of adhesive bandages. But the closest thing to medicine I have on me is ChapStick. At least the fresh air, while chilly, seems to be keeping the sneezing at bay.

"No antihistamine, but I just remembered I have a turkey sandwich in my bag. I don't cry at commercials—of any sort," I say, and Liam laughs. "But something to know about me is that I am always hungry. *Always*."

I pull out the squished foil-and-paper-wrapped packet, inside of which rests a formerly hot turkey, stuffing, and cranberry sandwich I picked up at the gas station. Opening the packet, I poke at the sandwich, then take a whiff. Seems fine.

"When did you get that?" Liam asks, glancing over and wrinkling his nose. Fair enough—it doesn't exactly look appetizing.

"A few hours ago," I say with a shrug. "Pepper's heat doesn't work well, though, so it should be okay."

"Pepper?"

"That's my car's name. I've had her for fourteen years. My longest relationship, by a long shot." I'm mildly embarrassed to have revealed both things so quickly, so I take a big bite of the sandwich to keep me from sharing more. It's cold and the cranberry has congealed in a gummy way, but otherwise it tastes good. I'm starving, so I take another bite, and offer him the other half.

"No, thanks," he says.

"Suit yourself," I reply through a mouthful of turkey and stuffing.

"So what brings you to Harmony Hills, Elizabeth?"

I swallow and am about to answer when a phone rings through the truck's speakers. He looks at the screen—*Call from Pops*—and frowns. "Do you mind if I take this?"

"Of course. Please," I reply, staring out the window and starting in on the second half of the sandwich while he answers the call. There's still no snow on the ground, which is odd for this time of year in Harmony Hills. We had more of a dusting when I left Toronto.

"Hey, Pops, I'm almost there," Liam says, keeping his eyes on the road.

"Crisis averted. No need to rush on over, I've got it under control." The voice is familiar, though I can't place it. I wonder what this guy's connection is to Harmony Hills, and who this "Pops" is.

Liam lets out a breath in obvious relief. "Great news. Okay, well,

I'm almost in town, so I'll come by regardless. I'm sure you could use another set of hands."

"If you mean someone else's hands, you bet!"

There's laughter from both, and then Liam says "bye" and ends the call.

"Starter emergency over?" I ask, crumpling up the paper-and-foil packet.

"Thankfully, yes," Liam replies, shooting me a smile. "How was the old and cold sandwich?"

"Delicious. I love a good turkey and cranberry sandwich." Though now it feels like a brick in my stomach. I ate too quickly, a hazard of my particular line of work. Always in a rush.

Liam slows the truck, pulling onto the main road that snakes through the tiny Harmony Hills. We pass the familiar sights—the town square with the giant evergreen, the sweets shop, the pharmacy and dry goods store, the library and redbrick school, the community centre that is the hub of the town—and nostalgia hits me, along with a wiggle of anxiety. I swallow hard and take a couple of breaths.

"You okay over there?" Liam asks, noting my discomfort.

"I'm fine," I reply, clearing my throat.

"So where can I drop you off, Elizabeth?"

"Anywhere here is fine. Thanks," I reply. My parents' house is only a couple minutes' walk from the downtown area. I'll figure out what to do about Pepper once I get there.

Liam pulls into a spot near the town square, puts the truck in park. "This okay?" he asks.

"Perfect." I'm gathering my stuff when Liam says, "Let me get the door for you."

I could easily open it myself but wait for him to walk to my side of the truck. This gesture reminds me where I am—in small towns like Harmony Hills people look out for one another. Opening doors, bringing casseroles over after injuries or illness, shoveling snowy driveways and raking leaves for neighbours, always having a minute to stop and chat rather than rushing by, eyes fixed to the sidewalk or, more likely, a phone.

For a moment we stand there, my arms full with my bag and boots, and Liam with hands again in his pockets. He smiles and I smile back, but I'm quite aware of the lengthening silence.

"So . . ." I take a quick glance around. "It's been a while since I've been back, but it doesn't seem like much has changed."

"That's one of the things I love most about this place," Liam says, making me wonder again what this guy's story is. But there's only so long you can stand outside a stranger's pickup truck before you need to make a move—one way or the other.

"Well, I should probably get going," I say, setting my duffel bag's strap across my chest. "I really appreciate you stopping, and I hope your day gets better."

"It already has." Liam's smile deepens (*hot damn*, those dimples!), and he holds out a hand. "It was nice meeting you, Elizabeth."

"You, too, Liam." I reach out to shake his hand, and he takes it with a warm, steady grip. Firm, but not too firm. I like that.

Just as I turn to go, he says, "Maybe I'll see you around town?"

I glance back and meet his sparkling green eyes. "That would be great," I say, as casually as I can. Then I start walking towards my parents' house, thinking maybe Harmony Hills isn't going to be the worst place to spend Christmas after all.

4

December 20

I'm sweaty and hot, in a nauseating way. When a patient says they feel like they've been "run over by a truck," well, lying here, I know exactly what they mean.

For a moment I think I'm in bed in my Toronto apartment, which is a twenty-minute brisk walk from the hospital. I adore my bed—it's king-sized and has layers of plush bedding on top of a memory-foam mattress, along with far too many pillows. Many nights I sleep in fits and bursts at the hospital, so at home I'm rigid about sleep hygiene. Austin's condo is closer to the hospital and bigger, so we often stayed there, but my bed is far comfier.

A memory settles in then, from when I caught a nasty virus earlier this year and was bedridden for days. Austin hadn't come by to check on me. He did send a soup delivery to make sure I was staying hydrated, but he said he couldn't risk catching it. "Surgery is packed this week. You know what a nightmare rescheduling is," he texted.

Later that day on FaceTime, as I gingerly sipped a cup of the delivered chicken-noodle soup, Austin asked, "Think you'll live?" with a teasing smile on his handsome face. Nary a wrinkle or blemish anywhere, despite his being forty-two years old, with ocean-blue eyes that were mesmerizing even through the phone's screen.

"I'll live. Thanks for the soup," I replied, my voice a painful squeak. I remember feeling grateful for the soup—even though I threw it up later—and for Austin's thoughtful gesture. I would have preferred him to lie in bed with me, watch a movie, replenish my glass of water, and make sure I medicated my fever. But I kept that wish to myself; Austin was busy, plus, I was a capable, independent adult.

The door creaks open and my dad walks in, opening the slat blinds before smiling at me as he takes my wrist in his fingers to check my pulse. I'm in my childhood bedroom, in my parents' two-level Craftsman house. A soft, warm quilt puddles around my feet on the double bed, the walls a vibrant yellow I still love. A whiteboard calendar hangs above a simple wooden desk. Squinting, I see it still holds the schedule for my final week of summer before I left for university. The entire room is like a museum exhibit of teenage me.

"Mom and I are about to head to the clinic," Dad says, perched on the edge of the bed. "Do you need anything before we go?"

My dad and I are peas in a pod, especially in appearance. The same honeyed-amber eyes, chestnut-brown hair that could be called "auburn" in certain lighting, a lean physique well suited to running. Something we used to enjoy doing together when I was younger. I still run a couple times a week to relieve stress, but I don't love dodging litter and dog waste not picked up by careless owners, or maneuvering through the endless traffic grid.

Now, lying here with a stomach that feels like it has really been through something, I suddenly remember the last twenty-four hours. My car broke down, and Liam—the handsome green-eyed stranger with killer dimples—gave me a lift into town. I ate that cold sandwich, which clearly explains my pathetic state. One might think that as a doctor I'm hypervigilant about food-borne illness. However, I spend so much time around sickness I rarely think about it outside the hospital setting. Which is unfortunate when one decides a turkey, stuffing, and cranberry gas-station sandwich sounds good.

I started feeling dizzy and nauseous shortly after dinner, so Amelia and Beckett went to get my car (Beckett's brother Chase has a towing company), and I spent the rest of the night on the bathroom floor. I give my dad a weak smile. "Sorry for the drama, Dad. I'm gross—a total disaster."

He waves the apology away. "I'm your dad, Libby. And a nurse to boot. This is my wheelhouse, honey. Besides, we're just thrilled you're home!"

My smile dims, guilt blooming, but I manage, "I'm glad to be home, too."

Dad feels my forehead with the back of his hand, the way he used to when I was little. My dad is—and has always been—the caregiver of our family. I learned a lot about doctoring from my mom, but everything I know about bedside manner has come from him. "You're not febrile. That's good."

Not febrile means no fever. In the Munro house medical terms are tossed about regularly. Even Amelia, who had eschewed anything related to a career in health care, can speak "medical-ese" without blinking an eye.

"Why don't I send Mila up with some flat ginger ale before she heads out for school? That should help settle things."

My sister still has breakfast with our parents Monday through Friday, as her school is closer to their place. Very occasionally, and typically only on the rare occasion I come back to Harmony Hills, I think about how easily I left home. Without so much as a backwards glance, while Amelia—who is seven years younger than me—stayed, ultimately forming an adult relationship with our parents. I feel more like the wet-behind-the-ears teenager I was when I left for university, versus the accomplished thirtysomething physician I am today.

I'm about to reply that ginger ale sounds great when the opening bars of "Jingle Bells" echoes down the hallway.

"Mom's current ringtone," Dad says. "You know how she gets this time of year."

I do know. Mom is "crackers for Christmas" (self-described) and always has been, or at least for as long as I can remember. The house is decked out for the holidays, with two fully decorated trees and four miniature villages complete with a working model Polar Express train that runs along ceiling-suspended tracks from one room to the next. There's fresh cedar garlands and pine wreaths on the doors and windows, and a family of lit-up snow people on the front lawn. Outdoors you'll find more of Mom's holiday spirit with twinkle lights wrapping around porch columns and fastidiously hung icicle lights lining the roofline. *Crackers for Christmas*, no question.

Tall and statuesque, with bright blue eyes and long silver hair that's always tied back in a ponytail, my mother, Dr. Monica Munro, is a striking woman. But she's also a total goofball with a wicked sense of humour. Evidenced today by the *Elf*-inspired one-piece jumpsuit she wears, and the plate of crispy bacon in hand.

"Thought you might be hungry after all the vomit drama last night," my mom says, raising one eyebrow teasingly.

"Mom, are you trying to make me throw up on my bed?" I groan, plugging my nose. Normally, a day that starts with a hand-delivered plate of bacon is a good one. Today is not that day.

Mom laughs, then reaches into the pocket of her onesie and

pulls out a blister pack. "Ondansetron, sweetheart. It will pair well with the flat ginger ale." Ondansetron is an antiemetic (anti-nausea) medication that works like a charm.

"Thank you," I say, letting the small pill dissolve under my tongue. I settle back against my pillow that Dad has kindly fluffed for me. "Now, I love you both, but please go to the clinic and leave me to my misery."

Closing my eyes, I remain horizontal, but point firmly with one hand in the general direction of the plate of bacon my mom set on the desk. "Don't you dare leave that in here, Mom."

"Wouldn't dream of it," she says, before adding, "Oh, Libby, I've planned on turkey and cranberry sandwiches for dinner tonight. We still have leftovers in the freezer from Thanksgiving. Okay, Stark, off we go."

I moan, covering my face with my pillow. As I will my stomach to behave, I hear Dad say, "Monica, you're bad," the two of them laughing lightly before shutting the door behind them.

5

"Flat ginger ale for the lady," Amelia announces, using her *Downton Abbey* English accent and a singsong tone. "Will you be joining us for luncheon in the drawing room?"

Amelia speaks French fluently and has a knack for accents. I have a basic knowledge of French, thanks to our elementary school's immersion program, but it's modest at best.

"Also, expect you're missing this?" She hands me my phone, which had fallen under the car seat.

"Oh! Thanks—and thanks for getting my car last night. Let me know what I owe Chase."

"He said you're family now, so no charge." Amelia jumps on the bed without waiting for an invitation, right onto my stretched-out legs.

"Hey!" I complain, before drawing up my legs to give Amelia more space. She leans forward and wraps her arms around my bent knees, giving them a hug.

"I'm glad you're home, even if you're sick." Amelia offers a wide smile, looking so much like our mom. She's willowy, too, taller than me by about an inch, her blond hair naturally wavy, like she's spent a day at the beach.

"Same," I reply, squeezing her forearm gently. I see the sparkling diamond eternity band on Amelia's left hand. "Nice *accoutrement* you've got there."

"Nice use of the word *accoutrement*," Amelia replies, in perfectly
accented French. Grinning, she holds her hand out so I can take a
closer look. "J'adore. Elle est l'une des bonnes."

"Sure, to whatever you just said." I sip the ginger ale. It's sweet,
warm, and soothing.

"I said, 'She's one of the good ones.'"

"Of course she is—you said yes." I'm truly happy for Amelia,
who is also *one of the good ones*.

"So Beckett Livery-Quinn is joining the Munro family, huh?
Does she know what she's getting into?"

Amelia nods, smiles. "She does."

"What about your number one rule?" I ask. "It seems to me
you broke it."

"I did not! My number one rule was to never marry a doctor
or a nurse," Amelia says, holding up a finger in correction. "I'm already surrounded, and you know medical stuff makes me feel icky."

"Clearly you made an exception," I reply. "Beckett *is* a doctor."

"An *animal doctor*—totally different! Turns out I'm not as
squeamish as I thought," Amelia says. "I even assisted when she
delivered a calf."

"Wow, that's progress. How was it?"

"The delivery?"

I nod, and a sudden sense of wistfulness hits hard, like a wicked
case of déjà vu. Between the well-used mug I'm holding, which has
carried many a servings of warm ginger ale over the years, and
the cozy Christmas decorations, to Amelia sitting cross-legged on
my bed, her elbows on her knees and chin in hands, it's like I'm
sixteen again.

"It was fine, and gross." Amelia grimaces, shakes her head, and I chuckle.

"Okay, off to school. Last day, so wish me luck—the kids are bananas this time of year." She stands, smoothing her black turtleneck and pleated silver skirt. "Oh, before I forget."

Amelia holds up two fingers, the way I expect she would for her students. "One, we need to go to a celebration of life service tonight, so get this sickness out of your system today."

"Celebration of life for who?"

Amelia mouths *for whom*, and I narrow my eyes.

"Sorry, force of habit," she says. "For Elsie Farrow."

"Oh no, Miss Elsie died? When? Why didn't anyone tell me?"

I'm heartbroken for Claire—my high-school best friend and Elsie's granddaughter—as well as for Harmony Hills more generally. Elsie is a beloved member of the town, running programs for seniors, chairing community events, and taking in every stray dog or cat that happened upon our village.

"She passed about six weeks ago?" Amelia replies. "I'm pretty sure Mom left you a voicemail."

My stomach clenches, guilt rearing up again. Six weeks ago, and I haven't reached out yet to Claire, which makes me eligible for the Worst Friend of the Year award. But I rarely check my voicemail. However, I can't blame this one on anyone but myself. I need to get better at checking my messages (*New Year's Resolution Number Two*).

"She died in her sleep, the day after her ninety-fourth birthday. Anyway, it's not meant to be a sad affair. We are to wear 'festive' attire."

Festive attire? To a memorial service? Though I shouldn't be surprised, having spent the first eighteen years of my life in Harmony Hills. The town and its residents take holidays, all of them, though especially Christmas, quite seriously. The town's motto is even written onto the welcome sign: HARMONY HILLS—WHERE EVERY DAY'S A HOLIDAY!

"I'll be there even if I have to bring this wastebasket with me," I say. Amelia's at the door now, and I add, "Wait, what's the second thing?"

"Oh, right!" She half turns, facing me again. "I'm almost twelve weeks pregnant. You're going to be an aunt."

My mouth drops open, my food-poisoned brain slow to catch up to this epic news she drops on me like she's merely telling me there's freshly brewed coffee in the kitchen.

"But, p.s., it's a secret, and I'm going to surprise everyone— Mom and Dad included—after the wedding, so zip it for now," she adds, before blowing me an air kiss and shutting my bedroom door.

By the time I get ahold of myself, calling out, "What do you mean *you're pregnant*?!" my sister is gone and the house is empty, the only sounds I hear are faint Christmas carols ("Little Drummer Boy": "Pa rum pum pum pum / Rum pum pum pum . . .") playing on the kitchen radio.

"Excuse me? Dr. Munro?"

There's a determined tug on my skirt—red, pleated satin, nearly identical to Amelia's silver one. I borrowed it from her closet, adding a sparkly silver belt and an enameled Christmas wreath pinned to my white blouse to meet the "festive attire" brief for the memorial service. I glance down into the curious wide eyes of the small person tugging at my skirt, and see deep blue eyes that are so familiar.

"Hi, Jonah." I crouch so I'm eye to eye with one of Claire's six-year-old twins. "You don't need to call me Dr. Munro—that's my mom's name. Elizabeth, or Libby, is just fine. What's up?"

He doesn't answer right away; instead, he glances at the ornately carved walnut box that holds his great-grandmother's ashes. It's on a table at the front of the funeral home's gathering room, which has been transformed to look more like a holiday office party setting than a sombre memorial. The room is full, crowded with so many conversations and people, shoulder to shoulder, the entire town here to celebrate Elsie Farrow's life.

A blinking, lit-up Christmas tree stands tall in one corner, with boxes wrapped in holiday paper nestled underneath, featuring candy canes, decorative bulbs, and Santa Claus wearing board shorts on a surfboard. Long boughs of pine garland frame doorways and windowsills, with bright and shiny decorations poking through the greenery. There's a low hum of lively chatter throughout the space, with holiday songs (currently an upbeat, a cappella version of "God Rest Ye Merry Gentlemen") streaming from built-in speakers. Guests enjoy spiked eggnog, nonalcoholic cranberry-soda punch, and trays of holiday-themed cookies. Jonah is holding a half-eaten Rudolph the Red-Nosed Reindeer sugar cookie in hand.

"So Gigi died, which is sad." He shifts his weight from one leg to the other. Then with his cookie-free hand he fiddles with the red sequined bow tie around his neck. Likely purchased from Everhart's Dry Goods down the street. People here don't shop online—they support the local businesses, and their neighbours.

"It *is* sad." I rub Jonah's back gently. The half-eaten sugar cookie's vanilla scent wafts into my nose, and for the first time since the sandwich incident, I'm hungry. A good sign.

"And Momma said Gigi is *in there*." Jonah whispers, pointing at the walnut box on the table.

"That's right," I say, keeping my tone gentle and open.

"But, um, I was wondering . . . Dr. Mun—Miss Elizabeth," he says, before lowering his voice even further. I lean in to hear him. "How did they fit Gigi into that little box?"

I resist the urge to laugh. Glancing over at Claire through the crowd, I see she's holding her youngest—a little girl named Lucy— tightly with one hand, and trying to pry something out of Jonah's twin sister Jasmine's hand. I can see at least two cookies grasped in Jasmine's hand, and her face is smeared with blue icing.

Then Jasmine suddenly darts away, giggling as she does, cookies still in her clutches. Claire sets a hand to her head (some blue icing transferring to her forehead, which I'll tell her about in a moment) and catches my eye. She gives me a crooked smile and shrugs as she picks up Lucy before following Jasmine.

Turning back to Jonah, I hold his hands so he faces me. Employing my doctor's tone—*confident but not cocky, clear but not emotionless, empathetic without being condescending*—I explain cremation as simply as I can.

"Do you understand?" I'm still holding his hands but stand to let the blood flow back into my screaming leg muscles. I wonder how moms adjust to these constant bent-over and crouched positions. I think then of Amelia and her bombshell news, which I've had no time to revisit because we haven't been alone all day. I have *a lot* of questions, starting with "Are you taking your folic acid?" and ending with "How did you know you were ready to be a mother?"

Jonah purses his lips, clearly deep in thought. *Maybe I went too far? Shoot, he doesn't need to know details about cremation, Elizabeth.* But then he gives the box a long look, and nods.

"That's what I thought," he says, with the confidence of someone four times his age. He hands me his half-eaten cookie. "You can have the rest. I'm gonna tell my sister about Gigi now."

"Oh, Jonah, hang on—" I turn to catch him before he takes off, but then someone steps on my foot and I gasp, pain exploding in my baby toe.

Cursing, I hop on one leg, then bend at the waist to try to catch my breath, the pain making me dizzy. A strong hand cups my elbow to support me.

"Oh my gosh, I'm so sorry. Are you okay?" The voice is deep but smooth, sort of like a country-song-crooning cowboy's. Or what I imagine that might sound like. Also? It's familiar. Very familiar.

I look up and right into Liam's green eyes. "Oh . . . hi," I say, still standing on one leg.

"This is not what I meant when I said I hoped to run into you around town," Liam says with a smile. The dimples are dimpling, but then his grin drops as he glances at my foot. "What's the damage? On a scale of one being barely a bruise to ten being I'm going to have to carry you out of here?"

"No real damage. I'm okay." I gingerly set my foot back on the ground. My toe throbs angrily, but a moment later goes numb—a bad sign for the likely swelling toe, but good news for the pain level. I'm embarrassed by all my hopping about, but also take a moment to imagine Liam lifting me into his *clearly very strong arms*.

"You sure?" He scans my face with those impossibly green eyes, which I now see are flecked with gold. I nod, attempting to smile through another wave of baby-toe pain. So much agony for such a tiny appendage. Just then Amelia appears, her expression concerned.

"What's wrong?" she asks. "Why were you all bent over?"

"It's nothing. Someone stepped on my foot," I reply, though I don't mention who. It's crowded in here, and Liam surely didn't mean to crush my baby toe. No need to make him feel worse than he obviously already does. "I'm fine."

"That's a relief. Thought you might need this." Amelia releases my arm, holding out a small bag covered in Christmas trees, eyebrows raised. She glances over at Liam. "My sister may be older, but she is definitely not wiser, at least when it comes to bad turkey sandwiches. There was quite a lot of"—she sets a hand to her stomach and blows out her cheeks—"last night."

Liam cringes, then laughs lightly as he turns my way. "Oh no ... the sandwich didn't love you back?"

I give Amelia a look that says *Stop talking NOW.* She shrugs but gets the message. "Love the sweater, Liam. I saw Mary has a similar one—so sweet. Everhart's?" she asks.

"Thanks, Mila. And of course." He's wearing a crazy Christmas sweater, red and green patchwork, with a gift on its front, wrapped in a large gold organza bow that actually ties up. Perhaps odd for a memorial service, unless you live in Christmas-obsessed Harmony Hills. Through the haze of pain I wonder who Mary is, and how she and Liam are connected, with their "sweet" matching Christmas sweaters.

"Oh, there's Becks," Amelia says, eyes only for her fiancée now. She doesn't even look at me when she asks, "You good?"

"I'm good. I'll come find you and Beckett later." Amelia nods, then is gone, swallowed up into the crowd.

"So you're Mila's sister, the famous Libby Munro?" Recognition dawns on his face. "I didn't put it together when you introduced yourself as Elizabeth."

"Definitely not 'famous,' and I haven't gone by Libby in years, but—" I'm so distracted by his adorable dimples (a matching set!)

that I don't notice what's beside me, getting closer to my hand, the one still holding Jonah's abandoned Rudolph cookie.

"Mary Piggins, *enough*," Liam's voice goes down another octave, the tone sterner. *Mary Piggins?* I quickly glance around. But before I can figure out who "Mary Piggins" is, the cookie is tugged out of my hand. I look down, confused, before promptly screaming when I see a potbellied pig—caramel and black fur, a black nose at the end of a whiteish-pink snout, and a sort of reverse mohawk of sand-coloured fur at the crown of her head. She's as tall as a large dog and as wide and round as a rain barrel. Mary's still got the cookie in her mouth as she darts off into the crowd.

A half-dozen people have turned our way with my scream, and, mortified, I say, "Oh, it's nothing! I'm so sorry. Everything's fine."

But is it . . . fine? There's a pig loose in the funeral home. I glance around for Mr. Covington, the home's director, but can't see him anywhere.

"Libby . . . Elizabeth, hey, so sorry about all this. She's still learning her manners. Uh, I'll just grab Mary . . . where the heck did she get to?" He glances around the room, sighing in obvious frustration. Then he turns his attention back my way and gives my elbow a little squeeze. "You sure you're okay? Mary isn't exactly light on her hooves."

"Of course. Yep, don't worry about me." I wave away the concern, blushing fiercely under his intense gaze. Only now realizing it wasn't Liam who stepped on my toe, but the cookie-stealing, Christmas-sweater-wearing potbellied pig. "You go get your . . . pig."

"Huh. I guess she *is* mine now," he says, placing his hands on his hips. He lets out a long breath, which turns into another sigh, like he isn't at all sure what to do next. Then he smiles at me again, his dimples settling in deeper (*hot damn*). "I'll be right back. With another cookie for you. You're always hungry, right?"

"Right." I nod, dazed from our interaction and forgetting for a moment all about my throbbing baby toe, and the fact there's a pig stealing sugar cookies from guests at a memorial service decorated for the holidays.

6

December 21

It's Saturday, Amelia is finished teaching for the year, and Christmas is only four days away. Which means the wedding is tomorrow, so this is about as down to the wire a bride trying on her wedding dress for the first time can get.

We're in Everhart's—whose owner, Rosalie, is also the town's seamstress. Only in small towns can you buy a wedding dress at the same place you get athletic socks, camping gear, and seasonal decorations. Plus, why not toss in novelty items like a "Lordy, Lordy, He's Forty!" gag gift and a box of superhero-themed bandages while you're at it? Everhart's Dry Goods is a one-stop shop that has served Harmony Hills for more than fifty years.

Amelia's trying on her long-sleeved white dress with a scoop neck and floor-length hemline. There's lace overlay, endless rows and swirls of crystal beading, and a thin gold belt cinching the waist. The dress shimmers with every swish of her hips.

"Can I pull this off?" Amelia asks, glancing in the mirror. "It's *a lot.*"

"Every day of the week, anywhere you want to go." She's stunning.

Amelia smiles, then lets out her breath. Suddenly, the belt pops open at the back.

"Here, I'll get it." But the belt won't latch. There's about half an inch of space between the two ends. I look around on the floor. "Did a piece come off?"

"No, I stopped sucking in." She rests her hands on her stomach, and I see it now—the tiny round of her belly, straining against the shimmering fabric, like she's had a too-big meal. A mix of emotions moves through me when I see her hands on her stomach: joy, sadness, envy, longing. None of which I plan to unpack at the moment.

"You don't need the belt," I say. "The dress is perfect without it."

"And more comfortable." Amelia gently taps her palms against her stomach. Then she catches my eye in the mirror.

"Hey, in case I haven't said it already, I'm really glad you're here. I wasn't sure you . . ." She shakes her head and tears up, which makes me tear up. I've developed a tough outer crust from years in medicine, but when someone I love cries, it's game over. "I wasn't sure you'd be able to get here in time."

For a moment, I say nothing. Then I'm annoyed, a quip about how demanding my job is on the tip of my tongue to alleviate the guilt I'm reluctant to admit. Yet I know what's behind her comment and that she's justified in making it. I left Harmony Hills without another thought, and haven't been great at showing up for my family in the years since. Regular communication hasn't been my strong suit.

"Mila, I wouldn't miss this *for anything*." Clearing my throat, I reach for a nearby box of tissues, which sits atop a shelf with silver and gold Christmas ornaments, a few bottles of bug spray left over from summertime, and a couple freeze-dried bags of astronaut ice cream sporting a thin layer of dust. Who knows how long those have been there.

"Okay, no more waterworks." I hand her a tissue. I use another to dab at my eyes. "You need to get out of that dress and write vows, and I have a maid of honour to-do list to tackle."

I glance at the list, written on actual paper because Amelia is old school like that. There are twelve items, enumerated to represent the importance of each. I quickly scan the list.

1. *Dress!*

That one gets crossed out with a flourish of my pen.

2. *Rehearsal breakfast—confirm with Season's Eatings*

I start walking, heading towards the diner on the other side of town, eyes on the list.

3. *Bûche de Noël cake???*

Reading number three, I stop midstride. *What do three question marks mean?* I reach for my phone in my coat pocket, dialing Amelia as I continue perusing the list.

4. *Pick up candy cane ribbons from—*

Voicemail. "Hey, Mila. I have a question about the list. The cake, specifically. There are three question marks, and I don't understand what— OH!" Something shoves into the back of my thigh, and I drop the list. I twist to get a better look and see it's the same pig that stole the sugar cookie from my hand last night. Tinny Christmas carols—"Here Comes Santa Claus," it sounds like—stream out of a flashing red-and-green-lit collar around the pig's expansive neck. Attached to the collar is a leash, held by none other than Liam, Mr. Dimples for Days.

"Libby, I'm so sorry," he says, reaching down to pick up the fallen list. As he hands it to me, I note that he smells like baking bread and fresh cedar shavings today. Heaven.

"It's okay," I reply. Mary snorts, and I glare at her.

"She's a good girl, but she's going through some stuff," he says. My irritation towards Mary Piggins thaws slightly.

"Aren't we all?" I say, my sigh involuntary. He gives me a curious look. "It's almost Christmas. The season of stress, right?"

Liam smiles, and my insides go melty, like marshmallows in hot chocolate. There's a moment of silence between us (why am I holding my breath?) before I break eye contact to look down at the paper in my hand.

"I should probably get back to this." I hold up the list. "Sister-of-the-bride duties call."

"Same, though in my case it's best-friend-of-the-other-bride duties," he says, then points to the paper in my hand. "How's the list coming?"

"Not bad. Dress at Everhart's, check." I mime a check mark. "Next up is Season's Eatings. Have to confirm the wedding-day breakfast-slash-rehearsal-party thing."

"Mind if I walk with you? I'm headed that way, too. I promise to keep Mary on a tight leash."

"Of course," I reply, because while I could do without Mary, Liam is an unexpected but pleasant addition to my morning. "What's on your list?"

"Slice of Life, for starters," Liam says.

"Ah. I've not been yet. My parents rave about it."

Liam smiles. "If you go, make sure you try the seven-grain sourdough. It's the best, in my opinion."

We set off, Mary thankfully walking on Liam's other side. Then Liam stops abruptly, looks down at my feet, his forehead creasing with concern. "Are you limping?"

I am, in fact, limping. My baby toe that Mary stepped on swelled up like a fat little Vienna sausage, and is now spectacularly purple. I buddy taped it to its neighbour toe, which helps, but it remains tender inside my boot. But I wave away his concern.

"Seriously, you barely need your baby toe. It's practically a vestigial appendage."

"Vestigial?" Liam brings his eyebrows together.

"Unnecessary," I add brightly, to show I'm truly fine. Even if it's a lie, about the baby toe being unnecessary. In fact, it's a crucial part of the complex mechanics of the foot, and so quite necessary despite how small and insignificant it may seem.

He nods at this, but his concerned look remains as he glances at the pig and lets out a quiet, "Mary, *good grief.*"

I smile, because it sounds more like something a grandfather and not a (seriously attractive, adorably earnest) guy would say. "Liam, please don't give it another thought. Toes heal in no time. This is a professional opinion, so you should trust it."

"Is it broken?" He doesn't acknowledge my assurances, looking from my face to my foot and back again.

"No! Of course not." *Oh, it's broken all right.* I'm 99.95 per cent certain. "Just a bruise. Barely even a bruise, really."

"Phew. Okay, good." He sets a hand to his forehead. "This pig is a snort-happy calamity."

This time I laugh out loud. *A snort-happy calamity.* An apt, colourful description for this creature. "So what's it like having a pet pig?" I ask, trying not to limp as we walk on.

Mary's collar continues to play "Here Comes Santa Claus" on a loop. It's cold though sunny, and the air smells chilled, like snow is on the way. The whole town is eager for the first snowfall, and it's unusual that it hasn't arrived yet.

"It's different, though not unlike having a big dog, I guess? But also, not what I planned. I'm more of a dog . . . and chickens and goats person." I glance over at him with an eyebrow raised. *Chickens and goats?*

"I have a lot of questions," I say.

"Honestly, me, too." Liam laughs. "What's the most pressing one?"

"Maybe, how did you end up with a pet pig if you're more a *chickens and goats* person?"

"Well, Mary Piggins was Miss Elsie's pet—she rescued her. Along with a squirrel, named Frank, and two cats—Sam and Dazey. Beckett found homes for the cats, and Frank is at a local wildlife centre. He's the star mascot, apparently."

Liam reaches down and scratches Mary behind one ear. She gives a snort and nuzzles into his hand. "I helped Miss Elsie out, taking Mary for walks and sometimes for weekends at my farm. Being a rescue, Mary has more quirks than average, I think? But I don't really know—she's my first pig."

What's an "average" potbellied pig like? I wonder.

"Miss Elsie asked me to look after Mary, when the time came. I was happy to do it."

Dazzling dimples *and* kindhearted? Who is this guy? "I'm not experienced in 'pig,' but it seems Mary adores you."

"She tries her best," he says, chuckling. "Except when sugar cookies are involved. Then all bets are off."

"No sugar cookies today." I pat both my pockets, proving they are empty. "But maybe it's me? Like, you know when someone is nervous around dogs, and the dog always seems to know?"

"Are you nervous, Libby?" Liam asks, his tone playful.

I don't say "Actually, I prefer Elizabeth," because I find that's not true in this case—I like how my nickname sounds in Liam's deep, measured drawl. My melty insides melt some more.

"I'm never nervous." I hold out one of my hands. "See? Emergency room steady."

"Impressive," Liam says, before chuckling lightly when Mary noses my calf from behind, causing me to let out a tiny yip of a scream.

7

"I'm so glad we're doing this," Claire says. We're at Beans & Brews, Harmony Hills' coffee shop that turns into a pub in the evenings, drinking Cranberry Ginger Sparklers. The cocktails are made with cranberry juice, vodka, ginger-infused simple syrup, and club soda, and have frozen cranberries floating on top, with a festive sprig of rosemary nestled amongst the berries.

"Me, too." I pluck out a frozen cranberry and pop it into my mouth, crunching the sour fruit.

We've already had a good hug and cry at her grandmother's memorial, but I'm looking forward to catching up properly. So far we've discussed the Cranberry Ginger Sparklers, the fact there's no snow yet, and the story of Mary Piggins at the memorial. "Rest in Peace, Libby's baby toe," Claire declared, after a solid minute of laughing at my reaction to Mary Piggins stealing Jonah's sugar cookie from my hand. ("She's really the sweetest thing," my friend assures me.)

"Fill me in on your life," I say now, stirring my drink with one finger. Claire laughs softly, watching me—she's nowhere near a germaphobe, impossible with three kids, but chooses the rosemary sprig to stir her own drink. "How's Kirby? The kids? I can't believe Jasmine and Jonah are already six."

"Tell me about it. And Lucy is almost two! It goes so fast. Well, that's not entirely true. The days are long but the years short." Claire sips her drink. "Kirby's great, though busy. He's on staff at Westhaven Memorial, plus doing a locum for a family doc who went back to England to look after her dad."

Claire's high-school-sweetheart husband, Kirby Kirkpatrick, like me, is double licensed in emergency medicine and family medicine, which allows him to work in the hospital and at a community clinic. They now live in Westhaven, which is about double the size of Harmony Hills and a thirty-minute drive away. Claire's an accountant who works freelance, though mostly she's busy with the kids these days.

"Is he looking to open his own practice?" I nibble at the bowl of nuts between us—cinnamon-sugar roasted cashews, and highly addictive.

"Maybe in a few years?" Claire replies. "We really hoped we could swing buying your parents' practice and come back here, but we just don't have the savings yet."

She glances at her phone, vibrating on the table, so doesn't see the look of confusion and shock on my face at her comment. "Uh-oh, it's Kirby's mom. She's watching the kids tonight."

Claire answers her phone, but I'm barely listening. *We really hoped we could swing buying your parents' practice, but we just don't have the savings yet.* What does that mean? Since when were my parents even considering selling Munro Medical?

"I'm on my way. Thanks, Charlotte," Claire says. She ends the call and slides her phone into her purse. "Libby, I'm so sorry but I have to run. Lucy has a fever."

She's calm, the way most parents of many kids are when they

come into the emergency room with fevers, or relentless stomach bugs, broken arms, mysterious rashes. I can always tell the experienced parents from the newbies.

"Let me know if you want me to take a look at her," I say. What I want is to pepper her with questions about my parents' clinic, but now's not the time.

Claire doesn't notice my angst, searching for her wallet in her large purse. I wave away her attempts to pay. "I've got this."

We hug goodbye, and then Claire is gone. Luckily, Kirby's parents live about two blocks from Beans & Brews, so it's a short walk.

"Oh, shoot," I murmur, remembering item number nine on Amelia's list: *Jonah & Jasmine, flower kids*? I'm typing out a text to Claire when someone says my name.

"Hey there, Libby."

I glance up from my text, find Liam standing next to the table.

"Oh, hey!" I set my phone down. He looks good in that effortless-yet-put-together way—distressed jeans, a salmon-pink T-shirt that fits exactly right under his dark brown corduroy trucker jacket with the faux shearling lining. His wavy hair is a touch mussed, likely from being under a toque. Luckily, the dimples still pop.

"Where's your calamitous sidekick tonight?" I'm feeling cheeky, and somewhat tipsy from the sparklers that may have had more vodka in them than I thought.

"Past her bedtime," Liam says with an easy smile. He gestures to Claire's cocktail glass, mostly full. "Big night for you, or am I interrupting something?"

"Claire was here, but she had to take off. Lucy has a fever."

"Poor kiddo," Liam says. "I can't imagine the stress of a sick kid—I get worked up when one of my animals isn't well."

"It helps when the dad's a doctor. Or a friend is, only a text away," I reply, tapping my phone. "I guess in your case, with the animals, a vet is more useful?"

Liam nods. "Becks has come through for me so many times."

He glances towards the back of the room, where I see a small group playing darts. Beckett is currently at the dartboard, removing her dart from the bull's-eye. She glances over at us, smiling, and waves. I return her smile. *That's my soon-to-be sister-in-law*, I think, still a touch stunned by how quickly this is all happening.

"We're having a little pre-wedding celebration," Liam says. "Want to join us?"

Yes. No. Yes. No.

I may be reading more into the ask than is there, but I also know I've had almost two sparklers (soon to be two and a half, if I finish Claire's drink, too), and I am not a big drinker. Tapping out at this stage is wise. The wedding's tomorrow, and I don't want anything—especially an avoidable hangover—to ruin Amelia's big day. "Rain check?"

"You got it," Liam says, rapping the table lightly with his knuckles, his smile deepening. "But probably a snow check, if the forecast is right."

It's so adorably cheesy that I can't help but grin, and I almost change my mind. Hangover be damned! I can hydrate, take something for the headache. But I need to avoid complicating things, even if said complication is this cute, funny, and charming guy.

"Snow check it is," I reply, feeling better than I have in a while. I know it's not only because of the Cranberry Ginger Sparklers.

8

December 22

"Libby, honey, there's a delivery for you!" Mom calls to me from the front door.

"For me?" I'm not expecting anything—especially not here.

It's still early, just after seven. We have about two hours before we need to be at Season's Eatings for the wedding rehearsal breakfast. Amelia's still asleep upstairs, Dad's making coffee, and Mom and I are finishing the final to-do item for the ceremony: tying ribbons onto candy canes and attaching miniature white note cards with *'Tis the Season to Be Married!* handwritten in calligraphy. Apparently, Beckett's craftswomanship.

"She's multitalented, my wife-to-be," Amelia said last night, as we were getting ready for bed, tracing the calligraphy with her finger. "I'm getting married tomorrow, Libby. *Tomorrow.*"

My heart had exploded then, and I vowed to do whatever I could to make Amelia's wedding perfect. Which began with getting up at five a.m. to finish the candy cane ribbons.

"Apparently you need to sign for it," Mom says, coming into the living room. She has an unfamiliar travel mug in hand.

"Who's that for?"

"Thomas," Mom replies, disappearing into the kitchen. She returns a moment later, pressing the lid firmly onto the mug.

"Who's Thomas?" I ask, focused on tying a knot in one of the ribbons.

"The deliveryman. It's chilly out there, and I offered him a top-up," she adds.

I smile and nod. *Only in Harmony Hills.* Following Mom to the front door, I hum along to the Christmas carol currently playing—"Hark! The Herald Angels Sing".

"This is Libby—Dr. Elizabeth Munro," Mom says, nudging me forward. Towards Thomas, who holds the refilled travel mug in one gloved hand, an envelope in the other, and has an awkward smile on his face.

"Where do you need me to sign?" I ask. Thomas is probably a decade younger than me, and it's all I can do not to roll my eyes at my mom's thinly veiled attempts to get me to flirt with him.

"Right here," he says, turning a tablet towards me for a digital signature. "Thanks again for the coffee, Monica, and Merry Christmas!"

"To you as well, Thomas," Mom says. "Stay warm out there."

He waves over his shoulder as he heads to his truck, and Mom waves back before shutting the door. "You know, honey, it wouldn't kill you to be a touch more . . . *joyful.* 'Tis the season, after all."

"Mother, please," I reply, laughing. "Thomas is barely out of his teens, for one thing. For another, like I've explained, I'm on a dating hiatus. Until further notice."

I turn the envelope over in my hands and see the sender's name. "Did the hospital call? Asking for your address?" My heart rate picks up. "I left your number in case they needed to reach me over the holidays."

"I didn't get a call," Mom says. "But maybe your dad answered?"

"It doesn't matter," I reply, tearing the strip from the cardboard envelope with impatient fingers. Inside is another envelope, covered in holly berries and ivy. I frown.

"A holiday card?" Mom says. "Strange to have it delivered so urgently. Who is it from?"

Inside the decorative envelope is a letter, folded in half, tucked into the generic holiday card with a "Season's Greetings!" message, stamped with signatures from the hospital's executive team. The hospital I've been waiting to hear back from after my interview.

But it's odd they've sent a card, unless I'm somehow already on the list of employees? An excited flutter fills me, and I turn to the letter, which is dated almost a week ago.

Dear Dr. Elizabeth Munro, it begins, *Thank you for your interest in the attending emergency physician position. You're an impressive and highly skilled candidate, and so it was an incredibly difficult decision. However, we've decided to go in another direction and hire internally for the role. We wish you the best with your search . . .*

Stunned, I hold the letter in trembling hands. I read it again, flip it over to see if there's any further explanation. There's a handwritten note on the back, which says they've been trying to reach me by telephone but my voicemail inbox is full.

Why didn't they send an email instead? I wonder. The next line explains it, with the excuse of circumventing "aggressive spam filters."

I sit down heavily on the small bench by the doorway, deflated. This was supposed to be my fresh start! A *new year, new you* opportunity. I never considered I wouldn't get the job—it seemed a perfect fit, and it couldn't have come at a better time.

With a sharp inhale, I grip the bench's edge as I reread the letter. *Thank you for your interest. Difficult decision. We wish you the best.* The phrases bounce around my mind like glitter in a shaken snow globe.

Mom takes the letter from my hand and quickly scans it. Then she folds it up and tucks it into her cardigan pocket, before nudging me over. It's a tight squeeze with both of us on the bench. "I didn't know you wanted to leave the hospital, Libby. I thought you were happy there."

"I am. Or I was," I say, with a shrug. Tears prick my eyes.

Here's what I don't say: I'm tired of avoiding my ex-boyfriend in the hallways, because seeing him makes me feel like a failure; things have started to feel monotonous, with the work less satisfying than it used to be, although I'm not sure why; and I thought a change of location might change *me*, for the better—unlike this haircut, which is currently pinned back with old bobby pins I found in my nightstand, and definitely one of my top regrets for the year.

"And now?" Mom asks.

"And now—" My voice catches as reality hits me like a rogue snowball. "Oh my God. I gave notice. I have no job." How irresponsible can I be? I still have loans; I have rent. Pepper apparently needs a new catalytic converter. *Do not panic, Elizabeth. Do not panic.* Too late—I'm panicking. I clutch my chest and twist towards my mom, which isn't easy on the narrow bench. "*I gave notice*, Mom. I don't have a job. Any job!"

"Don't panic, honey. Take a breath."

"I'm not panicking," I say, and Mom nods, kindly accepting the lie. "This is a calculated meltdown. It's fine. I'm—"

There's a loud wail upstairs, and Mom says, "I guess Amelia's up." Just then my sister appears on the stairs. Her hair is set in one of those heatless curling rods, the braided ends splaying out. She's in her robe, has moisturizing eye patches—bright pink—under her eyes, and is still wearing her retainer.

"My dress is *gone*. Mom, did someone move my dress?" Her words come in a lisp due to the retainer, and frantic—almost one syllable. "*Hasanyoneseenthedress?*"

"Mila, no one moved your dress. It's in our closet—left-hand side. Take a breath, honey."

Now Mila clutches her chest, and I almost laugh at the gesture, so similar to my own from a few moments ago.

"Mon Dieu. I had a nightmare I used the dress to make cutout snowflakes with my class, and when I couldn't find it this morning, I lost my mind for a second. Sorry to interrupt . . ." She's about to head back upstairs, but pauses, looking at me closely. "Are you okay? You don't look so hot."

"She's fine," Mom replies for me. "Go get ready. Dad's making pancakes."

"Perfect, I'm starving," Amelia replies before heading back upstairs. Some might find it odd to have breakfast before breakfast, but not if you're a Munro. Always being hungry is a genetic trait.

"This is not good," I mutter, holding my face in my hands. "Also? Who puts a letter like that—*bad news*—into a Christmas card?"

With a pat on my knee, Mom stands. "Whoever it was is clearly getting coal in his or her stocking this year. As for you, you'll be just fine. You'll see."

"Think if I chase Thomas down I'll find a better envelope in his truck? Ideally one with a signing bonus?" I groan lightly and hang my head.

"Maybe Santa will leave something nice under the tree?" Mom says, wrapping her arm around me and giving me a squeeze. "Now, can we put this—very justified—meltdown on hold? At least until the candy canes are finished?"

I nod, sullen. "My candy cane should read, "Tis the Season to Lower Your Expectations!'"

I'm still holding the holiday card. "What should I do with this?"

"I was thinking of starting a fire," Mom replies with a wink. I hand her the card as Dad calls out, "Pancakes are ready!" from the kitchen.

Amelia barrels down the stairs and into the living room. "Family . . . my cue-card vows are missing. *This is not a drill.*"

I've never seen my sister so disheveled and so disorganized. My first thought is, *Well, when you decide to get married with only a week to plan, what do you expect?* But then I remember the happy secret she's keeping, and I feel a bloom of sympathy for her.

"Where did you last see them?" I ask, keeping my voice calm.

"Last night. There." She points to the overstuffed easy chair closest to the Christmas tree. I check under the chair, slide my hands down the sides of the cushions, but come up empty.

"What if I can't find them?" Amelia moans.

"Are these the ones you practiced for us five times last night?" Dad, the fuss drawing him out of the kitchen, says. "You've memorized them, haven't you, kiddo?"

"That's not the point!" Amelia's close to tears.

"Mila, sweetheart, Dad made pancakes." Mom takes her hand. "Let's get something to eat, and then we'll attack this problem head-on."

"Is there apple cider?" Amelia asks, letting Mom lead her into the kitchen.

"Of course," Dad says, then adds, "I'm sure your sister will get you a mug, right, Libby?"

"Happy to," I reply, ladling some from the simmering pot on the stove. It's fragrant with cloves and cinnamon sticks and dried orange slices that bob on the surface, the way Dad has always made it. I set the steaming mug in front of my sister's seat, whispering, "I'm sorry I can't spike it."

"Moi aussi," Amelia replies as she sits down. An odd look comes over her face, and she stands again, sticking her hand in her robe's pocket.

"What?" I ask. Her expression is sheepish as she bites her bottom lip. She pulls the stack of cue cards, clipped neatly together with a rose-gold paper clip, from her pocket.

"See? Everything always works out," Mom says, but she looks at me as she says it. "One thing at a time. Starting with Dad's pancakes and too much syrup, because—"

"*We elves try to stick to the four main food groups: candy, candy canes, candy corn, and syrup,*" Amelia and I quote the movie *Elf* together, before laughing and then tucking into our breakfast.

Almost two hours later, I'm sitting alone in one of Season's Eatings' two-person booths, having given the excuse that I need to catch up on work emails. Instead, I'm ruminating about my recent bad news, pushing a bite of sausage around my syrup-laden plate and staring blankly at my inbox, when I hear "Waffle for your thoughts?"

Liam, in his BEST MAN T-shirt over a navy sweatshirt and jeans, extends a plate with a heart-shaped waffle my way. His look is teasing—eyebrows raised, dimples at midstrength with the restrained smile, head cocked to the side—but there's warmth to his tone, which suggests legitimate interest in the answer.

"They aren't worth the waffle," I reply, setting my phone down and giving a crooked smile. "But I appreciate the offer."

"Mind if I sit?" he asks, and I say, "Please do." Taking the seat across from me, Liam sets the plate between us. "In case you change your mind."

I nod, my polite smile fading as I continue pushing the sausage around with no intention of eating it. "Thanks, but this is my second breakfast, so the waffle's all yours."

"Ah, I'm not a waffle person," Liam replies. "Actually, I'm not a breakfast-food person. Period."

"Really?" I set my cutlery down, wipe my sticky hands with a napkin. "How come? Is it a time-restricted-eating thing?"

He laughs at this. "No, I like breakfast, just not typical breakfast food."

"Pancakes?" I ask. He shakes his head. "A nice granola and yogurt parfait?" Another shake of his head. "Eggs benedict?"

Liam scrunches his nose and whispers, "Can't do eggs."

So, not perfect after all, I think, oddly pleased to have discovered this flaw, however tiny.

"What about bacon?" I ask. "Everyone loves bacon."

"You remember Mary Piggins, right?" He winks. *Right*. Bacon comes from pigs. I cringe, offering an apology for my cluelessness.

"Don't be sorry. I used to eat bacon, so I know it's delicious."

I lean in, whispering animatedly, "It *is* delicious."

"That's better," he says. When I give a questioning look, he adds, "A legit smile. Which means whatever's got you skipping second breakfast isn't too dire."

"Oh, I wouldn't be so sure." I laugh, but it's mirthless. "Turns out I don't have a job to go back to. Happy holidays to me!"

"Ouch. I'm guessing this wasn't your choice?" he asks, leaning back against the red vinyl bench.

"No, it wasn't. Well, that's not quite true. I gave notice at my hospital, because I thought I was getting an attending position at another one. And then I got a Christmas card this morning with a lovely, festive letter telling me they've gone 'in another direction.'" I use air quotes and attempt a follow-up joke about being on Santa's naughty list, but it falls flat.

"They sent it in a Christmas card? That's shitty."

"I know! Like, 'Merry Christmas! Also, you're unemployed. Hope you enjoy the fruitcake!'" I say.

"I do love a good fruitcake." Liam starts laughing and shaking his head, and again I give him a quizzical look. "So remember when I picked you up, and you noted my, *ahem*, grumpiness?"

"I do."

"Well, right before I left my place that afternoon I received my own Merry-Christmas-slash-let-me-ruin-your-holidays card." Liam's fiddling with the cutlery at his place setting, aligning the knife up against the fork.

"Oh yeah? Who ruined Christmas for you this year?"

"An old friend whom I haven't spoken to in ages. Actually, a friend of my ex's." He sighs, though his smile remains intact. "Wishing us happy holidays and a congratulations on our wedding."

I stare at him, trying to piece it together. "Your . . . wedding?"

"Apparently my ex got married recently. My ex, who said she never wanted to get married, which was one of the main reasons things ended between us. And I guess this friend had her old address—my *current* address—and decided to pop a nice holiday card into the mail."

"Oh no!" I press my fingers to my mouth, crinkling my eyes in sympathy. "That might be worse."

"Nah, I think it's a tie," Liam says, and I laugh. "Now, tell me, Dr. Libby—what's the weirdest thing you've ever seen in the emergency room? I've got a strong stomach, unless I'm the injured one. Bonus points if the story involves heart-shaped waffles."

A burst of laughter ripples from one of the other tables.

Amelia's retelling the story of her morning meltdown and lost cue cards—she's animated, and quick-witted, like Mom—and it has everyone in stitches. I glance at her, radiant and glowing in a way that only someone in love can be, and then back at Liam.

"Nothing waffle-related," I say. "But give me a minute. There's a lot to choose from."

"Take your time," he says, his green and gold eyes holding mine. "We've got all day."

It's such a simple statement, but it hits me hard. I don't have a job pulling me back to the city. I don't have an urgent reason to rush away, once the wedding is behind us. For the first time in a long time, I feel untethered. Not lost, like I might have imagined, considering all the factors, but like this is exactly where I'm supposed to be.

9

Later that evening . . .

*E*verything is perfect.

This thought is, at first, met with relief. Somehow, in only three days' time, we've managed to pull off the wedding of my sister's dreams. It's a chilly evening, the way most evenings are here in December. The air holds the scent of coming snow, which forecasters have predicted will happen tonight. Three days before Christmas, so not a moment too soon for the impatient residents of Harmony Hills, for whom the holidays won't feel magical until the ground is thickly blanketed with the fluffy white stuff.

I glance over at Amelia, who's standing beside me. Her white dress glows iridescent, thanks to the moon's ambient lighting. "You look beautiful," I whisper.

"Thanks, Sissy," she replies in a hushed tone, smiling easily. Serene and calm—the opposite of how she was this morning, and how I'm feeling right now.

My left eye twitches, like it has been doing on and off since the letter arrived. The one letting me know I'm currently unemployed. I was hopeful the pre-ceremony "signature cocktail"—bourbon-spiked eggnog, which I don't enjoy but managed to choke down because: *alcohol*—would relax me and the tiny muscles around my eye. Two eggnogs later I'm full, nauseated from the sugary creaminess, and my left eye remains twitch-happy.

Mom and Dad are in the first row of guests, beside the Livery-Quinn family, and holding hands while Dad clearly fights back tears. A thrum of worry courses through me, which has as much to do with my sudden unemployment as it does my parents' clinic. My already-tenuous smile dims, thinking about my brief conversation with Mom after breakfast number two, when I enquired about the practice.

"It's business as usual, Libby—lots of work, very rewarding. Now let's focus on your sister and her big day, okay?" Mom said, telling me it was *case closed* on that conversation, at least for now.

I sense a shift beside me, as Amelia leans closer to her soon-to-be wife. She puts up a hand, whispers something to Beckett, who first nods, then grins before tipping her head back and laughing quietly, but enthusiastically. Beckett's dark brown hair is styled sleekly to her collarbones, the strands pin-straight, and her lips are painted a gorgeous red hue. The whole effect is stunning and classy, especially paired with Beckett's wedding outfit: white, wide-legged pants and a matching cropped wool jacket, adorned with shimmering gold buttons and a high neck. Once Beckett stops laughing, she presses the side of her head against Amelia's, and they clutch each other's hand, beaming smiles on their faces. It's as though they are the only two people here, completely lost in each other.

Liam, who's standing beside Beckett and Chase, the other "bridesman," looks my way, and I notice tears shining in his eyes. I pull a tissue from my coat pocket and hold it up, mouthing, "Need this?" He chuckles gently, nods, and reaches behind Beckett's back as I reach behind Amelia's to hand it to him. Our fingers touch, and he gives my hand a gentle squeeze.

"Thanks," he whispers, then he makes an animated face and mouths the words *too soft* as he points to himself. I hide a laugh behind my gloved hand. I've never met someone like Liam, who's so easily open and unapologetic about it. It's inspiring and, in his case, sexy as hell. Even if he's not a fan of breakfast foods.

A moment later the tree-lighting ceremony begins, a cacophony of voices echoing through the square as the wedding guests join in. "Twelve! Eleven! Ten! Nine! . . ."

A countdown starting at ten may be more common, but it has always been twelve in Harmony Hills, as a nod to "The Twelve Days of Christmas." Yet another quirk of this holiday-obsessed town. I add my voice to the mix, allowing the merriment of the moment to engulf me. We're facing the massive town-square evergreen, anticipating the lights illuminating only seconds from now. Suddenly, it begins snowing—the first few flakes falling as the crowd chants, "Four!"

There's a brief pause in the countdown, to allow for the surprised gasps that *finally* the first snowfall of the season is upon us. Liam and I lock eyes again, both of us grinning with the delight of it. A moment later the countdown continues. "Three! Two! One!"

The tree's lights illuminate, highlighting the rows of tinsel and garland, its branches dripping with ornaments. The falling snow begins sticking to our hair, our coats, the cobblestones under our feet.

"Harmony Hills, you know what this means . . . It's time to make a wish, and get ready for it to come true!" The voice that comes through the speakers set up on either side of the tree belongs to the wedding officiant, who also happens to be Beckett and Chase's dad, Charles. A mostly retired veterinarian—Beckett took over her dad's practice a year ago—he's holding a microphone and standing on the platform set up for the ceremony.

Amelia turns to give me a wide-eyed look. She reminds me of her six-year-old self now, full of wonder and unabashed delight.

"Can you even believe this is happening?" she asks. "Wish time, Libby." Then she closes her eyes and tilts her face up into the falling snow.

My eggnog-drenched brain isn't grasping the moment's significance, so I don't immediately close my eyes. Then Charles begins the rhyme as familiar as any other from my childhood.

"Gather 'round, young and old,
A wondrous sight, a tale to be told.
With sparkling lights and branches green,
A special wish for a festive scene.
As snowflakes fall on this glorious night,
Close your eyes; close them tight.
If you believe, just wait and see
What magic comes from the Christmas tree!"

"Libby, close your eyes," Amelia hisses. She gives me an impatient nod of her head.

I squeeze my eyes shut, but my mind is blank. *Make a wish, Elizabeth* ... I scrunch my eyes tighter, but my attempt to focus is interrupted by a loud grunt, immediately followed by Liam's voice. "Stay!"

My eyes pop open. I catch a glimpse of a sand-coloured mohawk braided with silver ribbon, attached to a rotund body covered in a red cable-knit pet sweater that reads HAPPY HOLIDAYS, HOLD THE BACON. As Mary Piggins races past me in her sweater, I feel guilty about the bacon I enjoyed this morning. Liam, about two feet behind Mary, is attempting to grab the leash that drags behind the quick-moving pig.

Mary runs in circles between guests, remarkably nimble for her shape, and continues to evade capture. She snorts exuberantly, digging her snout into the snow like she's shoveling a path through it. *Happy as a pig in . . . snow?* Liam has recruited help, including the brides and many of the adult guests. He's giving instructions to form a large circle around the snow-frolicking potbellied pig.

But then Amelia's long dress suddenly catches on the stone, and it's clear she's going to fall. She's off-balance and steps farther onto the hem, her feet tangling under her. Her mouth forms an *O*, and there's a split second of panic on her face as she tries to stop herself from going down.

"Be careful, Amelia! The baby!" The words are out so fast, and I can't reel them back in.

Elizabeth Mae Munro . . . What. Have. You. Done?

Everyone looks at me, then in unison heads whip towards Amelia, who has stayed on her feet, thanks to Beckett's quick reflexes. "Disaster averted!" Becks kisses Amelia's cheek, still holding her around the waist. The crowd lets out a collective sigh of relief, and then one little voice rings out. "Miss Munro, where's the baby? Is it okay?"

It's a young girl, I presume a student from Amelia's class. Her mouth is turned down into a frown, and her eyes are wide. Amelia reaches out to hold the girl's hands, before crouching to be at her level. "The baby is fine, Melodie."

She smiles then, and looks around at the guests—her neighbours, students, friends, and family. The entire town of Harmony Hills, plus me. "I'm pregnant, everyone. Becks and I are having a baby. Surprise!"

The cheer that goes up is epic—it's as heartwarming as a scene right out of a feel-good holiday movie. I'm about to join in the congratulatory hugs when something slams into me from the side.

My feet are knocked out from under me, and I hit the cobblestone stomach first, followed by a good knock to my forehead.

There's a ringing in my ears, and I can't breathe. Despite understanding what's happening (*phrenospasm*, or what we call "getting the wind knocked out of you"), panic courses through me. I roll over to lie on my back. My diaphragm spasms from the hit, and my lungs refuse to fill. It's like a vacuum has sucked all the air out of my body; it feels like I'm dying.

I slap my hands against my chest to encourage my lungs to inflate. Just then a face moves in and out of focus, hovering over me. Worried green eyes that are *so very* green—like mistletoe leaves—scan from the top of my head to my hands, which he reaches for and holds tightly. While he's handsome as ever, he also looks oh-so-serious. No sign of those glorious dimples.

"Libby! Can you hear me?" Liam kneels next to me in the fresh snow. I want to answer him but still can't speak.

"Don't move, okay? I've got you," he says, sounding breathless himself as he takes off his gloves, doubling them up to set under my head. He touches my forehead, his fingers gentle as he cringes.

"You're going to have a goose egg, but at least the skin isn't broken."

If I could speak, I would tell him a head contusion can be more serious than a laceration. His gloves are soft against the hard cobblestone, and I try to thank him. All that comes out is a wheezing sound, which makes the corners of his mouth turn down more. I miss the dimples.

"That's it. Try to relax," he says, as I finally take in a ragged breath. "I used to play rugby and have had the wind knocked out of me so many times. It always comes back."

He smiles now, and the dimples reveal themselves again. Liam's black wool coat is dusted with snowflakes, as is his thick, wavy hair. The lights from the town square Christmas tree create a halo effect behind him, making the snowflakes on his shoulders and crown of his head glimmer.

A crowd has gathered around us. I'm mortified and can't believe the ruckus I've caused at Amelia's beautiful wedding—first with my unfortunate outburst about the baby, and then with the knocked-off-my-feet drama.

Mom has her doctor hat on, and I respond to her questions as best I can. "Do you have pain anywhere besides your head?" *No.* "Can you feel your fingers and toes?" I wiggle them. *Yes.* "Do you know what day it is?" *December twenty-second.*

Finally, I'm able to sit up, with Liam and Mom's help, but I'm lightheaded. "Too dizzy," I mumble, and then see Liam's lips moving while Mom snaps her fingers in front of my face. I can't hear what Liam's saying, and while I see Mom's fingers snapping, there is no sound except for a loud ringing in my ears. Maybe I *am* dying?

A moment before I pass out, I have three clear thoughts:

First, *How is this the second time in nearly as many days that this pig has taken me out, in front of this guy?*

Then, *Speaking of . . . could he be any more gorgeous? (No, he could not.)*

Finally, *I wish I could erase the last five minutes, oh, and while we're at it, maybe the past year of my life . . .*

10

I wake up to an elbow jutting into my nose. Shock registers first, then searing pain. My eyes instantly start watering.

"Ouch!" I cup my tender nose with one hand, the other reaching out blindly in the dark room. It connects with something solid.

"What are you doing?" The voice is gravelly—sleepy, though irritable—and belongs to my sister. Why Amelia's annoyed is beyond me. I just took an elbow to the face!

"What am *I* doing?" I reach to turn on the bedside lamp, but all I find is emptiness. I shift closer to the edge of the bed, straining to find the lamp. A moment later I'm half lying on the floor, my legs and feet tangled up in the sheets.

A light snaps on, and I blink against the brightness. Amelia's on her stomach on the bed, peering at me over its edge. "Are you okay?" She bites her lip, a telltale sign she's holding back laughter. When I close my eyes and groan lightly, her tone changes. "Seriously, are you okay, Libby?"

It's then I hear "Let It Snow!"—the tune mechanical, music box–like—and I'm not sure where it's coming from. But then everything slows down, the way it does when you experience déjà vu.

That's the Christmas lamp.

I kick at the sheets entangling my feet before getting to my knees. On the other side of the bed is the illuminated, music-playing table lamp Amelia clicked on. It's made to look like an old-fashioned candy-cane-striped lamppost, with a faux candle inside and swirling snowflakes. It's playing the Christmas carol on a loop, and familiarity washes over me again.

"Where did that come from?" I ask Amelia.

She frowns, following my gaze. Her hair is in a messy bun atop her head, a satin scrunchie trying its best to keep the blond curls from falling out. It looks different, her hair, but I can't sort out why.

"The lamp? Mom, if I had to guess," she replies.

I take in the rest of the room, now understanding why I couldn't find the lamp's switch when I reached out. The bedside table it sits on, and everything else in the room, is in the wrong place. We're in Amelia's childhood bedroom. Our rooms are side by side, and mirror opposites.

"Did she buy a new one?" I walk over to the lamp. There's a price tag from Everhart's on its base. I scour the lamppost, looking for signs the ceramic has been Krazy Glued back together, but there's no damage. It's in perfect condition, nary a fleck of chipped paint or cracked ceramic.

"I don't think so . . ." Amelia watches me warily from the end of the bed. "What's wrong with you? Did you hit your head when you fell out of bed?"

"I *did* hit my head." I run fingers across my forehead, where the goose-egg lump should be. "After Mary Piggins ran around . . ."

My voice trails because there is no bump, nor can I find any point of soreness. Either I'm a super healer, or . . . *Or what, Elizabeth?*

"Mary Piggins?" Amelia asks. "What does that have to do with hitting your head?"

"I don't . . . What?" I reply, confused by her questions. The way Amelia looks at me—part incredulous, part anxious—is making me nervous.

"What do you mean, 'what'?" Her frown deepens. "Did something happen last night?"

Did something happen last night? My frown matches her. "You were there . . . though maybe you didn't see it? There was a lot going on. With the snow. And the tree lighting."

"Tree lighting . . . okay, you're clearly not fine," she replies, her voice going up an octave. "Maybe this is some vomiting-induced memory loss? Something to do with electrolytes?"

"Electrolytes?" *Vomiting-induced memory loss?* I scan my body. I feel fine. Normal, except for my racing heart and acute confusion.

Music-playing lamp still in hand, I pause to take a few deep breaths. The last thing I remember is the tree lighting ceremony, and Mary Piggins getting loose in the excitement of the snowfall, and then barrelling into me, and Amelia was about to get—

I spin towards her. "Why are you here with me, and not with Beckett?"

"Beckett Livery-Quinn? Why would I be with Beckett?" Her fingers tap against her tightly crossed arms. "And technically, you're here with *me*—this is my room. You upchucked all over your bed. Super dégoutant, d'ailleurs, Libby. Translation: super disgusting, by the way, Libby."

"Do I have the flu?" Upon reassessment, my head throbs mildly, but when I place a palm to my cheek, the skin is cool. Plus, my stomach is fine. No body aches. I may not be sick, but something is off here. *Very off.*

"Not the flu. Food poisoning. Bad sandwich, you said."

"Food poisoning . . ." Yes, right. I *did* come home with food poisoning. "But that was days ago. Before the wedding. I'm fine now."

Amelia's mouth drops open. "Wedding? Whose wedding?"

The words *your wedding* are preparing to come out, but I hold them back. I don't understand what's happening, but I have the sense that this is not the thing to say.

When I don't respond, Amelia gives a curt nod. "I'm getting our parents. They can deal with this," she says, before leaving her bedroom. I stay where I am and try to get ahold of myself. My breaths are shallow. My vision narrows, and I set the lamp down and sit on the bed.

"What is going on here?" I say out loud. Why does everything feel . . . off-kilter? Why was Amelia so weird when I brought up her wedding, and Beckett, for that matter? Did something happen after Mary Piggins knocked me off my feet last night? I can't make sense of anything.

"Let It Snow!" continues playing, and the sound of it grates on my last nerve. As I reach to turn off the lamp, I overshoot and knock it sideways. I try to grab it, but I'm not quick enough. I curse when I hear the sounds of ceramic breaking. Then curse again with panic when it dawns on me that this also happened *last year.*

See, this lamp made an appearance last Christmas, when I came home for those couple of days to check in on Mom after her ankle fracture. The lamppost did crack in half, but I wasn't the one who broke it . . . *Amelia did.* We were discussing how Mom and Dad should renovate our museum-like bedrooms, since it had been years since we left home.

"Turn them into a gym, or a reading room, or at the very least take down our teenage-crush posters and other paraphernalia so they can become guest rooms," I said, and Amelia laughed before replying, "Speak for yourself, Sissy. I still like seeing Bif Naked on my bedroom wall."

Mom's latest Christmas acquisition—the lamp I just broke— was on Amelia's nightstand, and we debated making it "disappear." With its relentless one-bar holiday song playing every time you turned it on (with no way to have light without the music), it was getting tedious.

Amelia picked up the lamp to pretend-smash it to the ground, but it slipped from her fingers and crashed to the floor. We stared at each other for a full five seconds, eyes wide the way only two sisters who just did something their mother would not be happy about can look. We confessed to Mom the lamp was "accidentally" dropped, and Amelia and I spent the afternoon meticulously Krazy Gluing the broken pieces back together.

So how could I have broken it again? The only explanation is that Mom replaced it, and this was a brand-new one. I'm staring at the lamp's ceramic base, cracked in half, when another Christmas carol begins playing. It takes me a few seconds to recognize the tune, but then I hear it: "White Christmas." Coming from my cell phone, resting on the windowsill.

The screen is lit up with an incoming call. But I never changed my ringtone, preferring the standard one that mimics an old-fashioned corded telephone. So why is my phone playing "White Christmas"? I wish Amelia would get back up here. I have a lot of questions.

Taking my still-ringing phone from the windowsill, I unplug the charging cord and glance at the screen: Austin 💜

I stop breathing, but my heart beats faster.

Should I answer it? Let it go to voicemail?

"Calm down, Elizabeth. *Calm down.*"

It doesn't work—I am decidedly less calm, if that's possible, and the only thing running through my mind is, *Why on earth is my ex-boyfriend calling me?*

11

"Hello?" My voice cracks, and the room spins. I clutch the duvet under me in a tight fist, trying to anchor my body and stay upright.

"Hey, babe, I wanted to catch you before surgery." He sounds just like Austin—baritone voice, smooth and confident.

"Austin?" My stomach flips. I'm not sick, but I could throw up right now.

"Is there someone else who calls you 'babe'?" His voice is teasing, and I can picture him: leaning against the wall outside the surgical suite, phone tucked into his neck and his strong biceps stretching his scrub T-shirt (his name and credentials, DR. AUSTIN WHITMORE, MD, MSC, FRCSC, PLASTICS & RECONSTRUCTION, embroidered above the chest pocket), as he crosses his arms over his chest. Dirty-blond hair cut close, chiseled jaw, blue eyes. He's a winker, too, and while that can be off-putting from the wrong person, I always found it endearing. He winks when he makes a joke, and I imagine he's doing it now even though I can't see him.

"You sound rough, babe," Austin says. "You okay?"

"I"—*I don't understand what is happening* is what I want to say, but instead finish with—"have food poisoning." My voice is weak, so it should be an easy-to-believe lie.

"Ah, babe, I'm sorry to hear that. You staying hydrated?" Austin replies. "So what got you this time?"

"Hydrated. Yes." There's a half-empty bottle of orange electrolyte-infused water on the bedside table. "A bad sandwich at a gas station, apparently."

He chuckles then. "You and your snacks. Well, I hope the worst is over. Need you all better for our trip."

Our trip? The one we took *last freaking Christmas*? "Right. Our trip. Uh ... when is that again?" We flew out last year on December twenty-second.

"Ha ha. Funny girl." Austin's tone is warm, which is confusing as well, because we are decidedly not warm with each other these days. In fact, we haven't spoken in months, unless you count a couple of tense but polite hallway hellos.

"Seriously, how many days until we leave?" My tone is not warm, sharpened by my impatience.

The briefest of pauses, then, "You *must* be sick. How high is your fever? The trip is all you've been talking about for weeks."

At this I frown, annoyed by this version of things. If anything, it was Austin who wouldn't stop talking about the trip ... which now I know had less to do with our spending vacation time together and more about the job he was courting.

"It's obviously the food poisoning. I'm not even sure what day it is today." I let out a quick laugh, which is forced, but hopefully effective. I need him to answer the question.

"Poor baby," Austin says, and I wrinkle my nose at this overly sweet tone. "It's December fourteenth. So just over a week until our flight."

Today's December 14? But I wasn't home last year on December 14. I didn't come home until after Mom had her fall, which happened on December 16.

My body goes numb, as the memory of this call with Austin suddenly lands in my mind. *We've already had this conversation.* Or a version of it. Because last year when we spoke I was not sick, did not wake up in Amelia's bed, did not have to ask what day it was or when we were leaving on our trip.

After my mom fell and broke her ankle, I raced home like the overbearing doctor daughter of a doctor that I am. Doctors make the worst patients, and I knew Dad would need help reining Mom in for her recovery. Initially, we thought she'd need surgery, but conservative care was deemed a reasonable option. I stayed in Harmony Hills for a couple of days to help get things in order, and then booted it back to Toronto in time to hop the plane to L.A. with Austin. *What's happening?* I press my hands against my temples and rub hard, as though that might fix the swirling confusion.

It was Amelia who broke the lamp that I just knocked off the table. I didn't have food poisoning last year, because I didn't stop for food, in my rush to get to Harmony Hills. When Austin called to check in, on December 18, I was happy to hear from him. Impatient to leave Harmony Hills, since Mom was doing fine, and anxious to get back to Toronto and to him. Excited about the trip that proved to be hugely disappointing.

"Be right there," Austin says now in what I recognize as his surgeon voice: more commanding, yet with smooth confidence. Probably talking to a surgical nurse, who has been sent to deliver the message that the patient is ready for him. "Do you need anything?"

When I don't immediately answer, because I think he's still talking to this other person, he says, "Babe? You there?"

"I'm here!" It comes out high-pitched. "I'm good. Or at least I don't think—"

"I have to run, babe," he interrupts. He sure calls me "babe" a lot . . . I didn't notice that before. "You keep those electrolytes up, okay? I'll call you after I'm done—a few hours, max."

"Okay . . . yeah. That sounds good," I reply, still reeling from the fact I'm speaking to my ex, but it's as though we never broke up. The discombobulation is extreme, and I clutch my phone to my ear. "Hope surgery goes well."

"Thanks, babe. Love you," he replies.

"Love you, too," I say, out of habit. The words feel strange now, like I'm speaking a foreign language.

After Austin hangs up, I turn, slowly, towards the bedroom door. It's open from when Amelia left, and so I half close it to look at myself in the hanging full-length mirror.

I look the same. Wait, no, I don't.

I'm wearing pyjamas I don't immediately recognize, and wonder if they're Amelia's. My nails are painted, and it's clearly a professional job. I'm an infrequent nail salon patron, because my hands take a beating in the emergency room, so it's generally a waste of money. But I had my nails done before our trip last year, choosing a colour called Napa Valley Red because it felt both holiday-like and California-themed.

My nails aren't Napa Valley Red now. They're plum-coloured, the tips lightly dusted with white shimmer. I hold up my hands, staring at my nails. *When did this happen?*

Staring back into the mirror, I also see that my hair is long. Well past my shoulders. This is my pre-breakup hair. It's *last* December's hair.

Okay, Elizabeth, think this through.

I should have awoken to December 23, *this year*.

The day after Amelia's wedding. Austin and I ended our relationship months ago. I've been gently flirting—yes, let's call it what it is—for days with Liam Young, the handsome stranger who cries at commercials and weddings, doesn't like waffles, and has the sexiest dimples. I'm newly and unfortunately unemployed; Mom's ankle is fine; and Amelia is pregnant and should be celebrating her first day as a newlywed.

At least that's what life looked like moments before Mary Piggins knocked me down, perhaps causing a head injury and the creation of this alternate reality. I whip off my sock to look at my toe. It should be buddy-taped, broken after Mary stepped on it . . . except it isn't. My baby toe appears as it did *before* Mary Piggins stomped on it at the memorial service. There's no bruise, zero swelling, no tape. I wiggle it—no pain.

My eyes shift to my phone. I'm holding it so tightly my fingers cramp. Touching the screen to wake it up, I take in the date illuminated front and centre (December 14). Despite Austin's confirmation, and my seeing it for myself, my mind still refuses to accept it.

"Make it make sense," I murmur, staring at my phone. "*Make it make sense, Elizabeth.*"

With shaking fingers I open my photos, checking the last picture. Me and Helena, at the hospital's Christmas party, which she did *not* attend this year because she was out of town, visiting her brother. Then I open my text inbox, looking at the top message. From Amelia, dated yesterday: "Can't wait for you to get home! THIS IS NOT A DRILL :)"

Finally, opening my calendar, I touch the Today button. My racing heart pounds in my ears. Yep. It's December 14. *Of last year.*

"This is not a drill," I whisper, choking on the words. I stare into the mirror. "This is *not a drill.*"

12

December 14, Christmas Past

I take the stairs slowly, clutching the holly-berry-garland-wrapped handrail. I'm out of breath, my thoughts frantic. *You hit your head, because someone—okay, Amelia—invited a potbellied pig to a wedding. You're unconscious. None of this is real. You have not travelled to an alternate reality, nor have you gone back in time. It's a fabrication of your mind, filling in the blanks because, again, you hit your head. You're unconscious. None of this is real. You have not travelled back in time...*

I murmur, "There's an explanation for everything. Even for this. Whatever *this* is."

"Is that you, Libby?" Mom's voice rings out. Stepping into the living room, I find my mom seated on the couch, her socked feet resting on an embroidered Santa Claus pillow on the coffee table. She's been reading, as evidenced by the book nesting in her lap. She pulls her glasses to the end of her nose and looks my way. The television is on in the background—Mom likes to multitask.

"What are you watching?" I ask.

"What am I watching?" Mom tilts her head, purses her lips. Her "Doc Munro" look—she's evaluating me, and I'm antsy under her gaze.

Chuckling nervously, I glance back at the television. "Kidding. Obviously, it's *Elf*. Which I've seen no fewer than a hundred times."

"For a moment there I wondered if you were sleepwalking," Mom says, tipping the readers atop her head.

"Ha ha, nope! Wide awake." My jaw hurts from my forced smile. Then I gesture towards the stairs, my arm moving somewhat wildly. "Also, sorry, but I broke a lamp. The Christmas one, that plays music? Do you have Krazy Glue?"

Mom raises her eyebrows at my frenetic pace, but before she can respond Amelia and Dad walk in. They're also wearing pyjamas—the same pattern—and when I look down, and then over at Mom, I notice we're in matching sets. *Of course.* The Munro holiday tradition of wearing family Christmas pjs, which begins the moment we're all under the same roof.

At first I don't recognize the pattern, which features melting snowmen against the soft flannel, and a matching long-sleeved jersey top. But then I remember these are *last year's* family pyjamas. Wrapped under the tree when I got home, with a tag in Mom's handwriting that read "Dearest Libby—Wishing You a Festive Meltdown!"

Except with all the chaos of Mom's injury, and my very brief trip home, I didn't open the present until after Austin and I got back from L.A. The pyjamas ended up stuffed into the back of a drawer in my Toronto apartment, never worn. And yet, somehow, here I am wearing them.

"Libby! There you are. Was just about to come up and check on you." Dad's wearing an apron over his pyjamas, and has two mugs in hand. The apron reads WE WHISK YOU A MERRY CHRISTMAS, and I would chuckle at the pun if I wasn't so freaked out.

He takes a sip from one of the mugs, and the smell of freshly brewed coffee hits my nose. I need caffeine and sugar in my system, STAT. He holds up the other mug. "Made you some flat ginger ale."

Well, at least it will take care of the sugar craving. "Thanks, Dad."

"How are you feeling now, honey?" Mom asks.

Confused? Alarmed? Having an existential crisis, thanks for asking?

"Weird. Really weird." My voice cracks, and my smile fades.

Amelia's looking at me as though my head is about to spin around, and Mom nibbles the arm of her glasses as she exchanges a glance with Dad. He sets the mugs down, as Amelia murmurs, "See? I told you something's up."

"Libby, let's sit." Dad leads me over to one of the overstuffed chairs across from the couch. I sink into the plush cushions, but my body won't relax. I'm wringing my hands, and then shove them under my thighs to hide my discomfort.

Dad crouches beside the chair, leaning on the armrest. His expression is neutral—no smile but also no frown; no worry lines between his eyes, the same colour as my own—as he checks my pulse. "A bit quick, but you're likely dehydrated. Let's give that ginger ale a try, eh?"

I nod, and take a small sip from the mug Dad hands me.

"What happened?" I ask, in my head adding, *Any idea how I travelled back in time to last Christmas? Anyone?*

"You ate a bad sandwich on the drive home, had severe emesis for a few hours, and woke up in a bit of a fuddle, it seems." Mom puts her book on the couch beside her. It's by her favourite horror writer, the cover black with bloodred slashes across it. I almost laugh—reading gory horror while watching the Christmas movie *Elf* . . . a tableau of contrasts.

"Bad sandwich," I say, mostly to myself. I'm running through

possible food-borne pathogens that might explain how I've hallucinated being a time traveller, but nothing comes to mind.

"I'd say this is more than a 'fuddle,'" Amelia says with a harsh
laugh. "Nutty as a fruitcake, is more like it. She was going on about
Mary Piggins, and some wedding?"

I gently tug my wrist out of Dad's hand. "Whatever it was, I feel
fine now."

At least physically, that's true. I lean forward and set the mug on
the coffee table, next to the embroidered pillow. Mom's legs cover
half of Santa's face, but one eye is visible. He's winking deeply,
crinkling the corner of his eye above a rosy full cheek, as though
he's in on the joke.

A thought bubbles to the surface . . . maybe this is a joke? I
wouldn't put it past them, especially Mom. She has a wicked sense
of humour and likes a good practical joke. A wave of relief moves
through me, and I stand and clap my hands together. "I don't know
how you pulled this off—changed my calendar, even—but good
one. You got me!"

I stare at my family, smiling, waiting for them to admit to my
joke theory. No one says anything. Buddy proclaims in the background, "I just like to smile. Smiling is my favourite!" As the quiet
stretches, I realize it's too much of a reach. A joke doesn't explain
how my hair is long again. Or how my nails are a colour I have
never before chosen at the salon. Or why my ex-boyfriend called
me, acting as though we never broke up.

"No one's messing with you, Libby," Mom says. Dad and Amelia
shake their heads.

"Oh, okay. Forget I said anything." I need some air. To escape
this living room, decorated floor to ceiling with Christmas merriment, and get away from my family's watchful gaze. "I think I'll
take a walk."

At my announcement Amelia throws her hands up in the air and mutters, "Doctors are the worst." Mom nods and says, "That's true," as Dad, who is closest to me, gives me a side hug. While other parents might say "Back to bed, young lady" after a bout of food poisoning—even when you're a full-grown adult—being a doctor's child means a blasé reaction to most illness and injury.

"Fresh air can do wonders," Dad says, proving the point.

"What if Libby hit her head when she fell out of the bed and has some sort of brain bleed?" Amelia looks between us, clearly agitated by how laid-back our parents are acting. "Do we all remember my wrist?"

When Amelia was eight she broke the scaphoid bone in her wrist falling off her bike, and it took my parents two weeks to get her an X-ray, despite their youngest's insistence something was wrong.

"Libby does not have a brain bleed, Amelia," Mom says.

"Well, you didn't think my wrist was broken, and it was, so . . ." Amelia replies, shrugging.

"Mila, Mom's right. I don't have a brain bleed," I say, hoping it's the truth.

"Oh, Libby." Mom turns towards me now, snapping her fingers. I remember her snapping her fingers in front of my face last night, before I passed out, and it unsettles me all over again. "Would you pick up a sourdough loaf while you're out? Toast with honey is exactly what the doctor ordered. Need to remind that stomach of yours that its job is to digest food, not reject it."

"Do we think eating anything is a good idea for Miss I Threw Up an Internal Organ Last Night?" Amelia asks. "Remember when you told me 'getting back on the bike is the only way to overcome the fear' after I fell, and then I did, and fell again and broke my wrist?"

"Darling, we've been apologizing for the wrist thing for *years*," Mom replies with a light sigh. But she gives Amelia a generous smile. "Maybe your Christmas present to us this year can be your letting it go?"

"Jamais," Amelia whispers, narrowing her eyes. *Never*—I know that one.

"So just the loaf?" I ask Mom, who follows me to the front door. I look around for my running shoes, a poor choice for the snowy conditions, but I need to get out of here. Frustration boils inside me. *Am I on the naughty list or something?* I think, silently adding in a few choice words. The answer is likely in the "or something."

"Just the loaf. Also, it's minus ten," Mom says. "There's an extra pair of boots in the closet." I see them when I open the closet door to grab my coat. They're black Sorels, fur lining slightly matted, definitely well loved.

"Thanks," I say, then realize I'm not wearing socks. But I'm not going back upstairs. Sockless, it is. I shove my feet into the boots.

When I open the front door, the frigid December air hits me. Mom's right—it's cold out here. My breath catches with the shift between the warm air inside the house and the frosty outdoors.

"Also, they're fully waterproof," Mom adds, as I'm readying to close the door behind me, my coat still undone and laces untied. "In case that ginger ale makes a comeback."

13

Maybe it is a brain bleed, I think, my feet sliding in Mom's boots as I walk. They're a half size too big, even though I've tied the laces as tightly as they go. The no-sock thing isn't helping, and there's something sharp (a decorative pine-cone barb, I learn later when I have to tweeze it out of my skin) that keeps stabbing my left sole. *Is it a coma? A fever-induced dream? One too many glasses of eggnog at the wedding? Or related, a brand-new dairy allergy?*

As a doctor, I make decisions based on evidence, and so I do a lightning-quick evaluation of the current situation. It feels all too real to be a coma-induced dream. I pinch the web of skin between my finger and thumb, and it hurts. I plunge my bare hand into the snow, and it prickles with the cold. I inhale deeply and catch scents of evergreen needles, until the inside of my nose freezes up and the scent fades. I'm definitely *here* … wherever, and whenever, here is. So that moves time travel to the top of the list, however unbelievable.

By the time I reach the town square, I'm no closer to untangling the mess I woke up into. Like, why am I here two days *before* mom's ankle fracture, which was the reason I returned to Harmony Hills last year? Why this date, in particular?

I attempt to recall anything special about December 14, not only last year but in other years past. *Nothing.* My mind is agonizingly blank and useless. I pull out my phone.

"Please be there, please be there," I murmur, and thankfully Helena picks up after one ring.

"Hey, you! How was your trip home?" she asks.

"Trip home was . . . uneventful."

"You sound weird," Helena says. "Are you okay?"

Definitely not okay. "I have food poisoning. I ate a sandwich from the gas station."

There's a sigh on the other end, which is sympathetic but tinged with exasperation. "Elizabeth, how many times do we have to talk about this? *Never eat anything from a gas station that isn't in a package,*" she says.

There's ambient sounds of traffic—horns, sirens, revving car engines—and I know she's outside the hospital, likely finishing her morning coffee before her shift starts. "Actually, never eat anything at a gas station. Maybe that should be the rule? No wiggle room."

"I know. I have a problem." This is not my first bout of road-trip food poisoning, and it likely won't be my last. But also, I have much bigger problems than my less-than-wise food choices.

"Ah, it's part of your charm. I'm sorry you're sick. Is Austin racing there to wipe your fevered brow?" Helena's tone is laced with sarcasm. She is not my ex-boyfriend's biggest fan, hence the quip. Helena, who, unlike Austin, did come by to check on me when I had the flu (she actually signed for his soup delivery), said, "Yes, it's a nice gesture . . . *for a coworker,* not the supposed love of your life."

"He can't make it," I reply now, ignoring Helena's mumbled "Surprise, surprise" reply. I think about how she responded to our breakup, with similar mumbling but with the words *good riddance* tacked on.

"But he's coming, isn't he?" she asks. "Before your trip, for an early Christmas with your family?"

"He can't. Surgeries. You know how it is." I swallow hard. "It's so last minute he can't reschedule anything."

"Surprise, surprise," Helena mutters again, less quietly this time. "That one is horny for surgeries."

I burst out laughing, and the release feels wonderful. A brief respite from whatever this new, inexplicable reality is. "Well, he *is* a surgeon, Helly. Being 'horny for surgery' is a good thing."

"Whatever, you know what I mean," Helena replies, her voice softening. I *do* know what she means. But Austin's lack of bedside manner is irrelevant now. As is how much the soup thing bothered me, even though I've never admitted it out loud.

"I need to ask you something." I sit heavily on a nearby bench and toe at the soft snow on the ground, remembering how last year there was plenty of pre-Christmas snow—a record, actually. More proof that I have in fact travelled back in time, or that I've lost it and hallucinated the end of my relationship, Amelia's wedding, Liam and Mary Piggins . . . I don't know if I want to laugh or cry at the incredulity of this.

"Sure. What's up?" Helena replies.

I pause for a beat, then, "How old is Adelaide?"

A matching pause on the other end before, "How sick *are* you exactly?"

"Please, Helly," I reply, my tone pleading. I'm reminded of my earlier conversation with Austin, and set my head in my hand, closing my eyes. "Just answer the question."

"She's two, Elizabeth, which of course you know because you were at her birthday party *a week ago*. Gave her that super-expensive doll I told you not to buy, but that is now her favourite thing on this planet, remember?"

But in my most recent memory, sweet Adelaide just had her *third* birthday. The doll from last year remains a beloved toy, and this year I gifted her accessories for it, including a plush show horse and an adorable mini–riding outfit for Adelaide. Helena rolled her eyes at this year's gift and nudged me hard with her elbow, whispering, "Thought we were besties; thanks for nothing, Aunt Elizabeth." They lug that doll everywhere they go, including to preschool, the park, even the grocery store. Now Adelaide insists the horse must come along as well.

"I need to tell you something, but don't freak out, okay?"

"I won't freak out," Helena replies, steady-voiced to prove it. "But are you about to tell me you're a spy or something? Is that it? *Are you a spy?*" She mock whispers the last part.

Helena is pragmatic, not prone to melodrama, and I'm positive she can handle anything thrown her way. However, this might be the exception. But I need to say it out loud—to tell someone what's happening. Besides, Helena knows me better than anyone. She *has* to believe me.

"Come on, Elizabeth," Helena continues, impatient with my prolonged silence. "Out with it."

I take a deep breath. "I think I've gone back in time. To *last* December."

"I bet!" Helena laughs. "Isn't that part of the Harmony Hills charm, though? 'It's like Christmas copied and pasted itself,' I think is how you put it."

"No, Helly, I'm serious. Not like, *This Christmas feels like every other Christmas* ... I'm living last Christmas season all over again. Like, *literally over again.*"

"Did your mom give you a pharmaceutical?" Helena asks. She's no longer laughing.

"No! Listen, I know this sounds . . . impossible . . . but something happened last night at Mila and Beckett's wedding, and I—"

"Hold on . . . Amelia's married?! Why didn't you tell me this was happening? Or was it a surprise? Holy shit, that's amazing, if so. Talk about burying the lede!" David, her ex, is a journalist at the *Star*, and she often uses this line.

"That's why I came home—for Amelia's wedding. Except when I woke up this morning, no one knew anything about a wedding. It was like I dreamt it, except I didn't," I reply, growing more agitated. I'm desperate for Helena to believe me, despite how far-fetched this all sounds. I walk back and forth in front of the bench as I try to explain the situation. My pacing creates a deep trough in the snow.

"I'm not following," she replies once I'm done.

"I'm sure I've told you about how we have this tree-lighting ceremony in Harmony Hills, and how if it snows right as the tree lights up, your wish will come true?"

Helena murmurs, "Yes, love that."

"Well, last night, when the tree lit up, it also started snowing— the first snowfall of the holiday season, which is a big deal in Harmony Hills—and Mr. Livery-Quinn—that's Beckett's dad— read the poem about the snowfall and wishes, and then Mary Piggins got loose and knocked me out cold, because I was on the ground one minute and the next waking up in Amelia's bedroom at our parents' house, but it was, or *is*, last Christmas, and nothing is—"

"Elizabeth, stop. Stop speaking." Helena's voice reminds me of how she talks to Adelaide when she needs the toddler to *pay attention, right this minute*.

I stop talking, shaking both from the cold and the burst of

adrenaline in recounting the impossible situation I've found myself in.

"Look, I have no idea what's going on with you—and I absolutely have questions about who Mary Piggins is—but ... I believe
you," Helena says.

"*Thank you.* I can't tell you how relieved I am!" I release
my breath with an audible whoosh. "I knew you'd believe me. I
thought, *Call Helly, she'll know what to do*, and you—"

"Hang on a second, friend. I believe *you believe* this is
happening."

It's like I've swallowed a snowball—my stomach goes ice-cold,
and my relief evaporates. "So wait ... you don't actually believe me?"

"I mean ... *you're a Christmas time traveller back from the future?*" Helena asks. "Would you believe me if I called you with a
similar story?"

I frown, dejected by this truth. "Unlikely."

"How would you respond? If I told you I had travelled through
time?" she asks, her tone gentle but no-nonsense.

Sighing, I reply, "I'd order a head CT, STAT."

"Exactly," Helena says. "So maybe get a head CT, STAT?"

Disappointment fills me, along with a fresh wave of fear, because of course what I'm saying is preposterous. If someone came
into my emergency room with this sort of claim, I would order a
full workup, plus call in a psych consult for good measure.

"You know, it's probably dehydration," I reply, keeping my voice
as steady as possible. "Don't worry about me—I promise I'm fine.
I know you have to get to work."

"I do have to get to work, but I will continue to worry about
you until you tell me you no longer think you've time-travelled,"
Helena says. "Keep me posted, and for the love of all things, get
some fluids in you, okay?"

I promise I will, then end the call. A moment later, it begins snowing. Gigantic, fluffy flakes that stay on your coat long enough to see each flake's unique and intricate pattern. I glance at the evergreen tree beside me, which is already partially decorated for the upcoming tree lighting. The twinkle lights are wrapped around the branches, but of course they haven't been illuminated yet—that tradition is saved for the ceremony.

Well, it's worth a try.

I close my eyes, tilting my head up to the sky, and whisper:

"Gather 'round, young and old,
A wondrous sight, a tale to be told.
With sparkling lights and branches green,
A special wish for a festive scene.
As snowflakes fall on this glorious night,
Close your eyes; close them tight.
If you believe, just wait and see
What magic comes from the Christmas tree!"

I take a breath, eyes still firmly closed, and add, "I wish for everything to be *exactly* as it was at last night's tree-lighting ceremony. The wedding, the snowfall, the—"

But my fervent wish is interrupted by a loud snort. My eyes snap open at the sound and, discombobulated, I lose my balance and fall dramatically into a soft mound of snow under the lowest branches of the evergreen.

14

*S*eriously, not again.

  This is the first thought I have, lying on the ground under the snow-laden branches of the tree, followed by *You obviously have to be MUCH clearer with your wishes, Elizabeth.*

"You okay?"

Looking up at the owner of the deep, drawling voice, I see it's Liam Green Eyes. He's crouched in front of me, cheeks rosy from the cold, his eyes a bright emerald with golden flecks, dark eyebrows raised in concern. One hand lifts a large evergreen bough so it no longer rests on my head. The other holds tightly to a leash, which is attached to none other than Mary Piggins, who's busy snuffling her snout in the snow.

"Liam! Hey, how are you?" I smile, raising a hand in greeting. With the other, I brush snow from the top of my head, off my shoulders. But I hit nearby branches as I do, and more snow tumbles onto me. With a barely audible sigh, I press my lips together, trying to appear as though *everything is just fine*, even though I want to scream "Everything is not fine!"

At my greeting, Liam gives me a curious look, head cocked,

smiling, but not wide enough to turn on the dimples. "Sorry, but have we met?"

My mouth parches at his question. He doesn't know who I am, because Liam and I have never met—at least not in this timeline. The urge to blurt out the truth nearly overtakes me, but if my best friend doesn't believe me, then there's no way Liam could.

"We have *not* met, officially anyway." I hold out my chilly hand to shake his gloved one. "I'm Elizabeth. Elizabeth Munro."

"Ah, Mila's sister, right? The ER physician from Toronto. Doc Munro's oldest daughter," Liam says, dimples engaged with his wide smile.

He doesn't take my outstretched hand, though, because he's still holding the branch up, and also Mary's leash. "How about we get you out from under the tree first?"

"Oh, right. Good idea." I scoot forward until I'm clear of the branch, which he releases, extending his now-freed-up hand. I take it and he pulls me effortlessly to my feet. I notice, as I hold on to his arm, that his bicep flexes when he lifts me. Pretty sure Liam works out—a lot. Also, he smells amazing (*like mulled apple cider*), and I inhale deeply before letting out a small sigh.

"All good?" Liam asks. I'm still clutching his arm, and so quickly release it and take a small step back, nodding. He smiles, then takes off his glove to shake my hand. His grip is warm, and it sends a pleasant jolt through me.

"Nice to meet you, Elizabeth. But I have to ask . . . what was it that gave me away?"

"Gave you away?"

"How did you know who I was?" He's still smiling, expression open and friendly.

Your green eyes, that spectacular head of hair, oh, and probably those knock-me-over-with-a-feather dimples?

"It was . . . the pig," I reply, grateful for a moment of quick thinking. "I suspect you're the only Liam in town with a pet pig?"

He laughs, looking over at Mary, who strains against her leash as she moves to the next patch of snow-covered cobblestone. "That would be absolutely true . . . if Mary Piggins was my pig. I'm just the walker and occasional pet sitter."

Right. In option B—Elizabeth Munro, modern-day Ebenezer Scrooge and Christmas time traveller—Mary belongs to Elsie Farrow.

"Cute pjs." Liam points to my legs, and I look down. Mortified that I forgot to change before I raced out of the house.

"I . . . uh, thanks . . . I'm supposed to be getting bread." Liam nods, and I realize this doesn't explain why I've left the house in my pyjamas. "One of my family's traditions is wearing matching Christmas pjs. It's nonnegotiable, even though I'm in my thirties and haven't lived at home for years."

I take in a breath, which is icy in my throat, thanks to today's windchill. "If you knew how seriously my mom takes all things Christmas, this would make more sense," I add.

Liam grins. "Fair enough."

"But I *assure you* that I don't make a habit of walking around Harmony Hills in flannel holiday pyjamas." I try to zip up my coat, my fingers numb and barely working due to the cold.

"*I'm having a meltdown*," Liam reads the message on my pyjama top out loud. He chuckles. "Is it true?"

"Is what true?" I ask, finally getting the zipper up.

"Are you having a meltdown?" One side of his mouth rises in a teasing smirk.

"Maybe the tiniest of meltdowns? I mean, would Christmastime be Christmastime without one? Who isn't having a meltdown these days, am I right?" I laugh to cover my nervousness. *For the love of gingerbread, stop talking.*

"'Tis the season,' as they say." Liam holds my gaze. The smile deepens, and I can't stop staring at the dimples. Or at those emerald eyes, with golden flecks. *Rein it in, Elizabeth.* It might be cold outside, but no question this sure feels like chemistry between us.

My attention snaps from Liam back to Mary, thanks to a sharp yank on my coat. Twisting, I see the pig with a section of the fabric in her mouth. She's tugging on it, as though trying to rip it away. Liam scolds Mary, pulling gently on her leash, but she's unrelenting, expressing her irritation with a sharp squeal.

"What does she want?" I ask Liam, my voice slightly shrill.

"I'm really sorry about this," he starts, finally managing to get Mary to release the coat. Liam draws up on her leash so she's tight against his side, a couple of feet away. But she continues to strain towards me.

"Any chance you have a candy cane in there?" He points to the coat pocket Mary was fixated on.

"A candy cane? I don't think so." I put my hand into the pocket to check. Soon my fingers find something that feels familiar. It's a mini candy cane—the cellophane partially ripped open—striped with white and a deep burgundy colour. "Wait, I take that back."

"Mystery solved," Liam says, chuckling. "Pigs have an excellent sense of smell. Candy canes are Mary's favourite treat. Is that cinnamon-flavoured?"

I smell it, and nod. Liam pulls a small paper bag out of his own coat pocket. He shakes the bag, and whatever's inside gets lightly tossed around. "This should help. Look, Mary, snacky-snacks!"

I'm dying at Liam's use of "snacky-snacks" and hide my smile behind my hand. He opens the bag and takes out a handful of popcorn, setting it on the snow in front of Mary Piggins.

"Popcorn, eh?" I say. "So pigs like candy canes and popcorn?"

"Seems so. Or at least Mary does," Liam replies.

"Must be complicated if popcorn string on the Christmas tree is your tradition. As a pig owner, I mean." I hand Liam the mini candy cane. "Here. She's welcome to it."

"Thanks," Liam says. "I'll save it for when I need to bribe her." He pockets the sweet treat.

"Well, I guess I better ... pick up the bread." *And figure out what the hell is going on, and how to fix it.* Also, I'm freezing. I can't stop the shivering that overtakes me.

"Mary Piggins has terrible manners, but mine aren't much better, apparently," Liam says, noticing my shivering. "Any chance I can tempt you with a hot chocolate to warm you up? Mary's treat."

"Um, well ..." *Say yes.* "Okay, sure. Sounds good."

"She's grateful for the second chance," Liam adds, with that dizzying, dimpled smile.

My teeth are chattering in earnest now, and I tighten my jaw, hoping that makes it less noticeable. *Clearly not*, I think, when Liam says, "You look really cold."

"I'mmm ... oooo-k-k-k-kaayyyy." The chattering makes it hard to speak.

Liam takes off his toque, a wool beanie. "May I?" He holds it out, clearly intending to place it on my head.

"Won't you be cold?" I ask. *Chatter-chatter-chatter* go my teeth. My jaw aches with the tension.

"Don't worry about me," Liam says. I nod, grateful for his offer, and he sets the toque atop my head. He pulls it down until it covers most of my ears. It's warm and smells of cedar and cloves. "Better?" he asks.

"Definitely. Thanks," I reply.

We start walking towards the coffee stall in the centre of town, when I abruptly stop. "Hang on," I say. Liam also stops, glancing my way. "Does Mary Piggins like hot chocolate?"

He laughs. "You're safe, but no promises on the marshmallows."

There's a flutter in my stomach that I'll write off as a remnant of the food poisoning I supposedly have, but I know it's something else altogether.

15

"Are you a peppermint-hot-chocolate person, or straight up?"
"Peppermint, with marshmallow foam, please."

"My order exactly," Liam says. "Mind holding the leash?"

"Happy to," I reply, which is not entirely true. I'm still wary of Mary Piggins, though it's hard to hold a grudge because she's wearing another festive Christmas sweater adorned with snowball pompoms. Holding tightly to the leash, I have anxious visions of her getting loose. Bolting, maybe chasing a poor soul with a box of sugar cookies, before making it to the main road.

Harmony Hills is a sleepy place much of the year, but during the holiday season, tourists descend, taking Sunday drives to see the lights, to pick up gingerbread-house-making supplies at the Cookie Cottage, which became semi-famous after a glowing write-up years ago in a national travel magazine.

"Please behave, Mary," I whisper, as Liam orders our hot chocolate. She wags her tail like a happy-go-lucky dog would. "You know, you have really pretty eyelashes."

As though understanding my compliment, her tail wags round and around, and she presses her head into my leg. I pat at her awkwardly, then scratch behind her ear the way Liam did.

"Don't make me regret this," I say, forcing my shoulders down. *Relax, Elizabeth. She's a cute potbellied pig in a holiday sweater— she's harmless.* Mary's hair is bristly, but she's warm and soft against my leg, letting out little contented grunts.

"You've done it now," Liam says. He hands me one of the take-out cups, then sits beside me on the bench.

I thank him, the warmth of the cup lovely against my cold hand. "And what have I done?"

He doesn't reply, simply smiles as he sips the hot chocolate. A ring of marshmallow foam clings to his five-o'clock-shadowed upper lip. However, my question is answered a moment later when Mary suddenly flops to the sidewalk. She lies on her side, frighteningly still.

"Is she okay?" My muscles tense up; I'm out of my depth. If a person collapsed, I'd know exactly what to do. But a potbellied pig? My medical skills are useless.

"She's fine. That's how she asks for a belly rub." Liam leans back and crosses one leg over his other knee. Compared to me, he's fully relaxed.

I glance down at Mary and her soft pink stomach, mottled with large brown spots and fine hair. "A belly rub?"

He takes another sip of hot chocolate, then, "Feel free to ignore the request. Teaching her that she can't always get what she wants is part of her training—if we can call it that. Sometimes it feels like *she's* training me."

I laugh, because I don't know if all potbellied pigs are like Mary, but she certainly seems determined to get her way.

"There's a reason the term *pigheaded* has *pig* in it," Liam adds.

"How do you deny her when she wags her tail like that?" I give her belly a little tap. "This is why I've never had a pet. They would be the boss of me."

"If Mary could talk, she would tell you she's the boss of *everyone*."

We laugh, then fall into an easy silence. But it's too quiet, and soon my thoughts threaten to overwhelm me. My mind flips between last year's memories and this year's realities, like a compass searching for its bearings. I need a distraction, and quick. "So what brought you to Harmony Hills?"

"Hmm. Do you want the short or long answer?" he replies.

"Whichever one you want to give." I point to my cup of hot chocolate, still mostly full. "I have this much time before my family notices I'm not back with the bread. To be clear, it's the bread they'll be worried about—not me. We're a family of carb lovers."

"Also a carb lover." Liam holds up his hand and smiles, which warms me faster than the hot chocolate has. If I *am* in some sort of coma-induced dream, this isn't the worst way to spend my time.

"I was in tech, and I built and then sold an app. Jaclyn, my girlfriend at the time, wanted us to leave Toronto—she was really into this cottagecore thing, and when she visited Harmony Hills with me, she fell in love with the vibe." He puts air quotes around the word *vibe*.

Jaclyn. That must be his ex? The one who gets married in a year's time and Liam finds out via an unfortunate Christmas card delivery. How can I know this? I shouldn't know this.

I need to stay in the present, which may actually be the past. *Good grief.* "Harmony Hills definitely is a vibe," I reply, hoping I sound more steady than I feel.

"Like nowhere else I've been," Liam says. "We bought a little hobby farm just outside of town, and started an animal sanctuary. Jaclyn's an animal lover—she was a communications director for the Humane Society before we moved. Anyway, the sanctuary is mostly for farm animals, though we did rescue two emus and an alpaca, and a dog named George. Oh, and Frida, a senior bearded dragon, who is a wise old soul. Jaclyn wasn't a huge fan of reptiles, but I can't imagine life without Frida."

There's a slight hint of something in his tone, but I can't tell if it's regret, or sadness, or maybe even relief? He referred to Jaclyn as a "girlfriend at the time," which reinforces my assumption it's his now-married ex.

The sanctuary part helps explain why Miss Elsie wanted Liam to take Mary Piggins. But I can't say this, so instead say, "The sanctuary must be so much work."

"It's busy and chaotic and definitely time-consuming, but I love it more than I thought I would. It was supposedly Jaclyn's dream, but I'm the one who's still here."

Again, there's something in his voice I can't pin down. Regardless, I understand what it's like to have dreams that get upended, and to feel a longing for new beginnings. Also? Breakups suck.

"And then Pops was looking for something to keep him busy, and he's an excellent baker, so we opened the boulangerie." He shakes his head, but he's smiling now.

"That's a bakery, right?"

"Yep. Jaclyn thought bakery was too old-fashioned sounding, though, and a 'boulangerie' is a bakery that specializes in bread, which is what we do. Anyway, now Pops and I run it together."

"Oh! So you own Slice of Life?" I remember Mom telling me when I was home last Christmas (*this* Christmas?) about a "nice young couple—Mr. Cutler's grandson and his girlfriend" who opened a bakery earlier that year. I didn't even know Mr. Cutler had a grandson, let alone one so . . . impressive and good-looking and, quite frankly, from what I've seen so far, pretty darn close to the whole package.

"Your granddad is Mr. Cutler?" Liam nods. "He taught me high-school mathematics—best teacher I ever had, hands down."

"Doesn't surprise me one bit," he says, smiling at the compliment. "Pops retired years ago, but I think he spends more hours in the bakery than he did at the school when he was teaching full time."

"Okay, let me get this straight." I lean back against the bench, now shoulder to shoulder with Liam. I turn towards him and enumerate with my fingers. "You were in tech and sold an app. You have a hobby farm and animal sanctuary. And you also run a bakery? Sorry, a *boulangerie*."

My French accent is terrible, and it sounds like I have a mouth full of marbles. "In case it wasn't abundantly clear, I do not speak French well. Amelia's the gifted one in that department in my family."

"Trust me, I get it—the rolling *r* is my downfall."

We smile at each other, our faces mere inches apart. Close enough I could just . . .

"The bakery has one deep, dark secret, though," Liam says, breaking eye contact to stare straight ahead. I abruptly shift my body back to centre, wondering how obvious the deep blush in my cheeks is.

"Oh yeah?" I focus on my hot chocolate cup, twisting the cardboard sleeve around. Sipping the spicy-sweet beverage, which is delightful, is making me homesick—even though I'm *in* Harmony Hills. With some trepidation I wonder what he's about to confess. Liam appears so serious, his jaw tight, no smile on his face, not looking my way.

"I opened a bread bakery but . . . I don't bake. Actually, scratch that. I *can't* bake." He tries to hold on to a grim expression, but the corner of his mouth twitches as a smile threatens to break through. It seems Liam Young doesn't have much of a poker face.

"Oh, wow," I reply, keeping my own expression solemn.

"Yup. Everything I touch is inedible. I'm more of a 'dough destroyer'—my granddad actually had a T-shirt made for me."

I'm partway through sipping my hot chocolate when he says this, and it goes down the wrong way. There are a few moments of dramatic coughing, and Liam taps at my back. "Sorry—didn't mean to make you choke."

I wave a hand around as if to say "Don't worry about it!," but the movement makes me cough harder.

"I don't have your medical skills, but I am prepared to do the Heimlich, if necessary," he says.

My throat feels raw, but I'm finally able to speak. "Dough destroyer, huh?" I clear my throat. "That's not the best when you, say, run a bakery."

"I know," Liam says, chuckling. "Pops, he's the genius behind Slice of Life. I couldn't do it without him."

His cheeks are rosy from the cold air, only adding to his attractiveness. I can't stop staring at him. But then he sighs, and there's a shift in energy. Less jovial, more thoughtful.

"Jaclyn and I broke up not long after the bakery opened, and she went back to the city. Turns out Harmony Hills wasn't her dream after all."

"I'm really sorry," I reply. "That's tough."

"Yeah, it is. Or was, I guess. Sometimes I wonder what I could have done differently, if I could go back in time and change things," he says. "Truthfully? That relationship should never have gone as far as it did. Hindsight is twenty-twenty, as they say."

I nod, any reply I might make stuck in my throat because I'm having a truly unhinged thought. *Is there any way Liam knows what's going on with me? Is this some sort of clue that maybe I'm not alone with this time-travel thing?*

"Say you could go back in time, what would you change?" I ask before I can stop myself.

"Good question," Liam says, flashing me a smile. *Damn, those dimples.* To use Mom's term, I'm all fuddled up again.

"Probably nothing? Sure, the breakup was messy and painful, like most breakups are when you've built a present—and anticipate a future—with that person." He shrugs, tips his cup of hot chocolate back to finish the last dregs. "But if I'm being honest, everything worked out for the best."

Immediately, I think of Austin. Of our breakup, and how, if we were still together, I wouldn't have driven Pepper home alone, wouldn't have had the car break down outside of town, wouldn't have had to catch a ride with Liam, wouldn't be sitting here having hot chocolate with him and Mary . . . in *any* timeline. As if understanding my thoughts, Mary leans heavily against my legs while resting her head on Liam's knee—he pets her ear, and she grunts softly. It's adorable, and I have to admit the pig is growing on me.

"What about you?" Liam asks, pulling me back from my thoughts.

What about me, indeed. I keep my eyes on the town square, which has started to fill up with passersby. Liam's being so forthright and honest, I'm afraid I'll do the same if I meet his gaze—it's destabilizing, his openness.

"What would you like to know?" I ask.

"Maybe why you left Harmony Hills. Big-city dreams?"

"That was definitely part of it. I like the energy of emergency medicine, especially in a city like Toronto. No two shifts are ever the same. Small-town doctoring felt . . ." I stop, unsure how to explain it.

"Small town?"

"Ha! Yeah. When you grow up somewhere like Harmony Hills, and everyone knows your name, well, I wanted to spread my wings. Have the opportunity for a more diverse career, I guess."

I always understood there was a fervent hope—just this side of a full-blown expectation—that after medical school, I would join the family practice. Fulfill the succession plan, taking over for Mom when my parents decided to retire.

When I chose to stay in Toronto, Amelia told me I broke my parents' hearts. I brushed the comment off as my little sister being melodramatic, as she was prone to be as a teenager. By then, I was chasing the attending job, and going back to Harmony Hills seemed unlikely. I was no longer Libby Munro, having adopted the more formal (and more professional, I believed) "Elizabeth" during med school. I told myself I couldn't possibly be fulfilled doing small-town medicine, and besides—Harmony Hills already had a doctor, my mom.

But only now do I consider the truth behind Amelia's comment. That perhaps it had less to do with an on-paper succession plan and more to do with remaining a close-knit family. There's a tightness in my chest I'm finding hard to breathe through.

"I grew up in the opposite of a small town," Liam says. "My mom lived here until my grandparents split up, then she moved with my grandmother to Halifax. She met my dad at university out there, and they got involved with the Global Affairs Program—sort of like a Canadian version of the Peace Corps," he adds, when I raise a brow, unfamiliar with the program.

"Then they had me and we travelled the world." He glances down at Mary, rubbing her head. "I never felt settled until I went to university, and then moved here. I like that everyone knows my name. Can't imagine living anywhere else now, and definitely not anywhere urban. Somehow it feels like I'm part of one big family."

"Libby, there you are!"

Speaking of family . . .

It's Amelia, and she has a determined look on her face that I recognize. I may be the older sibling, but Amelia can make me feel like she's the more mature one. She stops in front of us. "Hey, Liam. Hi, Mary Piggins."

"Hey, Mila," Liam says, standing to give her a hug. "Join us for some hot chocolate?"

"I'm good, thanks. Have to get back home." Then she turns towards me. "Our not-prone-to-worry parents sent me out here to find you. *This is not a drill*, Libby."

"What did I say about the bread? The Munros gets antsy without their carbs." I stage-whisper to Liam, so Amelia can hear me. She ignores my quip, while Liam laughs quietly.

Amelia reaches down to pet Mary's head but keeps her eyes on us. "Sorry to interrupt, but Mom said I needed to make sure you weren't passed out in a snowbank."

"Passed out in a snowbank?" Liam asks. "Sounds like there's a story here?"

"Munro melodrama, that's the story," I reply, with a semi-nervous laugh.

Amelia frowns, points to my cup. "Are you drinking hot chocolate? You must be feeling better."

"You're sick?" Liam turns towards me with an air of concern, which is sweet because I am a virtual stranger, and yet he obviously cares. *He's probably like this with everyone.* He's that type, I'm starting to see—bighearted and empathetic, noticing the little details.

"I *am* feeling better, which I already told you this morning,"

I reply to Amelia, before adding for Liam's benefit, "Apparently, I have food poisoning. Or had. I'm completely fine."

"Fine? You upchucked all over your bed at two in the morning, Libby," Amelia says.

"Yikes," Liam adds, and I can't look his way. This is not the sort of detail I would like Liam, with his incredible dimples and kind heart, to know.

"Thank you, dear sister, for that graphic and unnecessary update." I hook my arm through hers. "She's exaggerating, Liam."

He's obviously entertained by the back-and-forth between siblings, his smile intact.

"I assure you I am not," Amelia retorts. It's like we're kids again, and I resist the urge to have the last word.

"*Anyway,*" I say in a singsong voice, tugging on Amelia's arm, "we should get back before this escalates further."

"Glad you're feeling better," Liam says. "Food poisoning *blows.*"

I smile at both his kindness and witticism, but I'm impatient to move my sister along. "Thanks again for the hot chocolate."

"Sure hope we don't get an instant replay," Amelia mutters over her shoulder.

"Amelia Munro, *honestly,*" I whisper, pulling her away from Liam, who smiles at me once more before turning to walk the other direction, Mary Piggins ambling along beside him.

16

"Thanks for that, Amelia," I say, when we're far enough out of the town square that I'm sure Liam won't overhear us. "*You upchucked all over your bed?*"

"I had to move the goodbyes along," Amelia says. "With your topsy-turvy stomach now full of hot chocolate, I was obviously saving you from an even more embarrassing situation. *You're welcome*, Libby."

The look she gives me is pointed, but then we both burst out laughing.

We're back at our parents' house less than ten minutes later, which is when I realize I forgot to get the bread. I'm also still wearing Liam's toque. "Do you happen to have Liam's number?"

"Sure," Amelia replies, taking my coat and hanging it up. "How come?"

I hold up the wool beanie. "He loaned me this, but I forgot I was wearing it."

"You can drop it off at Slice of Life. He's there most days," Amelia replies. "Or I can give it to Beckett. I'm meeting her and some friends at Beans and Brews later."

Now I watch *her* carefully, trying to see if her face gives anything away when she mentions Beckett. But her cheeks are pink from the cold, and she's busying herself with the hangers, so I can't tell. They've been good friends for years, but I have no idea how they went from that status to getting married in less than a year.

Another example of what I gave up, relocating to Toronto: I'm out of the loop when it comes to what's going on with my family. Except I can't just blame the distance. I've been self-absorbed, laser-focused on my career, on my relationship with Austin—I can't even be bothered to check my voicemail most days. My conversation with Claire, about buying my parents' medical practice, comes to mind. The guilt heaps on.

"Hey, about this morning," Amelia says. "Whose wedding were you talking about?"

"I was hallucinating, obviously." The easiest explanation is usually the best one. "Dehydration can do wild things. I see it all the time in the emergency room."

She squints, not buying it. "I need you healthy, Libby. We have a lot to do to get ready for the *you know what*," she says, whispering the last part from behind her hand as she shuts the closet door. "Honestly, I don't know how you guys handle medical stuff. Good luck to me if I ever have a kid! One stomach flu or croupy cough and I'll probably lose it. Melodramatic Mila, right?"

Amelia's laughing at herself, but I've gone quiet—thinking of what she's just said. We have a lot to do to get ready for the *you know what*. No, Amelia, I *do* not *know what*.

Also? If this isn't all a dream, or some coma-induced hallucination, then Amelia *is* pregnant. Or will be this time next year. Yet standing here with me in the foyer of our parents' house, she has no clue what's to come. The lightheadedness returns, the energy leaving my body. *Do not pass out, Elizabeth. Don't you dare.*

"Libby? Are you okay?" Amelia holds out her hands, as though saying, "calm down, everyone calm down."

I don't respond, only shake my head.

"Is the hot chocolate looking for an exit plan?" she asks nervously. "Do you . . . need something?"

I don't like stressing her out, but it's easier to pretend I'm sick. My mind is a soupy mess, and it's stressing *me* out. I'm not used to feeling unmoored, as typically the more chaotic a situation is, the steadier I am. "You were right. Hot chocolate . . . bad idea."

I slap a hand to my mouth and race up the stairs, hearing Amelia shout, "Parents, we have a hot-chocolate situation! This is not a drill!"

I'm lying on my bed, pretending to be "napping," but I'm paralyzed with indecision. I'm afraid to do anything (what if I'm changing the future?) but also afraid to do nothing (what if I'm stuck here?), and the back-and-forth is giving me a tension headache. A buzzing interrupts the stillness, followed by the tune "White Christmas." It's Austin, and I answer right away. Might as well let this play out however it's going to.

"How are you feeling?" he asks.

"Better," I reply, but I'm distracted. I'm riffling through my overnight bag, looking for the bottle of ibuprofen I'm sure I tossed in. Though in *this* timeline I have no memory of packing the bag. Or why I'm home two days earlier. "My mom gave me ondansetron."

Wait. No, she didn't. That was in the *other* version of this home-for-Christmas mash-up. My heart beats faster as panic attempts to worm in. I glance at the contents of the duffel bag, now strewn across the bed. *Pair of jeans. Two sweaters. One of Austin's sweatshirts that he hasn't worn in ages, which I found at the back of the closet. Leggings. Three pairs of socks, none of them matching. Black bikini bottoms.* No ibuprofen.

I roll my eyes at the bikini bottoms, remembering how I thought they were underwear when I race-packed last year. I was exhausted after a long shift and worried about Mom. I ended up buying a package of Fruit of the Loom underwear—bright white, full coverage style—at Everhart's.

"Anyway, I feel more or less fine now." I continue sifting through the socks. Yep, none of them match.

"That's a relief. Those tickets were not cheap," Austin replies. I stop, a black sock in one hand, grey in the other. *Who says that, especially when the trip is a gift?* Then I try to recall if we had a conversation like this last year about the plane tickets, but can't. I probably would have laughed off his comment, despite its making me feel uncomfortable. Austin makes plenty of money, and he isn't typically one to scrimp on anything.

But in this bizarre moment in time I'm reliving for reasons unknown, his comment lands all wrong. I fight the urge to simply hang up.

"I've got back-to-back surgeries the day you get home, but I'll come over to your place after I'm finished," he continues. "That should give you enough time to pack. We can order in, and—"

"What?" I stare at the phone on my bedside table, and for a moment there's silence on his end as well.

"What do you mean, 'what'?" Austin finally says.

"I can't come *home*," I say. Oddly, it feels strange calling Toronto *home*, even though it *is* my home. "I need to stay here."

I'm petrified of leaving Harmony Hills right now. I still don't understand what's happened, or how permanent this time hop is going to be. For all I know, when I wake up tomorrow, I'll be back in the proper year, and Austin and I will be broken up, and Amelia will be married, and things will make sense again. I obviously can't *leave* with things as they are now.

"What are you talking about?" A hint of irritation in his voice. "You're supposed to drive back the morning after the party."

"Wait ... there's a party?" *Is that why I'm home early? For a party?*

"Babe, are you okay?" Austin asks, the irritation replaced with concern.

"Of course I'm okay!" *Easy, Elizabeth.* "Sure, the party. I'll be home the day after that."

Now I have to figure out what this party is, and what it has to do with me.

Austin starts talking about a recent surgery, and I mostly tune him out as I stuff the clothes back into the duffel bag. Austin's sweatshirt from his undergrad at Queen's falls out from the pile, and I reach for it. That's when I feel something solid and square stuck in the sleeve.

Snaking my fingers down the sweatshirt's arm, I touch the item, held in place by the cuff. I tug it out, then promptly drop it on the bedspread like it's burning hot.

The blue velvet box—the sort that holds something as sparkly as it is life-changing—rests in the folds of the quilt. Austin's voice drones on through speakerphone. He's shifted back to the trip. "Hopefully they'll upgrade us ... You should see the suites; you'll lose your mind ..."

The velvet is soft against my fingertips. With shaky hands, I slowly open the lid. The hinges are stiff, and it resists for a moment before releasing with a satisfying "pop." The gasp I let out is involuntary.

"Uh, Austin, I have to go." I'm abrupt, interrupting him as he's telling me about our hotel's rooftop pool. My insides buzz with what feels like electrical currents—I have to get off the phone *right now*. "I should lie down. I'm feeling sick again."

This part is true, but it has nothing to do with food poisoning and everything to do with what's nestled inside the velvet box.

"Okay, get some rest," he replies. "Feel better, babe. I'll call you later."

I hang up without saying goodbye. Sitting heavily on the bed, I stare at the ring.

I'm filled with an undeniable sense that this ring was intended for my finger. I also know, with absolute certainty, that a proposal never materialized. In *any* timeline.

17

I focus on the diamond. It's big and crystal clear, perched atop a dainty platinum band. Completely impractical for an emergency room physician, but definitely a showstopper. A ring that suits Austin's personality and lifestyle, which tends to be flashier than mine. So why did this ring never make it out of the box?

I think back to last Christmas—or *this* Christmas if I'm keeping track, which I am desperately trying to do. I was in Harmony Hills for two days, after my mom fell off the ladder hanging Christmas lights. There was no party, nothing celebratory about my time here. Once I knew Mom was okay, I drove back to Toronto, a full day before Austin and I flew to L.A.

I was exhausted after the long drive, and Austin offered to unpack for me. He was insistent on it, actually. Weirdly so, though at the time I chalked it up to his meticulous nature. Austin likes order in every aspect of life—I trend more messy and chaotic, including with my clothing, which is relevant in this memory. In my defense, what's the point of hangers or colour-coded systems when you wear scrubs every day, and your at-home uniform is leggings and sweaters?

When I arrived at Austin's condo that evening, I was wearing his sweatshirt—the one I just found the ring box tucked into. Now I recall Austin's reaction upon seeing me in that sweatshirt.

"Where did you get that?" he asked, his tone urgent. The navy sweatshirt has been washed so many times the gold letters were faded. It was far too big on me, so the sleeves were rolled and the hem hung below my hip creases. But it was comfortable and cozy, and made me think of him—which is why I packed it for my quick trip to Harmony Hills.

I looked down at the sweatshirt, then back at him. "This? It was in the back of the closet," I said. "I didn't think you'd mind. You haven't worn it in ages."

Something flickered across his face. Alarm, maybe? Odd, because Austin was always so measured. His Adam's apple bobbed, and he cleared his throat. I was confused by his reaction. He seemed angry with me, and I couldn't understand why. Especially if it had anything to do with this old sweatshirt.

"Let me just take it off, throw it in the wash. I only wore it for the drive," I said.

Austin's frown suddenly transformed into a smile. "Hey, don't worry about it. You look cute. Just surprised to see it, that's all."

"I should have asked. Sorry."

He waved the apology away. "Here, let me unpack for you. There's a bottle of red breathing on the counter, and I've ordered Thai. I'll join you in a few minutes—you go relax, babe."

He grasped my duffel bag and took it from me without waiting for me to answer, then headed into the primary bedroom. At the time I was tired and grateful, and so I'd padded to the kitchen to pour the wine. While I waited for him to finish and for our Thai to arrive, I noted how depressingly dull his condo was. Cool neutrals, not a stitch of holiday decor. A deep longing for

Harmony Hills filled me then, for the twinkling Christmas lights, tinsel-draped trees, snow-dusted rooftops, and the overall warmth of the season.

Now, coming back to the present, a ring I've never seen before today still pinched between my fingers, understanding bubbles to the surface. This ring was in my duffel bag the whole time. It came to Harmony Hills with me, accidentally, when I packed Austin's sweatshirt. He must have panicked when he saw me, which is why he offered to unpack—he was looking for the ring box, obviously no longer in the sweatshirt's sleeve. But most critical of all, he never gave me this ring. Not that Christmas, and not at any time during the following nine months, before our breakup.

I've made up my mind. Until I figure out what's going on— why I'm like Ebenezer Scrooge, in Christmas past—I can't leave Harmony Hills. Also, I need to dig into what's going on with my parents and the practice, in the present, or future, if I accept that I'm currently reliving the past.

I consider the possibility that this is some unbelievable second chance to repair whatever broke with Austin. To go back a year and do things differently, so maybe in the end he is my "happily ever after"? That this ring could end up on my finger after all. Maybe I would get married around the same time Amelia does . . .

The moment I think it, I'm sure that's not what I want. I can't forget where our relationship ended up, with the toilet paper incident being the last straw. It's past time to admit that Austin and I were like a gingerbread house put together with Marshmallow Fluff, rather than the far sturdier, break-your-teeth royal icing. It's clear to me now that we were never going to make it, our relationship doomed from that first date.

Our first date.

I go back in time again, but in my mind, to two Christmases ago. It was December 28, and the gorgeous plastic surgeon Dr. Whitmore, a friend of a coworker, asked me out. It was an easy yes. I dated, but infrequently, as there wasn't much time to nurture relationships with my demanding hours. Plus, dating coworkers was risky, because if things went south, you still had to work together.

But Austin and I were in different departments, and our paths rarely crossed. It—he—seemed a safe bet. Not to mention, he was handsome, funny, smart, and, truth be told, it had been, *ahem*, a long time.

We went out for dinner to Sotto Sotto, a restaurant beyond my typical dinner budget. It was fancy, dress-code enforced (I wore a fitted wrap dress and heels; Austin wore a dark suit and lavender tie). Sipping drinks while we waited for appetizers, I asked him to tell me three truths and a lie, a cutesy icebreaker dating game trending on social media.

"Hmm, three truths and a lie . . ." Austin smirked, setting his chin into his hands, his bluest of blue eyes holding mine. My heart actually pitter-pattered under his gaze that evening.

"I have one tattoo, of a Caduceus, but well hidden," he started.

"Interesting for a plastics guy, if true," I replied. "Okay, next."

"I have never had a pet of any kind," he said, then adding, "I speak three languages fluently."

"I'm impressed, if that's true," I replied, which I was.

"And because it's so close to Christmas, how about a holiday-themed one? Let's see . . . I don't believe we should tell kids that Santa Claus is real."

I laughed at this one, at the time fully believing it to be the lie. "Why not?"

"It's an outright fabrication." He leaned back, taking a sip of his drink. "What happens when your kids learn it's not true? They'll never trust you again."

I'd heard this argument before but didn't buy it. "My parents went all in on Santa Claus—they used to get a neighbour to record us a message on Christmas Eve, pretending to be Santa, and my dad always nibbled the carrots we left for the reindeer. I still trust my parents. Deeply."

"When was the last time you told them a secret? Something you didn't share with anyone else?"

"Umm . . ." I shrugged, sipping my Aperol Spritz. "I don't have secrets, I guess. And that better be the lie in our little game here, because I'm not sure I can go on a second date with someone who doesn't believe in the magic of Santa Claus."

Austin winked, raised his glass—a Green Monkey, made of absinthe, lime juice, and dry vermouth. "Well, this has been a lovely one and done, Dr. Elizabeth Munro."

"What?! That's *true*? What's the lie, then?"

It was about the pets—Austin had raised geckos as a kid and, growing up, had a family cat named Milkshake. Later that night I would discover the small tattoo on his ankle and be properly impressed when he showed off his fluency in English, German, and French when we weren't busy doing . . . other things.

"Should I get the cheque?" Austin asked. The menus were still open in front of us, as we'd only ordered appetizers. He was grinning, amused by how incredulous I was about the whole Santa Claus thing.

"Might be wise to cut our losses . . ." I replied. "But one more question, before we throw in the towel."

"Ask me anything," Austin said.

"What are your feelings about the Easter Bunny?"

He tipped his head back and laughed, hard, then gave me a

look I can only describe as *smoldering*. I was hooked, Santa Claus issue aside. *Of course* he would change his mind, maybe when he had a family of his own.

So when he answered, "That's a conversation best saved for the second date, Elizabeth," I nodded in agreement. After which I returned his smoldering look with one I hoped came off as flirtatious (closed-lipped smile, one eyebrow raised, deep eye contact), and said, "I'm free for New Year's . . ."

18

Waking up the next morning, I'm confused all over again. In the semi-dark room, I touch my hair, my fingers running through the strands. When they keep going past my chin, I know I'm still in Christmas past. I check the duffel bag for the ring. It's as glimmering and beautiful (and startling) as it was when I first discovered it. The date on my phone confirms it: December 15. Yep, Christmas past.

I head downstairs in search of coffee and find my parents already in the kitchen making breakfast. The scents of browned butter and freshly brewed coffee swirl together, and my stomach growls.

"Morning. That smells great," I say, giving my mom a kiss on her cheek and my dad a hug.

"Someone's chipper today!" Dad's assembling over-easy eggs onto smashed-avocado toast. He sprinkles on everything-bagel seasoning, chili oil, and sea salt, then sets the two plates down on the table. "How's the stomach?"

"Good. Back to normal." I pour steaming coffee into a mug from the cupboard. It's from a set we gifted our parents many

Christmases ago, each mug sporting a different quote from the movie *Elf*. I have the DOES SOMEONE NEED A HUG? one in hand.

"Excellent. In that case, there's creamer for you. Second shelf in the fridge," Mom says. My parents, and Amelia, take their coffees black, so the creamer was bought with only me in mind. I thank my mom and pull out the bottle of peppermint-mocha creamer.

I pour the creamer ("Why even drink coffee?" Austin used to say), then, thinking about his comment, add another slosh for good measure. After a quick stir, I set the spoon into the Mrs. Claus spoon rest, which might be as old as I am.

"So I ran into Liam Young and his pet pig in town—actually, Mary Piggins is Miss Elsie's pig, not Liam's." I need to keep my stories straight, but it's getting increasingly complicated.

"Ah yes, we know Mary well. She goes everywhere with Elsie, including to clinic appointments." Dad puts half his breakfast on a plate for me. I smile my thanks.

"She's a bit of a menace, that one. Cute, but a menace nonetheless," Mom adds, piercing the sunshine yellow yolk on her toast. "Mary Piggins, I mean. Not Elsie Farrow."

"Understood," I reply, with a chuckle. "I didn't realize Mr. Cutler had a grandson."

"Oh? I'm sure I told you that." Mom sips her black coffee from her favourite seasonal mug—it's a large, white ceramic one with a red-painted interior and has the words CHRISTMAS IS TOO TWINKLY . . . SAID NO ONE EVER written in green cursive.

"Maybe you did. I was just surprised I've never met him before." The coffee is restorative, a balm for my scattered mind, and I take another sip. "Anyway, he loaned me his toque yesterday, so I'm going to Slice of Life to drop it off. I'll get the sourdough at the same time."

"Grab a cinnamon-swirl loaf, too, would you? Mom has a hankering for French toast for dinner," Dad says. Breakfast for dinner was a frequent event in my house growing up. When you have parents who are a doctor and nurse, and run the town's only medical practice, there's not much time to whip up elaborate meals. At least that's what I used to think. Now I get that, like me, Mom has a sweet tooth ... Why have boring chicken when you can have French toast and syrup?

"Your wish is my command." I finish the coffee and half piece of toast and egg before placing my dishes into the dishwasher.

"Thanks, honey. Dad and I will be at the clinic for most of the day, and I want to get those lights up before dinner." Mom peels a clementine and hands it to Dad, without any communication between them, before starting on another for herself. I love seeing this rhythm to their relationship, nurtured both at home and at the clinic over all these years. *That's the dream*, I think, *to have such synergy with another person.*

"Shoot," Dad says, interrupting my musings. "I have to go to the Dempster farm after we close shop. I won't be able to give you a hand with the lights, Monica."

"Not to worry," Mom says, wiping her mouth with her napkin. "I can manage."

"No!" I shout, far too loud for our small kitchen. Both my parents immediately stop what they're doing, looking at me in surprise.

"Sorry—I think the caffeine and sugar hit my system all at once." I give a sheepish laugh, but it comes out strangled. *If I could go back in time and change things ...*

It's a brilliant idea, and I can't believe it's only coming to me now. I think back to the conversation I had with Liam. How this newfound time I'm reliving might be a second chance to change the past, and ultimately the future. Why would I not at least *try*?

"How about I do the lights for you?" I say to Mom. "I'm here for . . ." Actually, I don't know why I'm here—yet. I consider asking about this party I've supposedly come home for, but I hold off. ". . . a few more days. So please, put me to work."

If I do the lights, it means Mom won't be up on that ladder.

If she's not on the ladder, she won't fall and break her ankle. Which means everything that comes after—Mom being off work, the practice struggling in her absence, the quiet conversations about selling—won't happen either. I've been given an inexplicable opportunity to change the past, and I'd be a fool not to take advantage of that.

"That's sweet of you to offer, Libby. But you didn't come home to hang Christmas lights for your very capable mother," Mom says, clearing the table.

"Well, what *did* I come home for then?" My tone suggests I'm being easy, cheeky, versus what I *really* am—attempting once again to get an annoyingly hard-to-pin-down answer.

"Mostly to get through that jug of coffee creamer," Dad says, giving me a hug. "We're off. Have a great day, Libby."

"You, too," I reply. "And Mom, I insist. Let me handle the lights. Besides, I want to say hello to Miss Betty. I haven't been over to see her yet."

"You don't have to ask me twice. Fine, the lights are all yours!" Mom says cheerfully, before holding up her finger. "But remember, they need to—"

"—wrap around the posts and be ruler straight along the roofline." I laugh, for I have years of experience dealing with Monica Munro's Christmas-decorating rules. "This is not my first light-hanging rodeo."

"That it is not," Mom replies with a smile. "It's nice having you home, honey. Even if you have terrible taste in how you take your coffee." She wrinkles her nose at the creamer on the countertop.

"Hey! Don't knock it until you try it," I say, reaching out to hug her. "And it's nice to be home."

My voice is muffled because of how tightly I'm holding her. Tears prick at my eyes, and I don't even care about why this is happening to me—I'm just glad, at least for this moment, that it is.

19

On my way to Slice of Life, I start texting Amelia, but then call her instead. I need to move away from my reliance on messaging—especially with my family. But after only one ring, her voicemail picks up. She's likely already in class and has her phone on Do Not Disturb.

"Hey, Sissy, can you give me a call when you get this? I have a question for you. About . . . that *thing* I'm home for." I'm hoping when she calls back, she launches into whatever it is that has brought me home early—serendipitously, at least for my mom's ankle. Otherwise, I'm going to have to find a way to ask outright.

I turn onto Main Street and see the bakery up ahead. There's a flagpole outside with a hanging, bread-shaped sign that reads SLICE OF LIFE. The black awning over the door and front windows says BOULANGERIE in white cursive. Last night's storm left layers of fluffy white snow trapped between the building's red-brick crevices. The aesthetic is Christmas-village charming.

A bell chimes as I open the front door and step inside, where I'm hit with cozy warmth. It's a small space with display cases on either side of the bleached-wood countertops and high-top stools facing the windows. Sparkly, cutout snowflakes hang on clear fishing line down the windows, giving the impression they're float-ing. A Crock-Pot has a homemade sign taped to it that reads APPLE CIDER—ENJOY! The air is fragrant with cinnamon, sweet apples, and the irresistible scent of freshly baking bread, hot from the oven.

Mr. Cutler suddenly appears, popping up from behind one of the display cases when the bell chimes. "Well, if it isn't Miss Libby Munro. Hello!"

He looks exactly as I remember him—thick wavy hair (I see where Liam gets it), though now it's white instead of its former deep brown, along with soft hazel eyes and an easy, welcoming smile. Mr. Cutler's apron reads BAKE THE WORLD A BETTER PLACE, which makes me smile.

"Mr. Cutler, it is so nice to see you." He takes my outstretched hands, after wiping the flour from his own. "I can't get over how good it smells in here. You really should bottle it."

"Thank you, my dear," he says, beaming. "I'll put that one on the Blue Sky list Liam and I keep. Parfum au Pain . . . has a nice ring to it, doesn't it?" I agree it does, promising to be his first cus-tomer.

"I'm sorry to interrupt. Morning must be a busy time," I add, noting the row of lit-up ovens behind the swinging door's window. "But I wanted to return Liam's toque. Is he here?"

"He's in the back, cleaning up." Mr. Cutler gestures over his shoulder, and the corners of his mouth turn down. "We've had . . . an incident."

"Oh? Is everything okay?"

At that moment the door swings open and there's Liam. His eyebrows raise, and a brief shadow crosses his face, like he's an-noyed to find me at his bakery. I'm not sure what's going on, but there's charged energy in the room, and it's clear I'm somehow involved.

"Libby, hey. Nice to see you," Liam says, standing slightly behind his grandfather due to the lack of space. His tone is friendly enough, but he still seems displeased about something. "Sorry about this—I told Pops not to bother you."

"Bother me?" I glance between the two men, wholly confused.

"Liam mentioned you were recovering from a bout of food poisoning. Hope you're feeling better?" Mr. Cutler says.

Liam sighs audibly, and his grandfather turns his way, putting on his no-nonsense teacher voice, which I remember from high school. "Cool your jets. I didn't call Libby."

"I'm good as new," I tell Mr. Cutler, before addressing Liam. "No one called me or bothered me. Though now I have to ask, what about?"

Liam sighs again, then holds up his hand, which I hadn't noticed as it was hidden behind his grandfather. It's wrapped in a white bar towel, a line of red seeping through the fabric.

"Uh-oh," I say. "Is that a dough-destroyer injury?"

He grimaces. "More a dish-destroyer situation. I was washing up and sliced it on a knife. It was a stupid mistake."

"Ouch. Want me to take a look?"

"Becks is going to drive me over to urgent care in Westhaven after she's done with a sick horse," Liam replies. "But if it's not too much trouble, maybe you can tell me if you think it needs stitches?"

"You're going to need stitches," I say, calmly but without hesitation.

Mr. Cutler whistles under his breath. "I was distracted by the ovens. We're tripling up on bread for Christmas chili night, and it has been nonstop. On that note, I hope the party plans are coming together, Libby? You've only just arrived home, and now you've been ill. I'm sure your to-do list is the length of my arm."

Christmas chili night. It's a much-loved, annual event that brings the entire town together. It's always on December 18, exactly one week before Christmas. *Does this party have something to do with chili night?*

"Party plans . . . right. Yes, my to-do list." But before I can ask any follow-up questions about this party I'm supposedly planning, Mr. Cutler continues, "Liam here kindly tackled the washing up, but he didn't know I'd set a knife in the sink. Seems it tackled him right back," he says with a heavy sigh.

"Pops, it's not your fault," Liam says. "I'm a fully grown adult who should have known better than to stick my hand into a sink full of suds. So much for being helpful."

He looks pale, a slight sheen to his face, but otherwise handsome as ever. My stomach flips, and my palms go sweaty. I can't say exactly what it is, but something about Liam causes a visceral reaction in me. Like every cell in my body is magnetized, straining towards him.

"Accidents happen," I say. "I wouldn't have a job otherwise."

Smiling at Liam when I say the last part, I'm glad to see he returns it. I wipe my palms on my leggings, almost perplexed by my unfamiliar nervousness that has everything to do with the guy standing in front of me. But then he gives a subtle wince when he looks down at the bloodied towel, and that, along with his pallor, kicks me into doctor mode.

"Let's see the damage." I gesture towards the stools. Unzipping my coat, I hang it on the hook by the front door. "Please, take a seat in my clinic."

Liam's smile widens—dimples turned on—as he sits on a stool. "I like what you've done with the place," he says. "And that air freshener . . . what's the scent?"

"Sourdough Serenity, I think it's called."

He chuckles, and I use the moment to unwrap the towel from his hand. The cut, about two inches long, is clean—what I'd expect from a run-in with a sharp knife. But it's also deep, still bleeding. Definitely needs stitches. "Can you wiggle your thumb?"

He can, and I nod, satisfied there's no other damage. When I glance up at him, I notice he's white as a sheet. Then I remember our conversation at Season's Eatings on the day of Amelia's wedding. "Let me guess . . . you're not great with blood?" I say. "At least your own."

"No, I'm not," he replies, shaking his head. "But how did you know that?"

"Experience," I say in a breezy tone before meeting his eyes with a teasing smile. "What, do you think you're special?"

I rewrap the towel, and he holds it with his other hand. "Hold this tight for a minute while I get my coat on and tell you the most embarrassing story of my life.

"When I was in residency, I wiped out running, tripped over a curb. See, unlike you with this knife accident, I am legit prone to clumsiness."

"Nah, it's not you. Curbs have it out for all of us," he replies.

"That's kind of you to say, but I assure you I have two left feet." Liam laughs, glances down at my boots. "You've seen how many times I've been knocked off my feet."

He tilts his head, eyebrows coming together in confusion, because in this timeline it has happened only once—yesterday, when Mary Piggins's snort startled me. I wave a hand as if swatting away a pesky fly. *Get back on track.* "Anyway, the curb. Like I said, I tripped while running and smashed up my knee pretty badly."

"Sounds painful," Liam says.

"It was. I cried like a baby. My kneecap looked like a dog's breakfast—it was bloodied, full of gravel, a real mess," I reply, zipping up my coat. "I sat on the curb and cried so much I hyperventilated, then fainted. A Good Samaritan called 911, and I ended up taking an ambulance ride *to my own hospital*."

Liam cringes in sympathy.

"I would probably already be on the floor if this was my thumb. Just saying." I set my hands on top of his, and the towel.

"Libby, who's being kind now?" he says, before quickly adding, "Do you mind Libby, or do you prefer Elizabeth? I know you introduced yourself as Elizabeth, but everyone around here seems to call you Libby."

"Libby's fine. Libby's good." I stand quickly to put a bit of distance between us, because I'm getting that melty-centre, lightheaded feeling again. "Is this your coat?"

There's one other hanging on the hook by the door. He nods, and I hold it open for him, glad for the distraction. "Okay, you have two options. One, I'm happy to drive you over to Westhaven to urgent care. I'll hang out in the waiting room to avoid becoming one of those hovering doctors other doctors wish would wait outside the treatment room."

"I would happily have you hover," Liam says, and there's that familiar lift in my centre again. What is it about this guy—aside from those most-charming dimples, and wavy hair I wouldn't mind running my hands through, and those piercing eyes . . .

Snap out of it, Elizabeth. You are Dr. Munro right now. Also? You are in Christmas past and still have a boyfriend at the moment. In my memories he's my ex, of course, but in this strange present I am most definitely *not* single.

Whatever lift I had deflates with this thought. Followed by, *I absolutely need to deal with the Austin issue, and soon. You are not someone who cheats, Elizabeth Munro. Even if you're a time traveller, or in a coma.*

"And option two?" Liam asks, shrugging the coat over his shoulder.

I refocus on Liam, push thoughts of Austin to the side for now. "We can head to my parents' clinic, and I can stitch this up myself."

Just then Mr. Cutler returns from the back of the bakery. "So, Dr. Munro. What's the verdict?"

"Stitches, as expected," Liam replies, before turning my way. "You're sure you don't mind?"

"No problem at all," I reply. "I've been going a little stir crazy, so I should probably thank you and that sharp knife for spicing things up. Besides, you don't want to leave that cut too long, because it gets trickier to close."

"You'll be okay without me for a bit, Pops?" Liam asks his grandfather.

"I'll just have to suffer through," Mr. Cutler says, letting out an animated sigh.

Liam laughs. "What he's not saying is that I can be more trouble than helpful. As I've said, I'm not skilled when it comes to baking." He looks at his injured, towel-wrapped hand. "Or apparently even washing dishes."

"Nonsense," Mr. Cutler replies. "I would be lost without you."

He squeezes Liam's arm but gives me a look that suggests a hint of sarcasm in his words. But while there is much jest in the exchange, there's also truth to his statement. It's the way the two smile at each other, the way Liam sets his good hand on his grandfather's and squeezes back—they are family, and family sticks together through thick and thin.

"I'll get him stitched up and back in a jiffy. Though you'll have to keep that hand dry, so no dishwashing," I say, clearing my throat to try to move the choked-up feeling along. Thoughts of my own family swirl through my mind, and then I remember the promised cinnamon loaf.

"Oh! I also need some bread. Mom asked specifically for the cinnamon-swirl loaf—she has a French toast craving."

"Well, whatever Doc Munro wants, Doc Munro gets." Mr. Cutler reaches into the glass case and sets two loaves of cinnamon bread on the countertop.

"Quick question …" I start, then whisper from behind my hand and gesture towards Liam. "He didn't make any of these loaves, right?"

Mr. Cutler leans closer and whispers back, "You're safe—baked these myself this morning."

"I can hear you, you know," Liam says, in a semi-grumbling tone.

Mr. Cutler hands me the canvas tote, and it's full of freshly baked bread. The cinnamon scent drifts up, and I inhale deeply. "Thank you. What do I owe you?"

"On the house." I start to protest, and he holds up his hands. "Libby, this is nonnegotiable. Or as a former math teacher I might say, 'The probability of my taking your money is zero.'"

As we step outside into the crisp air, I steal a glance at Liam. He's standing beside me on the bakery's steps, his injured hand tucked carefully against his chest. There's a fine dusting of flour in his thick, dark hair, and his eyelashes are impossibly long from this vantage point. For a moment, the world feels still. Too still.

And that's when it hits me.

I shouldn't be here, at least not like this, thinking these thoughts. Not when I haven't handled the Austin situation yet—whatever that looks like. And definitely not while Liam is bleeding and pale, and far too charming for his own good—or mine. I clutch the tote tighter, then force myself to relax, so as not to squish the bread inside.

"Thanks for this," Liam says, glancing down at me with that easy smile, dimples and all. "I owe you one."

I tap the tote bag. "I think this cinnamon bread means we can call it even."

As we set off for the clinic, the knots in my stomach tighten. Here's the truth I can't ignore: I'm in no position to be falling for someone, not with the many unknowns and relationship loose ends I'm currently dealing with. Besides, Liam doesn't deserve to be anyone's distraction, least of all mine.

"All right, Dough Destroyer," I say, our boots crunching the fresh snow as we walk. "Let's see what we can do about getting you back in one piece."

But even as I say it, I know it's not only Liam who needs piecing back together—I do, too, and I have no idea where to start.

20

The Munro Medical clinic is housed in a cozy bungalow, painted in teals and creams, the door a glossy, deep magenta colour that also frames the windows. The exterior has a low-pitched, gabled roof and tapered square columns, with two outdoor rocking chairs set side by side. During the holidays, it's adorned with lights and decorations that complement the snow-capped roof, like something out of a Christmas tableau.

Focused on Liam, and his thumb, I've momentarily forgotten about the time-travel issue, along with worries about the clinic—and my parents. But as I start up the front steps, it all rushes back in, stopping me. Liam soon realizes I'm not beside him. "Libby? Everything okay?"

"Yes! I was . . . thinking about Christmas lights." I quickly head up the stairs, joining him. "I volunteered to do the outdoor lights. Don't want my parents up on ladders, especially when they're the only doctor and nurse in town."

"Luckily for me, there's another doctor in town today," Liam replies, casting a warm smile my way. We're at the front door, standing so close together our arms touch. Our winter coats provide a layer between us, but I'm hyperaware of his nearness. I take a second too long to react, and Liam's smile drops.

"You'd tell me if I was keeping you from something, right?" he asks. "I know you have a lot going on, with the party."

"I do . . . have a lot going on," I reply, reaching for the door handle. "But I'm happy to stitch you up."

Liam laughs, says, "Okay, then," and I add, "To be clear, I'm not happy you need stitches. But I am glad I can help."

I'm flustered, sweating with unfamiliar nervousness, and hide my awkwardness by stomping snow from my boots on the HEALTHY HOLIDAYS doormat. Liam follows suit before we head inside.

It's festive and warm, with exposed beams lining the ceiling, a stone hearth fireplace, which is lit and crackling, and a miniature Christmas village set up on the mantel. The air is scented with an orange-and-pine fragrance that I know Miss Betty—the clinic manager, who has been here from the beginning—makes at home. Candy-cane-fabric-covered pillows add holiday cheer to the waiting room chairs. Strands of tinsel garland cross the ceiling, from which hand-cut paper snowflakes hang, each bearing a name and age. I smile, figuring these snowflakes were made by Amelia's students, all of whom are also my parents' patients. Glancing around the space, I'm filled with unexpected pride. Not only is it merry and bright, it's also the most comfortable and calming waiting room I've ever been in.

"Proof the Munro family takes Christmas decorating as seriously as medicine," I say.

"And not just Christmas," Liam replies. "Don't forget Easter, Valentine's Day, Canada Day, and my favourite—outside of Christmas—Halloween, of course. Your parents go all out. They turn the clinic into a haunted house—but with friendly ghosts, for the kids." He throws a smile my way. "But you know all this."

I try to smile back, like, *Yes, I do know all of this*. But I'm struck with melancholy, reminded again how unaware I am now of the ebbs and flows of life here in Harmony Hills—a place I used to call home, but had no problem leaving. Along with everyone in it.

"Hello?" A woman's voice echoes down the hallway that leads to the back treatment rooms.

"Hi, Miss Betty—it's Libby," I call out. I haven't called myself Libby in over a decade, and yet it feels perfectly natural here.

"Welcome home, my darling girl!" Miss Betty envelops me in a hug. She's tinier than I am, but has impressive strength for a seventy-year-old. "Daily yoga and plenty of walking with a weighted vest," she told me last year when she came by the house to visit Mom after her fall. I shiver at the memory, at the bizarreness of knowing the future, which is supposed to be a mystery.

Miss Betty's silvery hair is styled in a chic pixie cut, and she's dressed in her usual—though unconventional—medical clinic uniform: hot pink leggings that match her lipstick, and a white linen button down that hangs loosely, with a Christmas light necklace and matching earrings. "You are a sight for sore eyes, young lady," she says, holding me at arm's length.

"I was just about to say the same to you," I reply, beaming. "The clinic looks wonderful."

"Thank you, honey," she says. "Only thing left is the Christmas tree. I think your dad is planning to get one in the next couple of days."

I nod, then say, "Oh, excuse my manners! Miss Betty, this is Liam. Liam Young."

"Of course I know Liam, Libby. He's responsible for my daily sourdough habit, and most of the Christmas trees in town."

"Oh?" I say, and Liam shrugs. "Harmony Hills is my best customer."

"He's being modest," Miss Betty says, setting her hands on her trim hips. "He doesn't charge a penny for those trees! The whole town visits the farm during the season."

Liam's cheeks redden. "I like Christmas, and this town," he says, smiling easily.

I wonder again if this guy has any flaws—aside from the quite minor breakfast foods thing, and a supposed inability to bake.

"And how's your granddad doing?" Miss Betty asks Liam.

It's possible I'm reading into her expression, but something changes in her face when she mentions Mr. Cutler. A slight rise of eyebrows, a deepening of her smile, a laser-sharp focus as she waits for Liam's response.

"He's well, Miss Betty," Liam replies. "Thanks for asking."

"Glad to hear it. Please tell him 'hello' for me," she replies. Then she notices Liam's hand, his coat shifting to reveal the towel, and purses her lips. "Hmm. The same can't be said for you, it seems?"

"A few stitches for our brave dishwasher here." I set a hand on Liam's arm, noting (again) his impressive muscles. *Now is not the time, Libby* ... My hands drops.

"The place is yours," Miss Betty replies. "It's going to be quiet for a couple of hours, until your mom and dad are back from house calls."

"Perfect." I shrug off my coat, as Miss Betty helps Liam with his. "Also, I'm going to hang the outdoor Christmas lights after this. Any chance you could pull them out for me?"

"Already done." Miss Betty points at a large storage tub near her desk. "Ladder is leaning against the side of the house. Give me a holler if you need anything. I'll be in the back, working on the photo collage."

"Photo collage? What's that for?"

Miss Betty gives me a curious look, then an exaggerated wink.

"Oh, you are good at secret keeping, Libby. I should take a page out of your book. I'm having a terrible time not spilling the beans."

"Wouldn't want to 'spill the beans.'" I wish desperately she would do just that.

"It's tough to have a surprise party if the surprise has been ruined," Miss Betty adds. "Too bad Austin can't join us, Libby. I was looking forward to finally meeting your beau. Next time, I guess!"

I nod and give a weak smile, my mind spinning. *Surprise party?* "Next time," I reply, my voice strained.

When I look at Liam, he's focused on the holiday decor, but there's a slight tension to his jaw—like he's clenching his teeth—which makes it seem he's about as pleased to hear Austin's name as I am.

21

"Feel free to sit, or lie down. Whichever you prefer," I say, pulling out a suture kit, antiseptic cleansers, a syringe, and some nitrile gloves.

"What's easiest for you?" Liam asks.

"It doesn't matter." I snap on a pair of gloves. "Not to brag, but I can do this with my eyes closed."

My tone is joking, and I expect some sort of response. But Liam seems lost in thought. His good hand rests in a tight fist on the exam table, his eyes locked on the syringe.

"What if, hypothetically, someone hates needles?" he asks.

"Liam, do *you* hate needles?" I casually place a gauze pad over the syringe.

"Well, *hate* is a strong word, but I can think of a thousand things I would rather do," he replies, his Adam's apple bobbing as he swallows.

"Why don't you lie down, okay?" He nods, before lying on the exam table, the paper crinkling under him. "Now, let's make that arm more comfortable."

I turn on the lamp and position the light so I have a clear view of the cut.

"So what *is* your favourite way to spend time?" I ask, holding the syringe with the numbing anesthetic out of view. "Just going to clean the area—it will feel cold for a second."

He nods, licks his lips, which are dry (definitely nervous—poor guy). "Winter or summer?"

"Let's do winter." I use an antiseptic wipe around the cut, then position the needle. "Now a few small pokes. Easy-peasy. Soon it will be gloriously frozen and you won't feel a thing."

Liam closes his eyes, lets his head rest back. "I'm a big fan of the snow, generally. Skiing, tobogganing, maple taffy."

"Maple taffy. I haven't had that in years." I remember how we used to make it every March, the water-like sap miraculously transformed first with heat, then by the snow. "Not the easiest to get in downtown Toronto."

Liam winces almost imperceptibly when I insert the needle. I'm thrust back to the last time I stitched up a hand—in the ER for Christmas-cake-maker Jennifer, who was not looking forward to the holidays. *How was that only a couple of days ago? But also . . . a year from now?*

"You okay?" I pause, forcing my shoulders down and telling myself to *relax*.

"I'm good." He releases a long breath. "Back to maple taffy—it's worth the drive, I think. From the city, I mean."

"Maybe I'll come back for the maple syrup festival." *March. Three months from now. What timeline will I be in then?* I breathe deeply through my nose, clearing the anxiety so I can focus. "So skiing, tobogganing, maple taffy . . . what else?"

"Snowshoeing. I used to think I hated it. It's just . . . walking through deep snow, right? But way more awkward, because you strap paddles to your feet." He grins, eyes still closed. I look at his face, seeing now under the bright lights a faint smattering of freckles across his nose.

"But turns out I love snowshoeing," he continues. He's more relaxed, the muscles and tendons in his outstretched arm releasing. "Pops and I try to go once a week."

I insert the needle a couple more times, plunging in the anesthetic in little bursts in the areas to be numbed. "I've actually never snowshoed, if you can believe it."

"You should go sometime. There are some great trails around here," Liam says. "Maybe before you head home?"

Home . . . a hint of panic fills me, remembering what's waiting for me in the present timeline. Or more accurately, what's *not* waiting: no relationship, no job, no idea what's next.

"Maybe . . . but remember the two-left-feet issue." I push back from the exam table and set the empty syringe down. "All done."

He lifts his head and opens his eyes. "Seriously?"

"The freezing part, anyway." I remove the gloves. I'll use a fresh pair for suturing. "Now we wait. A few minutes to let the anesthetic do its job."

I shift my rolling stool so when his head is turned it's easy for him to see me without changing position. "How about family holiday traditions?"

"We travelled around a lot, so we celebrated the traditions of wherever we happened to be during the holidays," Liam replies. "We spent two years in Venezuela. Did you know in Caracas they roller-skate to church for Mass during the holidays?"

"What do you mean . . . like, everyone? On actual roller skates?"

He laughs. "Everyone, young and old. With tie-up, retro roller skates. They even close the streets the week or so before Christmas to make it safer. It was a lot of fun, and definitely the most unique holiday tradition I've ever experienced."

"Wow. That's pretty cool," I reply. "Makes my family's traditions of matching Christmas pyjamas and leaving cookies and carrots out for Santa and the reindeer seem downright uninspired."

I test his hand. "Feel that?"

He shakes his head. "Nothing."

"It's go time." I give his shoulder a quick squeeze before pulling on new gloves. "Just take a few deep breaths. Won't take too long."

Liam closes his eyes again, and breathes in through his nose, out through his mouth.

"I'm jealous of your travelling. Of seeing so much of the world before you were even a teenager. I'm sure it wasn't always easy, or comfortable, but still. It's a fascinating way to grow up." I focus on tying off the first stitch, preparing for the second.

"It is. It was," Liam says. "Have you done much travelling?"

"Unfortunately, no. Medical school was all-consuming. Then residency. I've barely had time to think beyond my next shift, actually."

I continue stitching, my eyes trained on my work. "Still feel nothing?"

"Nothing! It's so strange, because how can I not feel this?"

"The benefits of modern medicine," I reply.

"It's not too late, you know," Liam says.

"Too late for what?" I'm concentrating on the final stitch, making sure the wound is closed and the skin isn't puckered.

"To travel. To see the world. You're not exactly 'over the hill,' as my pops would say."

"I'll be honest—sometimes it feels like I'm almost 'over the hill,'" I say, with a mirthless chuckle. "Or at least past the point of being able to make a big change."

"I don't believe that," Liam replies. "It's never too late to make a change. Look at my granddad. From math teacher to master bread baker and entrepreneur. At seventy-five years young."

Stitches complete, I turn off the light and set the magnifier glasses atop my head. "I've always wanted to volunteer somewhere, as a physician."

"Aside from the obvious, what's holding you back?" he asks, as I start to bandage his hand.

I pause, despite it not being a hard question to answer. I know what's holding me back: fear; discomfort; logistics, if I think practically. Also, before it became a nonissue, my relationship.

"Well, for one thing, my"—I'm about to say "my ex-boyfriend didn't share my dreams," before remembering I'm in the past and so do not yet have an ex—"*career* makes it hard to take that sort of time off."

"I'm sure," Liam says. "It's tough when things don't line up. For me, it was my relationship. Jaclyn and I had different goals, different values, even. At some point it was like a square peg and a round hole, you know?"

Nodding, I swallow hard. Austin and I were a square-peg-round-hole situation, too. I wish I could elaborate and commiserate with Liam, but it's best to keep it to myself.

"You're all set." I secure the bandage around Liam's hand. "Stitches can come out in about two weeks. Keep it dry, and watch for any signs of infection. Redness, swelling, weeping around the site."

"Will do, Doc. I can't thank you enough, Libby," Liam says, hopping down from the exam table. "Why don't I give you a hand with the lights?"

He smirks then, wriggling the fingers on his good hand. "Literally, *a* hand."

"Ha! Well, think you can hold a ladder steady?"

"*Not to brag, but I can do this with my eyes closed,*" Liam says, and I laugh hard, ignoring—yet again—the voice in my head that tells me if I want to make things less complicated, I should spend *less* time with Liam Young, not more.

22

I clutch the rungs so tightly my fingers tingle both with strain and the cold. I wish I was wearing gloves, but I need all the dexterity I can get. I hate heights, but this is the only way to ensure Mom doesn't break her ankle. My breath comes out in little gasps, creating frosty wisps.

"Did you know hanging Christmas lights leads to twenty thousand emergency room visits a year?" I say as I begin climbing up the creaking ladder. "I spend so much time suggesting people stay *off* ladders. Nothing like not taking your own advice."

"Someone should tell folks in Harmony Hills . . . this place lives for its holiday lights," Liam replies. "But we will not be adding to that number today, Libby. Promise."

Glancing cautiously over my shoulder, I see he's got one boot positioned against the ladder's base and is using both hands to hold it steady. "This ladder is not going anywhere. I've got you," he adds.

His voice is calm, assured, and I instantly feel less scared. He's not going to let the ladder slip—even with his bum hand. *I've got you.* Another shiver moves through me, unrelated to the temperature. I lessen my grip just enough to stop the tingling in my fingers. "Appreciate it. Can you pass me the lights?"

There are already hooks along the roofline, from years past, so all I need to do is string the lights from hook to hook, one section at a time. I'm maybe halfway up the ladder now, and hold on with one hand while reaching down with the other for the lights. It's a stretch, my shoulder and neck muscles protesting, and then our fingers touch. Our eyes lock, and I can tell he's feeling this thing between us as fiercely as I am.

I have a sudden urge to blurt everything out. The time travel, the truth about Austin, this undeniable energy between Liam and me that I haven't felt in a long time, if ever. The words are at the back of my throat, but then Liam breaks eye contact. His hand drops from mine and returns to hold the ladder again. Then I remember he believes I'm in a relationship. Because technically I *am*—I have a "beau." And Liam Young, with his perfect dimples and generous heart, is not the sort to step over a line like that.

After about twenty minutes I'm more comfortable going up and down the ladder, Liam has, as promised, kept it steady, and there have been no hiccups with the Christmas lights. They look perfect, and I know Mom will be pleased.

Ever since our locking-eyes moment, we have done a good job at keeping the mood light and cheerful, not veering into any topics of conversation that are overly personal. Work stuff (it's odd to talk about the job I no longer have), rescue-farm stuff, our favourite Christmas cookie (whipped shortbread, we agree). Then the weather, always a popular topic in these parts. We finish by wrapping a couple of strands around the porch posts for added cheer.

We carry the ladder—me on one end, Liam the other—to the side of the house, then walk back to the porch steps. "Thanks again," I say, rubbing my hands together to warm them.

"You're welcome, *again*," Liam replies, dimples shining with his smile. We're standing just over a foot apart, and I should create more space between us, but I don't want to. I like being close to Liam—he makes me feel safe, and like I can handle anything. Plus, those eyes . . . those dimples. *Sigh.*

"Glad I was able to help. Even with this." Liam lifts his bandaged hand.

"Remember, keep that dry. Doctor's orders."

He nods, and I glance at the clinic's front door. "I should check in with Miss Betty. To see if I can do anything else for her while I'm here."

"Of course. Don't let me keep you," Liam says. He turns to go, then pauses. "See you Monday night?"

"Monday night?" I'm trying to remember what day it is. *Friday?* I think. Yes, Amelia's working, and we're having Friday-night French toast for dinner.

"For the party? And Christmas chili night?"

"The party. Chili night, yes," I reply, though whether I'll still be here—in Christmas past—in three days' time in anyone's guess. Also, I had better figure out what this party is about and STAT.

As I'm contemplating my next move to get more information, Liam takes a step towards me and hugs me. It's friendly and warm, but I'm not expecting it and so my arms stay at my sides.

I inhale the heady scent of his shampoo, or aftershave, or whatever it is that makes him smell so damn good. He releases me just as I've managed to get my arms to work, attempting to return the hug, but I'm a second too late.

"Sorry, Libby," he starts, as I stare at him slightly slack-jawed. He bites his lower lip, looking mildly concerned. "I'm a hugger. I forget not everyone else is."

"No, it's fine. I'm a hugger, too!" I reply, but my shrill tone isn't convincing. I wish I could explain that my behaviour has nothing to do with the actual hug—which I quite enjoyed—but because I'm endlessly one step behind since waking up in another timeline.

"Trust me, it's not you, Liam. I'm—" I sigh deeply, try to smile, but I can't. "I'm having *a week*, that's all."

Liam cocks his head. "Everything okay?"

I'm flustered by the attention, by his considerate tone. Being a physician often means putting myself last, because the people I look after are having far worse days. A pounding headache from lack of sleep or the upset of a breakup is nothing compared to a scary case of pneumonia in a child, or a grandmother's stroke, or a family involved in a devastating car accident.

Unexpectedly, I start crying, which is embarrassing though unavoidable. A mini breakdown was inevitable, based on the chaos of what's happened in the past couple of days, but I would prefer to be having it alone. Without an audience—especially *this* audience.

"I'm so sorry," I mumble, willing my eyes to stop tearing up. I wipe at them with my gloves, try to laugh off my poorly timed show of emotion. "It appears I am, in fact, having a meltdown. My life is sort of falling apart at the moment."

"Don't be sorry," Liam says. He puts a hand to my shoulder and smiles warmly, his green eyes holding mine. "The holidays can be tough."

I sniff, and nod. My nose starts running, and I long for a tissue. As though reading my mind, Liam pulls a small packet from inside his coat pocket. The tissues have snowmen on them, and I hiccup and chuckle all at once. This is getting more embarrassing by the second.

"These are almost too cute to use," I say, sniffling again as I pull out one of the tissues. "Everhart's?"

"The only place I shop," Liam replies. "So look. We don't know each other well, but can I tell you something?"

"What's that?" I'm stuffed up, but have thankfully stopped crying.

Liam leans towards me, lowering his voice conspiratorially. "I suck at baking, and apparently at washing dishes. But I'm an excellent listener. If you're interested."

Oh, Liam—you have no idea how much I wish I could take you up on that.

I look down at my hands and the tissue I've balled up, noting the tiny paper flecks on my black gloves. "What do you do when things don't turn out how you hoped? When everything you thought was real . . . isn't?"

Shifting my gaze to Liam's face, I see he's taking my question to heart, and he nods his understanding. "Been there. Most recently with my ex, Jaclyn. It wasn't fun."

"Relationships are *not* easy," I reply. Then the next words are out before I consider the implications. "Austin and I broke up."

His eyebrows rise. "Sorry to hear that. I'm guessing it was recent?"

"Sort of," I say, all the while knowing this confession is a terrible idea. In this wacky timeline everyone, including my family and Austin himself, believes we are very much together. "It was coming for a while. One of those death-by-a-thousand-paper-cuts sort of things."

I almost laugh, thinking about paper cuts, and toilet paper, and the ridiculousness of our actual breakup.

"Everyone says not to sweat the small stuff. But everything that happened with Jaclyn made me realize the small stuff—those daily choices—are what matter most," Liam says.

"How so?" Despite how unsettled I currently am, my curiosity about what happened with Liam and Jaclyn is piqued.

"I mean, you need to choose that person again and again, every day. Which sounds like a lot of work, maybe, but I think if you've found the right person, it only gets easier to handle the small stuff. And the big stuff, too."

I almost start crying again. "I don't think I'm great at choosing the right person the first time."

Liam sighs. "I can relate. And it has nothing to do with Jaclyn, or who she was. It was about me, not understanding who *I* was, if that makes sense?"

"It makes sense. So much sense, actually." And it does. Throughout my nearly two-year relationship with Austin, I had moments of doubt, but also plenty of excuses to brush them aside.

Now, when I think back to the two of us, I am not sure how we got past the honeymoon phase of dating. The things I thought made us a good match—our career ambitions, our understanding of what it means to work in medicine, his love of city life and my desire to escape my small town, our physical chemistry— worked on paper. But there were many red flags I ignored, like his hunger for status, his lacklustre interest in family, and his need for control. Our values and goals weren't aligned, not even at the start.

I wanted to make a difference, whether it was in my emergency room, or somewhere else, like with Doctors Without Borders. I longed for community, I see that now—to be a part of something bigger than myself. Austin expected everything and everyone, including me, to revolve around his goals. Our trip to L.A. made that crystal clear.

These realizations land without a moment to catch my breath, and I go weak in the knees. I reach for the porch step railing to keep myself from falling.

"Whoa, Libby." Liam's grabs me by my waist as I stumble. "Why don't we sit for a second?"

He brushes off the bottom step to clear the fine dusting of snow, and my heart pitter-patters at the sweet gesture.

"Thanks—I'm okay," I reply. We sit on the bottom step. Liam sets elbows on his bent knees and looks my way, waiting until I'm ready to talk.

"So when you're having a bad day, what do you do to make it better? Looking for tips, in case that wasn't clear," I say.

He sets a finger to his chin, miming deep concentration. "Hmm. First, I have a good cry—obviously."

I laugh, hold up the disintegrating snowman tissue. "Check."

"Then I eat something. Food is the best distractor. My go-to is heaps of nachos with extra jalapeños and sharp cheddar, or my granddad's cinnamon-raisin bread, toasted, with butter and honey from the farm."

"Those are solid choices. And after the food coma wears off?"

He gives me a smirk. "I sing Christmas carols."

"Christmas carols? You mean if you're trying to cheer up during the holidays?"

Liam shakes his head. "I mean, *anytime* I'm trying to cheer up. Holidays, springtime, summer, fall . . . doesn't matter. They just make me happy."

He says this so easily, without disclaimer. "They just make me happy." Well, if I wasn't already charmed.

"Which is your favourite carol?" I ask. "For mood-boosting."

"That's tough," Liam replies. "'Jingle Bells' is a solid contender. So is 'Up on the Housetop,' 'Deck the Halls,' 'Rockin' Around the

Christmas Tree'..." I nod with each one, agreeing with his choices. "Maybe we should try it?"

"Try what? Singing?" I shake my head. "You don't want to hear me sing. We'll both be miserable."

"You can't be worse than me. I am a truly awful singer. I failed the vocal portion of music class in elementary school." He mimics a stern, teacher-like voice. "*Liam works hard in class, but is unable to hold a tune. He is unfortunately not musically inclined, and would be wise to pursue other academic endeavours in the future.*"

"They did not say that!" I laugh.

"I'm paraphrasing, but the teacher was not wrong."

"Well then, we can be truly terrible together. Because I think *that* might cheer me up," I reply, feeling lighter by the second. I'm beginning to learn it's hard to be sad, or upset, when you're with Liam. "Besides, I don't believe you're that bad—let's hear it."

"This is a safe space, right? No judgement?" Liam asks.

"No judgement," I reply.

He clears his throat in dramatic fashion, then starts singing. "'You better watch out / You better not cry . . .'" He pauses, raises an eyebrow.

"Touché," I murmur.

"You better not pout / I'm telling you why," Liam sings. He may be great at many things, but this is not one of them: he's so out of tune it's almost hard to tell what the song is, if you didn't know the lyrics. But he gives it his all for the next verse, his voice rising, and I join in.

"He's making a list / And checking it twice . . ." Our voices mingle together, and I'm only marginally better at singing than Liam is.

Soon I'm grinning ear to ear, feeling warm and flushed and happy. The tears are long gone, until I laugh so hard I cry when Liam tries to hit a falsetto note on the final chorus.

"I told you I can't sing," Liam says. "But where are we, on a scale of cheerfulness? One being bah humbug, and ten being Santa Claus on Christmas Eve."

"I'm a solid nine," I reply.

"Then my work here is done." Liam raises a hand, and I high-five it.

For a moment we sit quietly, side by side on the step, the warmth of our bodies comforting in the chilly air. Then he asks, "What's your position on Christmas trees? Real or fake?"

"Real. There isn't another option as far as I'm concerned."

"I was hoping you would say that," Liam says with a definitive nod. "So I know you're good with needles. But how are you with a hacksaw?"

23

"I wanted to ask you about the party." I busy myself with the coffee maker, measuring scoops with precision and counting in my head as I go. Except I lose count after the first two, focused on Miss Betty's response.

"What about it?" Miss Betty asks, adding another log to the fire. Liam has gone back to Slice of Life, but not before asking if I want to visit the farm and see the animals, maybe pick out a tree for the clinic. I don't tell him I have a low-key fear of large animals, and instead share my skills with a hacksaw (I have cut down many a Christmas tree with my parents over the years). I'm already feeling that anticipatory nervousness, and excitement, of seeing him again.

As I try to formulate my question about the party, I add another scoop to the basket. This pot is either going to be too weak, or gasoline-level strong. Either way, not great.

"Libby? What's your question?"

"So I was wondering if you've seen a to-do list lying around? For the party? I . . . I've misplaced mine." I pour the water into the coffee maker's reservoir, waiting for her answer.

"I do have an extra one, actually—Mila dropped a paper

copy off a week ago, but I prefer to use my phone. Let me grab it for you."

As Miss Betty heads off to retrieve this list, I sit in one of the waiting room's chairs, marveling at how cozy everything is. It's the sort of place in which you wouldn't mind waiting to see the doctor—homey and inviting, with plenty of natural light, warm wood, and comfortable chairs. Contrast that to the waiting room of any Toronto hospital, with their bright fluorescent lights, cracked plastic chairs, scuff-marked linoleum flooring . . . no comparison. Also, my shoulders are relaxed, I don't have a headache, and my eyes don't sting from the antiseptic cleaning smells. For a moment I consider what it would be like to work here, permanently, alongside my parents.

Do I love emergency medicine as much as I think I do? I'm not sure anymore. Sometimes you get so used to a specific narrative you stop checking in to make sure it's still accurate.

Either way, I'm pretty sure I'm burned out. Most docs I know, particularly those in the emergency room, are working on a half-full battery all the time. So where do I see myself in ten years? What do I want?

It's about the small things, Liam said. He was referring to relationships, but I'm starting to see how it applies to all areas of life. The small things, like freshly brewed coffee and soft cushions, homemade air fresheners, and a kind ear when you need someone to listen—those are the things that matter.

"Here you go," Miss Betty says. She hands me a piece of lined paper from a school notebook. It hasn't been ripped out, but rather a ruler has been used to make a clean edge, free of tears. The check boxes are perfect squares; the handwriting pristine. It has Amelia's signature style all over it, and I'm grateful to my little sister for her fastidiousness when it comes to to-do lists, among other things.

"Staying Alive! Munro Medical Turns Silver" is written at the top of the list.

Oh my goodness. Of course.

My parents opened the clinic twenty-five years ago this Christmas. This surprise party is *an anniversary* party, scheduled for the same night and venue as chili night to make sure my parents—who wouldn't miss this annual event—are none the wiser.

"Amazing, isn't it?" Miss Betty says. She's behind me, and she sets her hands on my shoulders. "Where has the time gone?"

"I have no idea," I reply, also realizing there was no such party last year. *What happened?* Mom's ankle, for one thing. But if this party was scheduled—even if it was cancelled in the end—why didn't I know about it? Why didn't my sister ask for my help? I would have stayed for this milestone event, no question.

Truth time, Libby. Okay, I would have come home for the party, but I would have presumed Amelia would handle the planning—and she definitely would have anticipated that, so she may not have involved me.

I'm so far away ... schedule is insane ... you're much better at this than I am, I likely would have said when she floated the idea of an anniversary party. I may also have argued that Mom and Dad took oaths as health custodians for the community, and therefore wouldn't need, nor frankly want, this sort of fanfare (a not-so-subtle attempt to eliminate the need to be involved—if there's no party, there's nothing to plan!).

I would have been wrong, though, on all counts—except the one about my sister's party-planning skills eclipsing mine. Yes, our parents serve Harmony Hills, but the town that relies on them would want to express gratitude and honour the clinic's legacy. A legacy that will end with my parents, because without a successor there are only two options: sell the practice, or end up with an underserved Harmony Hills. I well up, considering all of this.

"You all right, Libby?" Miss Betty asks, rubbing my shoulders.

"Never better," I reply, but my tone is strained. "Just overwhelmed that it has been so long. It's a big deal."

"Sure is, honey. Now, let's take a look at what's left to do." Miss Betty pulls out her phone, uses her finger to scan her digital list.

"Check, check, check, check . . . looks like most things are handled. Just my photo collage and the cookies are left. Oh, and the party gifts need to have the tags attached. Have you seen them yet?"

I shake my head, having no idea what the gifts are.

"They are so cute—turned out really well. Monica's book club made them all, bless those bookish ladies and gents! The gift tag is clever, too. Let me try to remember . . ." Miss Betty taps a finger to the side of her face, then holds it up, her face brightening. "*Twenty-five years of sleighing sickness—ho, ho, healthy!*"

I laugh at the festive pun. "I'll do the tags," I say, now seeing the item about halfway down the list. Ah, the party gifts are ornament-shaped bath bombs. Cute.

"It's lovely the two of you are doing this for your parents. They work hard. Too hard, I think. But what's the option?" A shadow passes over Miss Betty's face, and I long to ask, *Is everything okay, with my parents and the clinic?*

But before I can, the clinic's phone rings. "Excuse me, Libby. I should get that."

"Please, don't let me stop you. I was about to head out anyway."

"Munro Medical, this is Betty." There's a pause as she listens to whoever is on the other end of the phone. I start gathering my things. Miss Betty clicks into her laptop, eyes scanning the screen. "I can squeeze you in this afternoon. How about two o'clock?"

I slide my arms into my coat sleeves and zip it up; then, with a last wave and smile to Miss Betty, I open the door, Christmas bells chiming as I do.

Glancing into the kitchen, I see Mom and Dad side by side at the butcher block island, chopping veggies for the salad and whisking dressing. We're having a green salad with our cinnamon French toast, because: *balance*. Mom used to make us eat carrots and celery with our birthday cakes, always found a way to add zucchini to every baked good, and a piece of fruit was paired with rare take-out French fries. Dad's singing along to Christmas carols, and Mom nods her head to the beat.

I've always taken their solid marriage for granted. My parents make it look easy, which perhaps was part of my issue with Austin. I assumed it should be easy, which was naive. Success takes hard work, whether it's a career or a relationship.

Amelia and I are setting the dinner table, and I know our parents can't hear us with the music playing. "Mila, how about I do the tags for the party favours?"

She looks up at me, slight surprise on her face. "Oh, great. That would be a big help. I have all the supplies at my place, if you're okay to do it there?"

"I'll do it tomorrow," I reply, laying out the cutlery. "Miss Betty gave me her extra list."

I swallow hard, embarrassed by my lack of awareness. I should have remembered this anniversary without any reminders. I'm hoping what I say next doesn't sound accusatory, considering how much work my sister has clearly done for the party. "Why didn't you ask for my help earlier? I would have been glad to do more. You took on a lot, it looks like."

Amelia stares at me, arm poised with the water jug mid-pour. "Libby, I did. Don't you remember? We talked about it briefly, last month. I asked you to come home early, and you said you couldn't."

I stare back, feeling the frown settle onto my face. I have no memory of this. I suddenly realize I'll never know what happened to the party last year—there's no way, and no one, for me to ask, because the future is currently being rewritten.

Glancing back into the kitchen again, I watch Dad and Mom bump hips to the music, laughing as they do. I have thought very little about my parents, the clinic, and how integral they have been to the community here. Shame fills me, soon followed by melancholy.

Amelia continues filling the water glasses. "You said you'd be there for the party but couldn't leave work much before that. And then, weirdly, you showed up early anyway. Like, *days* early . . ." She shrugs, eyes on the water glasses.

My hands shake lightly as I set the forks onto folded napkins. I'm glad she's not making eye contact, because I am struggling to hold a neutral expression.

"You said you took a few extra days off work, and I should take advantage of your empty schedule. But then you got sick, and, well, truth be told, everything was already mostly done. Miss Betty was a huge help. Becks, too—she did the invites. Did you know she does beautiful calligraphy? Hand addressed all of them for me. For us."

I watch Amelia's lips turn up into a subtle smile. "Huh, wow," I reply, thinking about the wedding note cards Mom and I attached to the candy canes, and how a year from now Amelia and Beckett will be starting a life together. "She's a good friend."

"She is." Amelia sets the water jug on the sideboard, puts the salt, pepper, and maple syrup in the middle of the table. "It's going to be awesome, seeing their expressions. I can't believe we've kept the secret."

Her voice is lowered, but Dad—who suddenly appears in the dining room, salad in hand—catches the tail end of her comment. "Kept what secret?" he asks.

Amelia and I exchange a quick glance, then I say, "Your salad dressing. We've never asked about your secret ingredient . . ."

Dad places his hands on the tablecloth, which is covered in silver bells, leaning towards us. "Nutritional yeast," he whispers. "Flakes of gold. But don't tell your mother—she thinks it's vile stuff."

Amelia and I burst out laughing, silently crossing our hearts and pressing our finger to our lips in a vow of silence.

24

December 18

It's a few hours before the party, and Christmas chili night, and everything is ready. The checklist double-checked, things seemingly on track. Amelia's already at the community centre, getting started on the setup. She made up some bogus end-of-year teachers' meeting so Mom and Dad don't catch on.

My parents are currently finishing up paperwork, nibbling on sugar cookies, and drinking lukewarm coffee at the kitchen table. I'm scattered and stress-eating my second slice of leftover cinnamon-bread French toast when the doorbell rings.

"I'll get it." Popping a last piece of syrup-drenched French toast into my mouth, I wipe my hands with a napkin and head through the living room. Christmas bells nestled into a decorative wreath jingle when I open the front door.

Elsie Farrow stands on the other side, a quilted bag in one hand and a leash in the other, attached to none other than Mary Piggins. For a moment I'm shocked, because in my recent memory I just attended her memorial service. It's mind-blowing to stand here across from her, seeing her so vibrant and healthy. So full of life. I'm afraid I might cry, and I try to get ahold of myself.

It's Mary who brings me back to the present, with a series of happy snuffles and snorts. I clear my throat and smile brightly. "Miss Elsie, hello! Happy holidays!"

"Hello, Libby, and happy holidays to you," she says, her blue eyes—that are so much like Claire's—holding mine. "I had an extra casserole, and something just told me I should drop it off for your mom and dad, especially knowing you're home visiting."

"That's so kind of you." I step back and gesture inside. "Would you like to come in? Mom and Dad are in the kitchen, finishing some work before we head to *chili night*." I give an exaggerated wink, and Miss Elsie smiles knowingly.

"Looking forward to it," she says, winking back. "But I won't come in—thank you, though. Mary here does best outdoors. She can be a bit of a handful, as sweet as she is."

Miss Elsie casts an adoring smile towards Mary Piggins, and it makes me both happy and sad, seeing how much she clearly loves this troublemaking potbellied pig—who feels the same about her, based on how Mary snuggles into her owner's leg.

"Mary and I have met a couple of times now, and 'bit of a handful' seems fitting." Another snort, and I bend so I can give her a little scratch behind her ear.

Miss Elsie holds out the quilted bag. "Macaroni and cheese soup—a family recipe—tell your mom and dad to keep the Tupperware, reuse it however they like. Now, I can tell by your face you're wary of this delicacy, Libby, but you'll have to trust me. It's the best comfort food there is."

I laugh lightly at being called out for my reaction—a subtle eyebrow lift, probably a mild grimace. Miss Elsie misses nothing.

"Well, I've never met a macaroni and cheese I didn't love, so I can't wait to try the Farrow family soup version." I take the bag in hand, noting its weight. I'm impressed that she's carried this over from her place, while also walking Mary—her fitness and strength must be excellent.

Again, I'm subdued and saddened by the reality that a year from now she will no longer be here. "Thank you so much. This was very thoughtful of you."

"Give them a hug for me, and I'll see the three of you soon." Miss Elsie reaches for my hand and gives a squeeze. I almost cry again, wishing I wasn't privy to the future. "You're a good girl for coming home for this. I know they miss you."

Now I do start to cry, but Miss Elsie makes no mention of the tears that blur my vision. She leans in to give me a hug, her wool coat scratchy against my chin, smelling of lavender and something softly peppery—winter mint, maybe.

"Time to go, Mary," she says, and the pig lets out a snort that reminds me of a toddler who has no interest in—nor intention of—doing as her parent asks. "Young lady, we need to get our steps in; otherwise, there will be no candy cane as a little treat, all right?"

"See you soon," I reply, giving a short wave. "Bye, Miss Elsie. Bye, Mary Piggins."

I'm shutting the door, bag of soup in hand, when my phone buzzes. Walking back into the kitchen, I take a quick glance at the screen.

Austin. Anxiety, mixed with a sense of obligation, moves through me, and I sigh.

"Everything okay?" Mom asks.

I decline the call—I'll check my voicemail later. "Just a work thing. Nothing urgent."

My tone isn't as convincing as I would like, but Mom lets it go.

"Was that Elsie Farrow I heard? Did you invite her in?" Dad asks.

"It was, and I did. But she had Mary Piggins with her." I set the bag on the countertop, and then reach inside to pull out the large, round Tupperware container from its depths.

"Macaroni and cheese *soup*. It also comes with a hug, for both of you—and she said you can keep the container."

"Mac and cheese soup?" Dad glances at the container. The contents look like a watered-down casserole, and we share a semi-concerned look.

"A family recipe, apparently," I say with a shrug.

"Knowing Elsie, I'm sure it's outstanding," Mom replies. "Why don't you put it in the fridge, Libby? We'll have it tomorrow for lunch or dinner."

I find a spot in the fridge and am shutting the door when my phone vibrates again. I grumble under my breath, but it's not Austin. It's Helena, and it's a video call.

Shoot. I forgot to get back to her, and three texts and a voice-mail later she's tracking me down, the way a good friend does.

"Helly, hi!" I say, answering the call. "Give me a sec."

I put up a finger for Mom and Dad, and then point to the living room. They've started doing the holiday-themed crossword from today's paper.

"What's a five-letter word for part of the mistletoe?" Dad asks, after nodding in acknowledgement of my gesture.

"Berry," Mom replies. "Or sprig?"

Their voices fade as I head through the living room, sitting sideways on the second to last stair so my socked feet and back rest on the pickets. It's how I used to sit as a teenager when I was on our corded landline, which is long gone now.

"I'm here," I say to Helena. She's dressed in a strange mash-up: a white Santa Claus beard, the elastic loops around her ears stretched so the beard sits below her chin; a butterfly antenna headband; and dinosaur stickers on her cheeks and nose—all surely the work of her toddler.

"Nice outfit, by the way. Very eclectic fashion choices. So how are you, Helly?"

"How am I? *How am I?*" She's mad, her frown deepening. "You call me to tell me you've travelled through time, like Marty McFly, and then I don't hear from you for over forty-eight hours? We text each other every night. *Every night*, Elizabeth. No exceptions—even if you think you're a time traveller, or whatever. Do you know how worried I've been?"

I shush her, because my parents are only one room away. Taking the stairs two at a time until I reach my bedroom, I close the door firmly behind me.

"I'm so sorry, Helly. I didn't mean to worry you. It's been . . . strange," I reply. I turn on the lantern light that I borrowed from Amelia's room, after Krazy Gluing it back together. "Let It Snow!" begins playing, creating the ambient noise I'm hoping will help muffle the conversation if my parents come upstairs.

Helena sighs in irritation. "Don't make me count to three," she says.

"Um . . . are you talking to me?"

"One . . ." she says, ignoring the question. She holds up a finger. "Two . . ." Another finger goes up, and her tone becomes more serious. "Good girl. Thank you, Dells."

"Phew. For a moment there, I thought I was about to get the wrath of Momma Helena."

She laughs, eyes back on me. "Adelaide is obsessed with the tree. We have these hand-painted-present ornaments that David's mom sent from Finland, super fancy. Dells unwrapped half of them! So now we have six tiny Styrofoam blocks hanging from the tree, which is not at all festive. Anyway, she was about to start on the others, and I'm trying to teach a lesson and not endure the wrath of my mother-in-law, who believes children are easily trained."

"'Have a kid,' they said," I reply, in my best Helena voice—slightly higher than my own—with perfect enunciation. Her mother was an elementary-school English teacher.

"'It will be fun—and quite easy!'—they said," she adds, with a half-decent Finnish accent to mimic her mother-in-law, and we both laugh. Then she abruptly stops, her brown eyes narrowing and her lips pursing. Her dark curls frame her face, and I wish I could reach through the screen and give her a hug.

"Hmm . . . you look okay to me. How are you feeling?" she asks.

"Perfect. Never better." A stretch, maybe. However, not completely untrue, despite the events of the past couple of days.

Another pause. "Do you still think you're in Christmas past?"

I hesitate. Chew the inside of my lip.

"Elizabeth . . ." Helena begins, impatience coming back into her voice.

"Yes, okay, *yes*. I am still in Christmas past." I throw up my hand, the one not holding the phone. "I don't understand what's happening, or why, and I know you're probably about ready to come here and drive me to the nearest CT scanner—"

"Correct," she replies, nodding emphatically. One of the dinosaur stickers falls off her cheek.

"But you just have to trust me. I'm okay. I can't explain it, but I also know I don't need a CT scan."

"You're sure?"

"I'm sure," I reply, repeating myself to, I hope, reassure her.

Helena sits back in her chair, crosses her arms, then looks to the side and blows out a long breath before facing the camera again. "I need to tell you something."

I'm thrown for a moment, wondering what she's referring to. She seems nervous, her fingers tapping against her crossed arms. Now I'm worried. Something must be wrong. I think back to last year, to anything that happened that might explain this shift in her. But I can't come up with a thing. Everything was fine last Christmas. Yes, she and David were recently separated, but it was as copacetic as a separation could be. Adelaide was healthy, work was fine.

"What? What's going on?" I ask.

She suddenly changes her position, leaning her elbows onto the table and looking right into the camera. "I *may* have done something you're not going to like."

"What did you do?" I have no clue what it could be, but my heart rate increases in anticipation. By the tone of her voice, the sheepish look she's now sporting, it's clear that, whatever it is, she's right: I'm not going to like it.

"Let It Snow!" continues playing on a loop, and it's distracting. I reach over and turn the lamp off so the room is silent again. Now I hear Adelaide faintly in the background, singing "You better watch out / You better not cry! / You better not pout . . ." in her adorable two-year-old, lisp-heavy voice. I think of Liam and our cheer-me-up singing outside the clinic.

"So you might be getting a visitor. Soon." Helena scrunches up her nose, and a second dinosaur sticker falls off.

"Who? What are you talking about?"

Just then the doorbell rings. I ignore it, turn my attention back to Helena.

"Sorry, doorbell just rang. My parents will get it."

"Um . . . shit. Ooops. Yes, Dells. I know that was a swear. Sorry, Elizabeth," Helena says, before adding, "I told Austin."

"You told Austin what?" But I'm distracted because Dad is

calling my name up the stairs. I go to the door and open it, then shout down, "Be right there."

To Helena I say, "I have to go. My dad needs me for something."

She waves, seems relieved the conversation is ending so abruptly. "Go, go. It can wait."

"Helena—wait . . . What did you tell Austin?"

It comes out in a rush. "I told him I was worried about you. That you were sick, which he knew, but also that you seemed to be *confused*. Like, in a bad way. Maybe in a pathological way?"

"Oh no . . ." Suddenly I wonder who's at the door. Why Dad is calling me to come downstairs. Surely not for another neighbour, nor a casserole. Now I wish I'd answered Austin's phone calls, because I'm realizing there's a good chance he's standing on the other side of my parents' front door. "What did he say?"

"I did a good job convincing him something was really wrong, let's put it that way." At the look on my face, she says, "I'm sorry! You legit scared the hell out of me. And then I ran into him at work, and one thing led to another, and . . ."

She stops, sighs with resignation. "He said he was coming to get you. Probably on his way there. May even be there already?"

"Helly, this is bad." My heart rate ratchets up further. My eyes dart to my closed bedroom door, and my throat feels tight. There is no way this isn't going to blow up in my face. Austin will tell my parents something is very wrong, everyone will freak out, I'll be forced to . . . I don't even know. But it won't be good. And we're T-minus two hours until the surprise party kicks off. Good grief, what am I supposed to do?

"Again, I am so, so sorry." Helena bites her bottom lip, utterly distressed.

"No, it's fine, Helly," I reply. "I would probably have done the same thing. I'll . . . figure it out."

There are footsteps on the stairs, and I almost can't breathe. Then, a knock at my bedroom door. "I have to go," I squeak out.

Another light knock, and my heart rate goes up a few more beats.

"Talk soon?" Helena asks, and I nod before hitting End Call.

Then I look at myself in my mirror on the back of the door, smooth down my long, last-Christmas hair, and take a deep breath before opening the bedroom door.

25

I t's Claire. Oh my goodness . . . *the relief.*

"Hey, you!" she says, leaning in to give me a hug. I tackle-hug her back, giddy with release that it's not Austin on the other side of the door.

"Uh . . . this is nice, Libby, but I can't breathe," she says in a strangled voice, followed by a short laugh.

I let her go quickly. "I'm so glad to see you. Come on in."

We sit on my bed, and Claire tucks her legs up under her. I think back to when we were in high school. I can still picture teenage Claire, with the blond fishtail braid she always wore and the metal braces she hated so much. Now her teeth are perfectly straight and her blond hair is shoulder-length, slightly waved, with layers framing her blue eyes.

"Sorry for the pop-in, but we're back for Christmas chili night. Staying at Kirby's parents' place, which means the kids get a lot of grandparent time, and I can hear myself think again."

"I don't know how you do it." My voice carries my genuine awe. "I would not look this gorgeous—that's for sure."

"I have applesauce in my hair, and if you smell hot chocolate, it's because I'm wearing half of Jonah's." She lifts one brow. "But thank you for the much-needed compliment."

"Here for you," I say, before it occurs to me that I haven't been there for Claire for years. The list of things I need to work on, to change, grows by the day.

"Anyway, I wanted to check in to see if you and Amelia need help setting up? I am sans enfants for now, so I'm all yours."

"We would love that," I reply. "But how did you know I was here?"

"Saw Gigi walking Mary. Told me she dropped off her mac and cheese soup—I know, it sounds awful, but it is divine." She crosses her heart.

"Well, I trust you," I say. "And I was just about to head out, so your timing is perfect."

We walk downstairs and into the kitchen.

"Is the cough productive, or is it dry?" Mom is talking to a patient on her phone, so I lower my voice.

"Dad, Claire and I are going over to the community centre."

Mom glances up at Claire and her face lights up; she offers an enthusiastic wave and smile. Claire was always a favourite in our house, and she continues to solidify that reputation by pulling a package out of her purse and handing it to my dad. "My mother-in-law has been baking—whipped shortbreads."

"Lucky us!" Dad replies softly, as the three of us move to the front hallway to avoid distracting Mom. "We'll thank Charlotte when we see her tonight. I assume she's going?"

"She wouldn't miss it," Claire replies.

"You guys okay? Is there anything you or Mom need, before I head out?" I ask, pulling on the Sorel boots and grabbing my coat from the closet.

"We'll see you there once we finish up here—shouldn't be too long."

"You'll let me know, right?" I slide my arms into my coat sleeves. "If you need help? Here, at the clinic, whatever, with Christmas stuff—happy to do anything."

Last year, I didn't make any such speech, and while I offered my help, it was limited by my very short trip. I'm ashamed by how self-centred I was, and I'm determined to handle things differently this time.

"Your presence is the only present we need, honey," Dad replies, with a grin that warms me to my core. "Plus, you have to head back tomorrow for your trip. Don't go worrying about us on your last night. We're fine."

A wave of panic crests at his mention of the trip, and what Helena confessed. I need to call Austin, to make sure he's not driving here and to let him know . . . what, exactly? That I'm not coming back tomorrow, because I'm in an alternate timeline? No—what I need to tell him is that I can't get on that plane with him because our relationship has run its course, at least for me. I have to deal with this, with Austin, before it gets more complicated. I reach for my phone in my pocket, but it's not there.

"One sec," I say to Claire. "Forgot my phone in my room."

I take off my boots and race upstairs. The phone is on my bed, and it's illuminated with a text message. "Call me back. Need to know you're okay. Worried."

Speaking of Austin . . .

Then, a series of texts, which came in two minutes later.

"Where are you?"

"You okay??"

"Do you need me to come and get you? I can leave tonight. No surgery tomorrow."

My heart races as I quickly type back a message.

"I'm okay! Helly said you guys ran into each other. No need to worry, I'm fine. Aftereffects of the food poisoning, I think. I was a bit of a mess when we chatted. Sorry about that. lol."

I hit Send. Moments later, three squiggly dots. I don't wait for his message, wanting to stay on top of the narrative. "Busy with stuff for my parents right now. Promise we'll chat soon," I type out.

The dots disappear. My finger hovers, the desire to confess it all overwhelming. I start typing again. "I also can't leave right now. I'll explain later when I . . ."

Sighing, I hit Delete. I'm struggling with the cognitive dissonance of trying to manage present-time Austin, when I know in a year we'll merely be part of each other's history. So while it would be deliciously easy to give myself an out via text message, it's not the right way to have the conversation—regardless of what the future holds.

So instead I type: "I'll call soon. Heading out the door—the party's tonight!"

Austin replies, "Hope it goes well—wish your parents well for me. And don't overdo it, if you're not 100 per cent. Talk soon. Love you."

I stare at his text, knowing past Elizabeth would reply with a "Love you, too." Instead, I double click his message to leave a heart emoji response, then turn my phone to Do Not Disturb, and head back downstairs.

26

The community centre has been transformed, decked out for the upcoming holiday: a giant blow-up Santa and his sleigh are parked near the front door; multicoloured twinkle lights are draped across the ceiling; tinsel garland frames every doorway and window frame; mini lit-up Christmas trees line the walls, waiting to be adorned by ornaments guests will make tonight. There's mulled wine for the adults and sweet apple cider with cinnamon for the younger set; those scents compete with the savoury-spicy smells of bubbling chili in dozens of Crock-Pots.

While Slice of Life donates bread to go with the chili, the main meal is contributed by the families of Harmony Hills. Each participating family has a secret recipe, and there's an annual competition amongst the chili makers for the Best of the Season trophy (a golden kidney bean).

Amelia, Claire, and I have just finished the surprise party portion of the decorating. Clusters of helium balloons dot the stage, with the number 25 printed in glitter on the white ones, and shimmery snowflakes on the silver ones to match the rest of the holiday decor. The photo collage is on a stand to one side, for people to peruse at their leisure, along with a large, wrapped gift.

The cellophane-and-ribbon-packaged bath bombs—shaped like candy-cane ornaments and scented with vanilla and peppermint oil—are nestled in a bin made to look like a gift box. The sign reads SOAK AWAY HOLIDAY STRESS! THANKS FOR 25 HEALTHY YEARS!

Amelia's smiling, but she looks tired—her ponytail mussed up, black mascara flecks on her cheeks, her eyes slightly bloodshot. "I can't believe we pulled this off."

"*You* pulled this off, Mila, nearly single-handedly." I wipe the mascara flecks from her cheeks. "I'm sorry I wasn't more help."

"Don't worry about it. I had loads of help, and you were busy saving lives." Her tone reveals nothing but kindness and understanding. I see my lack of commitment to the party was not something that needed to be forgiven, in Amelia's eyes. However, that doesn't change the fact that I no longer want to be that disconnected sister, daughter, or friend again.

"Everything looks perfect," Miss Elsie says, coming up to us. Claire links arms with her grandmother, who admires the party setup. "Well done, girls."

"Oh, this was all Mila," I say.

"It would never have all come together without a lot of help, especially from Libby and Claire tonight," my sister replies.

"It's a delight, having you both back in town. We all miss seeing you. Thick as thieves you were, in high school," Miss Elsie says to Claire and me.

"A much-needed blast from the past," Claire says. I catch her eye and we grin, remembering our shenanigans from those days. She still wears her signature scent, warmed vanilla sugar perfume, and I get a sudden waft of it—the increasingly present nostalgia crippling me again.

"Are you . . . crying?" Claire whispers, shifting to look me in the face. Miss Elsie and Amelia are discussing the gift, and when it will be presented to our parents.

I quickly wipe at my eyes, laughing. "Maybe? This place, during the holidays especially . . . I'm feeling all the feels."

Claire nods, smiling. "I know. Me, too."

"There's something in the air here that makes all the good memories bubble right to the surface," I say.

"My personal theory is that the city council pumps peppermint candy and hot chocolate with marshmallow scents through the heat vents," Claire says with a bemused look.

"I miss you, Claire. I miss . . . *this*." I wave an arm around. "I have Helena, of course—you need to meet her, you two will hit it off—and a few work friends, but it's not the same. You knew first-generation Libby."

"I loved first-generation Libby!" Claire replies. "Well, it's decided. I'm going to visit you in the new year. Leave the kids with Kirby's mom, or my parents. Three under six isn't that tough." She rolls her eyes at this.

"Besides, I need to finally meet the dashing Dr. Whitmore," she adds.

Claire never ended up meeting Austin. Last year when I was in Harmony Hills for those couple of days, she was still in Westhaven. We never had this conversation, and our communications have been entirely digital this past year. I sent her a text on her birthday in March; she sent me one on my birthday in June. Then we lamented, over a couple more texts, about how we needed to catch up on the phone, which never happened.

Hearing her enthusiasm about meeting Austin reminds me of the ring tucked in my overnight bag, wrapped up in his sweatshirt. I think of the ways my life might have turned out differently, had he given me that ring and asked the ever-important question, "Will you marry me?"

I consider all the ways I'm not only changing the past, but maybe also *the future* with these conversations and interactions. It's easy to believe I'm making things better (hanging holiday lights and saving Mom's ankle) . . . but what if I'm wrong?

I can't think straight. It's suddenly too loud, and I need to find a quiet place to regroup. "I'm going to the washroom. Want me to grab some mulled wine on my way back?" I ask Claire, antsy for an escape.

For a moment, I think she sees I'm not okay. There's a slight shift in her expression, a question mark in the subtle lift of her brows. But then Kirby's beside us, Lucy in his arms. The baby's wriggling, crying in great distress, and has a fistful of Kirby's long dark hair clutched in her little fingers.

"Hey, Libby!" Kirby says, trying to wrest his hair out of Lucy's grip. He's quite relaxed, considering the tornado of a child in his arms. "We'll have to catch up, after we tame the wild beast here."

To Claire, he says, "She's changed and dry, so I'm guessing she's hangry."

"Looks like you have your hands full," I start, gesturing over my shoulder. "I'll get us some wine. Kirby?"

"I'm good, thanks," he says, handing Lucy to Claire. "On call later, so it's an apple-cider party for me."

I give a thumbs-up and a crooked half smile, then turn and make my way through the groups of townspeople, who are chatting and celebrating. It's slow going, and I grow progressively more dizzy and anxious with each step. My lungs begin resisting deep breaths. *Am I having a panic attack?* I've seen plenty but have never experienced one myself.

"Excuse me, excuse me, oh, hello there . . . Very happy to be home for the holidays . . . Amelia will have them back in about half an hour . . . Yes, gout can be *awful*, I'm glad you're doing better."

This last comment is directed towards Millicent Mueller, a two-doors-down neighbour of my parents who used to babysit my sister and me, always serving this hot ham casserole that she boasted contained "an entire jar of mayo-nnaise!" *Hot mayonnaise mixed with ham* . . . ugh, no.

I make it to the other side of the main room, and then duck through the doorway, hoping for some privacy to catch my breath. But my plan's soon thwarted.

"Hey, Libby!" It's Beckett Livery-Quinn—the vet, Liam's best friend, and, most importantly, my soon-to-be sister-in-law.

Beckett's small-framed—about four inches shorter than I am—and has retained the compact, muscled figure from her former elite gymnast days. Her deep brown hair hangs neatly past her shoulders, with enviable bangs (I can't pull off bangs, more than one stylist has informed me). Dark eyes behind large-framed black glasses, which make her look like an investigative journalist on assignment, or an advertising executive.

We hug, and I hope she doesn't feel me shaking. "Beckett, so nice to see you. How are things?"

Black spots dot my vision. *Uh-oh.* I press my back against the wall, then pinch the skin between my thumb and pointer finger. Beckett's still talking, telling me a story about how my dad assisted her with a surgery because her vet technician had the flu. I nod and smile, appropriately timed, I hope, to her story. I'm barely paying attention though, trying to stay vertical.

"Anyway, I'm manning the family chili station tonight so need to get back on duty. Chase is the chef, but I'm the designated server." Beckett's a fourth-generation resident of Harmony Hills, and her great-grandfather, Arthur Livery-Quinn, was the town's first mayor. Her eyes dart over my shoulder. "Is Mila here?"

Her delivery of the question doesn't give anything away, but the look on her face does. Anticipation, with a hint of . . . hopefulness.

"She's gone to get Mom and Dad," I reply. "Speaking of my parents, I should hit the ladies' room before my own job begins. Surprise is set for . . ." I glance at my phone. "Seven on the nose. I have nineteen minutes. Mila was very clear we are to be ready to shout 'surprise' exactly five minutes early."

Beckett chuckles. "She's adorably uptight, that sister of yours." I catch her blush, watch her drop her eyes as her hands slide into her jeans' back pockets. She has always struck me as one of those women with confidence to spare, so this tiny act of what I presume is managing nerves fills me with a sort of sisterly adoration.

"That she is, and we all love her for it," I reply. Beckett's eyes come up to mine, and we exchange a smile. "Mila said you did the invites by hand. They're gorgeous—thanks for that. I know she appreciated it. We both do."

"Ah, I was happy to do it. Your parents and that clinic are the backbone of this community," Beckett says, pulling her hands from her pockets. They're steady now. "See you out there, Libby."

"See you," I reply, as Beckett steps past me through the doorway. *I should get back out there, too*, I think, turning to follow Beckett. But I don't get far, colliding with someone who happens to be coming through the doorway at that precise moment.

We bump together with some force—enough to make me gasp—then simultaneously throw our hands out, clutching each other's arms, to avoid stumbling. It takes me only a split second to realize who I've run into, and when he smiles down at me, those dazzling green-gold eyes on mine, and says, "Hi there," I'm light-headed all over again.

27

"I figured I'd *run into you* tonight," Liam says, his tone playful.

I laugh, too hard, and am then self-conscious. Especially because I'm still holding on to his arms, though his hands have already dropped. I quickly follow suit and take a small step back, so our bodies are no longer pressed together.

"How's that doing?" I glance at his bandaged hand. I'm grateful to be able to switch into doctor mode for a moment, to focus on something other than those dimples and piercing green eyes.

"All good," he says, the corners of said eyes crinkling with his smile. "I had a great doctor. Dr. Elizabeth Munro, do you know her?"

My cheeks grow warm, and I'm glad we're standing in the semi-dark so he won't notice.

"I've heard she's excellent," I reply, playing along. My blush deepens. "But it's easy when you have a great patient."

Easy, Libby. Stop flirting with Liam Young in Christmas past (even if it feels like the most natural thing).

"So how was the French toast?" Liam asks.

"Delicious. That bread is so cinnamony."

Cinnamony? Inwardly, I sigh, for I'm as awkward as a second-year medical-school student trying to put in an IV under the scrutinizing gaze of a charge nurse.

"I've never understood cinnamon loaf that wasn't super cinnamony," he replies. "What's the point?"

"Exactly. Without the cinnamon, it's just . . . bread." There's a pause as Liam says, "That's true," and my mind scrambles for a segue. There's only so long you can banter about bread, after all.

Thankfully, the silence is shattered by a series of ringing bells, the sound coming through the ceiling's speakers. My phone buzzes two seconds later. It's Amelia.

"Leaving the house in five—this is not a drill!"

"My parents are on their way." Glancing past Liam into the crowded, noisy main room, I cringe. This isn't going to be easy.

Liam looks over his shoulder. "Do you have a megaphone?"

"I do not. That would have been a good idea, actually."

"Come on," Liam says, reaching for my hand with his bandage-free one. For a split second I don't know what to do. Give him my hand, or pretend like I don't notice the gesture? The decision is made for me when his fingers find mine. His hand is warm, his grip both gentle and firm enough that I know he isn't going to let go, unless I do first.

We walk back into the main room, hand in hand. I have the wherewithal to realize that not only should I *not* be holding his hand, I shouldn't be holding it in front of the entire town of Harmony Hills. But by then we've made our way to the main stage. I clear my throat, readying my voice to quiet the noisy crowd.

Liam releases my hand first, to allow us to climb the narrow stairs single file. However, I can still feel the ghost of his grip—the comfort of his hand in mine. My limbs feel wiggly, or what we refer to in the ER—when dealing with an injury like a dislocation or a fracture—as "loosey-goosey."

After walking to the front of the stage Liam stops and, using the fingers of his good hand, lets out an earsplitting whistle. It's shrill and so loud I instinctively cover my ears. The room falls silent.

"The stage is yours, Libby." He invites me forward with the swoop of his hand, like he's presenting me to the audience after a show.

"Thank you," I whisper, as I take a spot centre stage. *Flutter-flutter-flutter* goes my heart, and it's pounding hard enough I'm sure he must hear it.

Between the last few minutes with Liam, the glare of the spotlight shining in my eyes, and the relentless pounding of my heart, all thoughts drain from my mind. A moment of panic ensues as the entire town watches me, waiting.

Say something ... Say anything ...

Liam, shifting closer, reaches out and gives my forearm a gentle squeeze. His touch snaps me back into my body. With a deep breath, I refocus on the crowd, pushing out thoughts of the impossibly sweet—and impossibly handsome—guy to my left.

Then I say the first thing that comes to mind. "Merry Christmas!"

My voice is loud—a few decibels below what one might refer to as a proper shout. I'm sweating, and wipe a hand across my forehead. *Merry Christmas?* Christmas is still days away.

"And to you, Libby!" An equally loud voice says. Scanning the crowd, I see it belongs to Miss Elsie—Mary Piggins sitting beside her. *That pig has an impressive social life.* Miss Elsie, in the front row, nods her head in encouragement. Then there's a slight murmur of "Merry Christmas" from a few others in the audience, as the crowd waits for me to continue.

I clear my throat. "First, thanks, Liam, for that most impressive whistle. If we ever need to call Santa's reindeer, we know who to ask!"

There's scattered laughter, and a few whistles sound off through the room.

"I think most of you already know me, but I'm Elizabeth . . . Libby . . . Munro, and my sister Amelia and I are so glad you're all here to celebrate the clinic's anniversary, and our parents." More cheers from the crowd.

"They're arriving soon, so we need to be quick. If everyone can form a semicircle in front of the main doors . . . you can stand in rows, as many as we need . . . Yes, like that—perfect," I say, watching as the townspeople move into formation. "Can we dim the lights?"

Miss Betty, at the light switch's panel, gives me a wave.

"Thanks, Miss Betty," I say when the lights go down. The room glows with the many holiday bulbs, which twinkle softly through the space. The ambiance is spot-on, the room instantly cozier.

My phone buzzes again. "They're parking," I say to the crowd, who are in place now—minus a couple of the kids who wander about, the way young children do.

"As soon as they walk through the door, Miss Betty, if you could put up the houselights, and then we'll all shout—in unison, ideally—'Surprise! Holiday cheers for twenty-five years!'" I take a breath, then ask, "Everyone ready?"

There are murmurs and nodding heads. Then, Amelia's voice can be heard outside the main doors. She's obviously speaking loudly, to give us a few seconds of warning. The door handle clicks, Mom and Dad walk in, Miss Betty hits the lights, and the crowd shouts "Surprise!" (All together, which is impressive for this number of people). Immediately followed by, "Holiday cheers for twenty-five years!" slightly less in unison.

Mom slaps a hand to her chest, smiling through the shocked expression on her face, while Dad begins to tear up, clapping his hands together with delight. Amelia and I make eye contact, and she pumps her fist in the air three times and grins. I smile at her, taking in the moment, as the crowd engulfs our parents in well-wishes and hugs.

"Mission accomplished," Liam says, leaning close to my ear, for the room is loud once again. I sense as much as feel his breath on the sensitive skin of my neck, and know if I turn my head, our lips will be in perfect position to—"Did you sign up for the ginger-bread house competition?"

"What?" I ask, rattled by my own thoughts.

"The gingerbread competition? Are you doing it?"

This is one of the highlights of chili night, and the whole town takes it quite seriously.

"Yes. Yes, of course," I reply, still not fully recovered. "The Munros are fierce competitors—we have the trophies to prove it."

Liam raises a brow. "'Trophies' plural, eh? Should I be scared?"

"Probably," I reply, and he laughs. "Did you sign up?"

He nods. "Pops doesn't look it, but he's pretty competitive about gingerbread decorating. Maybe it's a Harmony Hills thing?"

"Oh, it's *definitely* a Harmony Hills thing," I say emphatically.

I notice my parents snaking slowly through the crowd, getting closer to the stage, where they'll accept the gift. Liam notices as well and, before he leaves the stage, says, "See you soon for some friendly competition?"

"Not if I see you first!" My guts contract uncomfortably with my eagerness. It's perplexing what Liam does to my nervous system. Somehow both calming it down and working it up. I've never met anyone who has quite this effect on me. Normally I'm fairly level-headed, might even be described as "laid-back" by my colleagues. It takes a lot to get a reaction out of me, good or bad.

As I'm contemplating the nature of our chemistry, Liam jumps the short distance from stage to ground, because Claire and Kirby's twins are running up and down the stairs. He pauses to wish my parents well, giving them both hugs. It stops me, seeing the warmth between them, until I remember that Liam has his own relationship with my parents. Like everyone else in Harmony Hills, he will have visited the clinic during the time he's lived here. Attended events alongside them—from Christmas tree lightings to chili nights to memorial services to other gatherings, like the Harvest Festival and Easter picnic.

In some ways, I'm more the outsider here. I frown, thinking of all I've missed in the pursuit of . . . *of what, Libby?* But I don't have time to wallow further, because my parents have reached the stairs—the twins having been removed from the steps by Kirby and Claire, who are doing their best to contain their rambunctiousness.

Dad still has tears in his eyes, his cheeks rosy from emotion, and Mom, grinning ear to ear, is one step behind him. She gathers her long, flowing skirt in her hands as she starts up the stairs. Then, a billow of fabric gets caught under her shoe. For one heart-stopping moment I watch as she attempts to regain her balance—her smile replaced by a look of alarm, eyes wide and mouth open.

She's going to fall! Panic paralyzes me. Suddenly, I understand I didn't avert disaster by hanging those Christmas lights—I merely postponed it. Maybe you can't actually change the future, even if you've gone back to the past.

I shout, "Mom!," and my dad turns quickly—but he's more than an arm's length away and can't reach her. My mom falls backwards down the stairs in dramatic fashion, and there's nothing I can do to stop it this time.

28

Thank goodness for Kirby, who darts around Jasmine and catches Mom before she hits the ground. A second later the drama's over, my parents and Amelia thanking Kirby profusely.

"These two here have given me lightning-fast reflexes," he jokes, pointing at Jasmine and Jonah, who now run tight circles around him, caught up in their own game. People nearby have begun clapping, and Mom holds up Kirby's hand and the two give a bow—as though the entire thing was part of a rehearsed act.

I can't stop shaking. Adrenaline pumps through me, and my hands are still clenched in fists.

Liam, standing directly in front of me on the floor, catches my eye. *You okay?* he mouths. Relaxing my hands, I nod my response, then repeat it in my head: *Mom's okay. I'm okay.* I force a smile as my parents make their way onstage, Dad a half step behind Mom this time.

We share a long hug before I join Amelia stage left, where we watch them open the gift (a new clinic sign, made of laser-cut bronze) and give an impromptu speech to the receptive, appreciative audience.

"That was too close. So glad there was no broken ankle this

time," I whisper to Amelia, as Dad wraps up the thank-you speech. I'm still wobbly from the adrenaline crash, but grateful Kirby was in the right place at the right moment.

"What do you mean, *this time*?" Amelia asks, also whispering.

Shoot. I scramble to cover my misstep. "Nothing. Just that I'm glad she didn't hurt herself."

"But you specified a broken ankle . . . and *this time*. Like it has happened before." Amelia likes clarity—it's the teacher in her. "When did Mom break her ankle?"

She frowns, as though trying to recall a story she's forgotten.

"Never, I don't think," I reply, still whispering. "Broken ankles are just common injuries. From falls, stairs or otherwise."

I take a deep breath, glance at Amelia to see if this is mollifying her. "She's lucky Kirby was there."

Amelia nods. "Look at them, Libby. They're so happy." Emotion makes her voice crack. "This hasn't been the easiest year for them," she adds, more softly.

I stare at my sister. "How so?"

She shakes her head. "Don't worry about it. We can talk later."

I want to push, but then our parents finish speaking and the crowd erupts. Beaming, Mom and Dad hold the sign up, waiting for the applause to ebb.

After the anniversary surprise, it's chili time, and Beckett's family wins the golden kidney bean trophy. Soon, Christmas carol karaoke is in full swing, as Miss Betty and Mr. Cutler sing "Jingle Bell Rock" as a duet (clearly Liam didn't inherit his granddad's lovely singing voice). On the stage, kids take turns sitting on Santa's knee while parents and grandparents snap photographs. I'm nursing my mulled wine—a heady concoction made of zesty orange, cinnamon, cloves, and a deep burgundy red—while I take it all in. *Why was I so eager to leave this?*

In the emergency room I see much heartbreak and despair, as well as plenty of lonely, isolated people. It's the opposite here in Harmony Hills. Sure, there's some gossip—when you live in a tight-knit community, there's a sense that all problems are shared, and all joys are celebrated together—but people show up for one another. It's a rare thing, and I'm only now realizing the power of it.

"For your sweet tooth," Dad says, appearing beside me. He holds out a cellophane-wrapped candy cane.

"Thanks, Dad." I take the candy cane—noting it's cinnamon-flavoured. I think about Mary Piggins, which makes me think about Liam, and I smile, a warm flush moving through me that inwardly I blame on the wine.

"That's nice to see," he says, noticing the smile. "You were looking a little forlorn, over here by yourself. Everything okay, honey?"

Not really. "Everything's great."

How I wish I could confide in my dad, who I know would tell me he believes every wild detail of my story. Even if he had doubts, he would be steady with his support, the way the best dads are.

"Mom looks like she's in her element." She's currently accepting a gift bag from Rosalie Everhart, adding it to the others already in hand.

"After it took us thirty minutes to move two feet, I told her I needed a walkabout," Dad says, chuckling. "You know your mom—the epitome of a social butterfly. But also very beloved by everyone."

I nod, watching how Mom's face lights up every time someone comes over to say "hello." She always shakes hands, or returns a hug, and has generous and genuine smiles for all.

"Looks like an early Christmas for you two," I say, pointing to the bags in Dad's hands that have piles of tissue paper poking out the tops, and curly-cue ribbons.

"Everyone outdid themselves, and many are edible, too! A

banana-chocolate-chip loaf, some homemade granola, Christmas cakes, a bag of oranges—the fancy kind, with the stems and leaves still attached," Dad says, his tone indicating he's impressed. "A couple of casseroles, for the freezer, that Amelia already put in the car."

"Wow. You guys won't need to cook for a month," I reply. "That's really nice of everyone."

Dad smiles. "That's Harmony Hills for you, Libby."

"It sure is," I murmur, again seeing my hometown through a different filter. I unwrap the candy cane and pop a piece in my mouth. It's spicy and sweet enough that my teeth ache.

"So where were you a minute ago?" Dad asks. "You seemed lost in thought."

I suck on the candy cane, taking a moment. "I was thinking about how nice it is to be home. It's been years since I came to a chili night."

"And we have loved having you home, honey. Both of us, and I know Amelia really appreciated your arriving earlier than expected. The two of you, pulling off this surprise . . ." Dad's voice catches. I reach out and rub his arm, and he smiles at me. "It means the world to your mom and me, Libby."

"I'm glad to be here, Dad."

"I'm not anxious for you to leave, but when do you expect you have to head back to the city?" he asks. Another urge to confide in my dad grips me. *Tell him everything, Libby.*

Yet, I can't form the words. "Not sure yet. Sorting a few things out."

But this may be the opportunity I've been looking for. To get more information about the clinic, and what's really going on. "I may stick around a bit longer. A few more days, at least."

"Oh?" Dad's eyebrows go up. "What about your trip with Austin?"

"It's no big deal if I can't go." Austin most certainly would not agree. "He has some work stuff to handle. I was just tagging along for a dose of sunshine."

I never told my family the trip was an early Christmas gift from Austin, and I don't mention it now. Though I wonder, *Why not?* It seems like the sort of thing you'd be excited to tell everyone—that your boyfriend is whisking you to sunny L.A. for a magical Christmas holiday.

"But enough about me. How is everything with you and Mom?" I ask, seizing my chance. "With the clinic? Twenty-five years . . . that's really something."

The briefest of pauses, and his lips press together. But then a second later I wonder if I imagined the hesitation, because he's smiling again.

"Twenty-five years. Amazing, isn't it?" Then he glances at his watch. "Oh, look at that. Almost gingerbread house time. Let's go extricate your mom from her loyal fans."

I follow him, watching his steady stride. The candy cane melts on my tongue and my mind lingers on that brief pause in his answer, on the momentary shadow that crossed his face. There's something unspoken here—something I can't put my finger on. But if there's one thing I know for sure, it's that a secret doesn't last long in Harmony Hills. I just need to stick around long enough to figure out what it is.

29

"Do I need to go over the rules of play again?" Mom asks, and the group of us murmurs no, focused on the task in front of us. We've participated as a family in the gingerbread house decorating contest for years—the rules haven't changed, and they're seared into our collective memory.

Decorating stations have been set up on the long dining tables—one house per every four chairs. I sit beside Amelia, who sits across from Mom, who sits beside Dad, in our usual formation. Kids on one side, parents on the other. Two of Amelia's best friends from high school, Miriam Scoville and Evie Hunt, whose family owns the Cookie Cottage and provided the gingerbread tonight, are next to us, with their significant others across from them.

I gaze down the long table and realize I recognize everyone. Remember babysitting some, or being babysat by others. There are former teachers, school friends, owners of businesses in town, some of which have passed from one generation to the next over the years. I think back to how Austin laughed when I told him how seriously townspeople take gingerbread house decorating. "Like, with candy and icing? Isn't that more a kid thing?"

It's an *everyone* thing in Harmony Hills, I'd responded, somewhat icily.

Amelia is restless beside me now, tapping her fingers against the tabletop as we wait for "go" time. The incessant tapping pulls me back to reality. "You okay?"

"What's taking so long?" she grumble-whispers, and I shush her lightly. Unless you know her well, or have witnessed it firsthand, you might not believe Amelia is cutthroat competitive. I once watched her speed-eat a pumpkin pie during Harvest Festival to win the title of Pie Queen. A feat made more impressive because pumpkin pie is one of Amelia's most-loathed foods. "It's thick and slimy, and tastes like licking the bottom of someone's feet after they've walked in mud!"

My sister starts bouncing her legs, her chair pushed back slightly to offer better maneuverability once the timer begins. *Competitive mode unlocked.* I chuckle quietly.

Along with the gingerbread, multiple bowls have been placed down the centre of each table, filled with red and white peppermint swirl candies, sprinkle-frosted chocolates, miniature silver balls, and sugar-topped gumdrops. Piping bags of royal icing sit at the ready beside each gingerbread house. There's a large clock—a Christmas bell, which is on display at Season's Eatings during the holidays—with a built-in timer used to keep tabs on competitors' progress. Miss Elsie is on clock duty this evening, sitting on the stage with Mary Piggins, who looks fast asleep on a cushy dog bed beside her.

"Hey, Libby. Are you in the zone?" Amelia asks, nudging me.

"You bet. Ready to go." I have every intention of winning tonight. Amelia and I may not look alike, and we probably have more personality differences than similarities, but we both inherited the Munro competitive gene.

Mom goes over the rules again, hurriedly, despite our prior assurances we don't need a recap. "Whoever decorates fastest wins first prize," she says, leaning her elbows on the table and locking eyes with me, then Amelia. "But you have to use every single candy at your station." We nod, already knowing the rules by heart but playing along for Mom's benefit. When I said Amelia and I inherited the competitive gene . . . it didn't come from Dad.

"Then, the independent panel of judges does the final review for second place: the most festive—I know Kirby's parents and Miss Betty are on the panel, but I'm not sure who else," Amelia says, taking over where Mom left off.

"Millicent Mueller, too. Colleen Rice, and Art Piney," Dad adds. Colleen Rice is the town's librarian, and Art Piney is a real estate lawyer. I see the judges sitting onstage, chatting while they wait for the event to begin.

"Did I miss anything?" Mom looks at each of us again, and we shake our heads. "Okay, c'est du gâteau! We've got this."

"'C'est du gâteau?'" I say to Amelia. "Something-something cake?"

"Hush," Mom says, at the same time Amelia says, "Piece of cake."

"Competitors ready?" Miss Elsie asks. She's standing beside the clock now, about to press the timer button. Mary Piggins continues snoozing, oblivious to the rising excitement in the hall.

"Ready!" The competitors shout as a group. Liam's at the next table over, but directly in my sightline. There's a crease between his brows as he concentrates on the dish of candy a few inches from his outstretched, at-the-ready hand. He looks up, sees me, and grins. He's on a team with Beckett (who is also grinning but has locked eyes with Amelia), his grandfather, and Beckett's dad.

The timer rings, and the room explodes with activity. Excitement rises as royal icing is quickly piped on and teams strategize in semi-hushed tones. Christmas carols stream through the speakers, adding to the energetic vibe.

I've opted to use plastic craft tweezers to apply my candies to the one side of the roof. Amelia's split the candy up and is applying it simultaneously with both hands, almost as quickly as Dad is piping on a hatch-design meant to look like shingles. I don't pay attention to the others, because the ticking clock is ticking, and my adrenaline has taken over. But my sister has decided it's time for some smack talk.

"Might as well give up now," she calls out to Beckett's team, not breaking focus or lifting her eyes.

"Was about to say the same to you, Mila," Beckett replies, her voice relaxed but teasing. I glance over at Amelia and see she's smiling as she continues applying candies with both hands—it's impressive, the dexterity and rhythm she has going. I need to get back to work.

"Now, let's keep things civil," Mom says. "We're going to win, but let's do it with Munro grace, girls."

Dad chuckles. He's used to this from the three of us, and always manages to appear unruffled by our intensity.

"And . . . done!" Miriam Scoville, who's seated beside Amelia, holds her hands straight up in the air, her auburn braids falling over her shoulders. The rest of her family sits back in their chairs, clapping hands and whistling. Miss Elsie notes the time, just as Amelia and I stammer, "What? How?"

We look at each other in confusion, before snapping eyes to the Scoville family's fully decorated gingerbread house. Sure enough, they've used every decoration, choosing a brilliantly simple design with no obvious pattern, but somehow the colours and shapes work beautifully together. I glance at the kids—two boys, around six and seven years old—and then lean over, holding up a hand. They take turns high-fiving me. "Nice one, you guys."

"Have you two forgotten Most Festive is still up for grabs?" Mom asks, not stopping her own decorating. We jump back in, matching her pace.

Evie Hunt—who's seated beside Beckett and Liam's team, and has no competitive streak to speak of—is only half finished, though her design is by far the most complex. Swirls are placed with precision, the colours alternating in a perfectly harmonized pattern. She and her family are going to be tough to beat for "most festive." They appear nonplussed by the tension of competition, methodically working away.

"Look at everyone, all relaxed," Amelia says, with a sharp, mirthless laugh. "As though this is only about 'fun.'" Beckett laughs, and Liam hides a smirk. I shrug as if to say, "Told you so."

The rest of the night is a blur. The gingerbread winners are declared, and we take second place (the prize is our family name on a plaque displayed year-round at the Cookie Cottage). Amelia is expectedly displeased. "Second place means you're the winner of the losers," she mutters after the judge's final tallies, and we all laugh—Amelia included. Chili stations are dismantled, and a skeleton crew, including me, Amelia, Liam, Chase, Beckett, and a few of the town's teenagers with energy to spare, handle the final cleanup. There's not much time to chat, but I catch Liam looking my way more than once, with an unabashed smile.

I'm not sure what to do about Liam, or our clear chemistry that I know is not one-sided. What if I wake up back in the present tomorrow? What if I don't remember any of this, or him? What if we never get the chance to see where this might go?

What if this was just a dream, after all?

It's almost midnight by the time Amelia and I get back to Mom and Dad's. The four of us—still buzzing from the evening and tired, though not yet ready for bed—settle into the living room for slices of homemade gingerbread cake with vanilla-bean ice cream.

It's cozy; Mom started a fire that glows brightly in the stone hearth, and we're snuggled up under soft blankets, enjoying the cake and easy chitchat. It has been years since we've done this. The sudden lump in my throat forces me to put down my half-eaten cake. I'm different in this timeline; I like who I am in Christmas past.

Mom smiles, noting the subtle shimmer of tears in my eyes. Family has always been her everything—for my dad, too—and I recognize these last few days, all of us together, have likely left a mark on her as well.

If only you knew what's coming, Mom, I think, returning the smile. I imagine her cooing over her first grandchild, who will be born less than two years from now. *It's even better than this, just wait.*

Mom nods gently, as though hearing my internal thoughts, and then the moment is broken by Dad, excitedly talking about the new sign. It leans against the living room wall, and we all look at it.

"Absolutely perfect," he says. "What a thoughtful gift."

"And imagine how gorgeous it will be in a few years," I reply. "Bronze gets better with age."

My parents glance at each other, and Amelia's eyes drop to her plate, where the ice cream has melted around the cake. The silence lingers, before Amelia picks up her spoon and starts eating again. Whatever spell settled over my family is broken, but I feel evermore like an outsider looking in.

Soon after, Amelia and I get ready for bed—she's decided to spend the night rather than go back to her own place. Brushing our teeth in our tiny, shared bathroom, like old times, we each stand at a corner of the sink and alternate spitting and rinsing. I had every intention of waiting until morning to ask her about what happened earlier, but I can't hold back any longer.

"Is everything okay with Mom and Dad?" I mumble, through a mouthful of foamy peppermint toothpaste.

"Hmm?" Amelia asks, leaning over to spit.

Our eyes connect in the mirror above the sink. I ask again, "Are they okay?," and she frowns before looking down to rinse her toothbrush. I turn the water off once she's done.

"What do you mean, *Are they okay?*" She wipes her hands on the towel hanging on the bar. The towel has a snowman on it, sitting on an old-fashioned sled. There are similar hand towels in all three bathrooms in the house.

"When we were talking earlier about the sign, it seemed to strike a nerve, and Claire mentioned that—"

Amelia's eyes go wide, and she slaps a hand to her forehead. "I can't believe I forgot to ask Claire about the twins."

"What about them?" I'm momentarily distracted from my own line of questioning.

"I was hoping they'd help my students hand out candy canes at the tree lighting." Amelia puts both hands to her face, tugging her skin down in her distress. "What's wrong with me? I'm never this forgetful."

"Give yourself a break." I tug on her arm until she drops her hands from her face. Then I put on my best bedside-manner voice. Calm, confident, infused with warmth.

"You single-handedly planned our parents' surprise party. Don't even bother saying it, Mila—this was all you." I smile, and she returns it.

"Plus, finishing up school for the year. It's a lot, and would make even the most organized planner in the universe a little wobbly."

Amelia sighs. "It has been a lot, quite honestly."

"I'm sorry I wasn't here to help out more." I mean more than just the party. Amelia's expression tells me she understands the scope of my apology.

"I'll text Claire," I add. "I'm sure the twins will be happy to take part."

"Thanks, Sissy." Amelia pulls me into a hug. "I know it wasn't easy for you to get home, with your schedule. Love you, Libby."

I can't extricate myself to look at her, because she's still holding me tightly, but I say, "There's nowhere else I would rather be. Love you, too."

The loud crash, and subsequent shout of pain, wrenches us apart, and we stare at each other for a split second, before Amelia says, "Libby . . . *Mom*," her voice tremulous and low. Then she tears out of the bathroom, with me on her heels, and together we race down the stairs.

30

December 21

The doorbell rings for the third time this morning, likely another kind neighbour dropping something off. The fridge and freezer are full, and there's little room left for any more "get well soon" casseroles. Amelia's started putting casseroles in her freezer.

The contrast between city life and living in Harmony Hills is stark: the former offers anonymity; the latter is like being at the centre of a giant group hug. Even though none of this is particularly revelatory, every time that doorbell rings, I have a pensive moment of reflection on what I have given up.

Also, it has been confirmed. Despite my best efforts, I can't change the past (or the future, probably). It happened on a different day, in a different way, but Mom still got hurt.

The crash Amelia and I heard, the night of the surprise party, was Mom falling from a wobbly stool when she tried to hang the bath bomb ornament onto the Christmas tree. The room was dark, and one of the stool's legs was on the carpet while the rest were on the hardwood, making it unstable. Even though she's tall, she was on her tiptoes trying reach the tree's top branches.

She said one moment she was hooking the ornament's string over the branch, and the next she was on the floor with her ankle crumpled underneath her. I've felt sick since it happened and wish again that I had someone, anyone, to confide in. Thankfully, the fracture didn't require surgery—a cast for six to eight weeks, and then physiotherapy. Regardless, not ideal when you're the only doctor in town.

"Would you mind getting the door, honey?" Mom asks, settled comfortably on the living room couch in her silk candy-cane-adorned pajamas. Her leg, encased to the knee in a pink fibreglass cast, is propped up on the embroidered Santa Claus pillow. *Scrooged* plays on the television, and I've been watching carefully, searching for clues about how to handle my own time-hopping Christmas situation. But in the end, it's simply a fictional movie with a well-oiled plot, and I can't glean anything helpful from it.

"Sure." I tighten the nail polish bottle's lid, having just finished painting Mom's toenails, then head to the front door. Millicent Mueller stands on the other side, donning a wide smile and a sage-green plaid quilted winter coat, with a matching hat that barely covers her springy, grey curls. In her hands is a rectangular glass casserole dish, which is covered in tinfoil held tightly with a series of elastic bands.

"Hi, Miss Millicent, how are you?"

"Hello, Libby! I'm well," she says, in a cheerful, singsong tone. She thrusts the casserole dish towards me, and I take it from her, noting that it's still warm to the touch.

"Wanted to drop this off, so no one has to think about dinner tonight," she says. "My chopped-ham-and-pea casserole. Just put it in at three seventy-five for about twenty minutes, until it's bubbling."

"Oh, thank you. This was . . . very kind of you," I say, knowing from past experience that this is the casserole with the jar of mayonnaise in it, and that not a forkful of it will pass my lips. Ham, yes (though now I can't help but think of Mary Piggins with a slight wiggle of guilt). Peas, of course. "Bubbling" hot mayonnaise? No, thank you.

"It's the least I could do, honey," she says, wringing her gloved hands, her lips turning down in a frown. "Your poor mother, with that pesky leg. How is she feeling?"

Millicent Mueller, being not at all subtle, peers around me, craning her head to look into the living room.

"Why don't you come in for a coffee?" I step to the side. "Mom will appreciate the company. Especially someone who isn't a hovering doctor or nurse." I smile at this last part, knowing that Mom probably needs us less than we need to take care of her.

"Oh, I wouldn't want to be a bother," she says, but then she's through the doorway and taking off her hat. She looks around the foyer entrance wide-eyed, taking in all the holiday touches. "Monica always does such a lovely job with the decorating. It's so festive and cheerful!"

Fresh cedar garland frames the front door's interior, with white twinkle lights and pine cones nestled into the branches. Two miniature Christmas trees stand on either side of the front-hall closet. A blooming red poinsettia is on a pot stand by the stairwell, with a trio of faux candle-lit lanterns beside it. Then, there's a red-green-and-white-plaid runner for snow-covered shoes and boots by the door. Finally, decorative stockings hang on the coat hooks that line the wall opposite the closet.

"She loves doing it." I shift the warm casserole dish in my hands. It has some weight to it, and thinking about the ingredients makes my stomach lurch. "Head on into the living room, and I'll make coffee. You can hang your coat in the closet if you like."

"Thanks, Libby," she replies, tucking her gloves into her coat's pocket, which she hangs up. Then she straightens her forest-green slacks and cream cardigan, which has a small, jeweled wreath pinned to it, and heads into the living room. "Just lovely. Lovely! Look at that tree, my word . . ."

I smile as I head to the kitchen, listening to Miss Millicent fawn over Mom. "Oh, Monica, you poor thing. Let me fluff that pillow for you. There, isn't that better?"

In the kitchen I open the fridge and start moving containers and dishes around, trying to find a spot for the large glass dish.

"This is like Tetris," I mumble, shifting and stacking until I create a spot. Dad's packing a lunch for his afternoon at the clinic and turns from the sink, where he's washing a bright red apple. "What did Millicent bring over?"

"Hot ham casserole, with *mayo-nnaise*." I shudder, close the fridge door, and press my hands to my stomach.

Dad laughs. "It's actually pretty tasty, honey. Don't you remember? You liked it when you were little."

I frown. "I did? Are you sure?" I don't share this memory, and I can't believe there was ever a time I liked anything with warm mayonnaise. I think it's the worst condiment out there, by a long shot.

"You and Amelia always asked for seconds," he says, tucking the apple into his reusable lunch bag, and setting a freezer pack on top.

"Do you need me today, at the clinic?" I ask. "Millicent is having coffee and a visit with Mom—but she said she could stay most of the day, if needed. I could give you a hand? I'm sure things have piled up these past couple of days."

"I just made a pot of coffee, so you don't need to start a fresh one. And the gingersnaps are in that tin," he says, pointing to a mistletoe-adorned cookie tin on the countertop. "The clinic isn't busy today, so I can handle the load. Why don't you go do something with Amelia? It's your last day in town, honey. Make the most of it. I cleaned Pepper off after last night's snow. She's all ready for your drive back."

"Thanks, Dad. You didn't have to do that." I pour coffee from the steaming carafe, my chest constricting with emotion. "Maybe Amelia and I will do something later. We'll see. Mom seems okay, right? Do you think she's okay?"

"She's okay, Libby." He takes a last sip of his coffee and puts the mug into the dishwasher.

"I'm just glad it wasn't worse," I reply, arranging a few cookies on a plate and picking up a small stack of napkins.

"Me, too, honey. I think I aged about ten years, seeing her on the ground like that." He shakes his head, his mouth a tight line.

I rub his arm, give him the biggest, brightest smile I can. "Like you said, she's okay. Let's not worry about what could have been."

We walk into the living room, him carrying the plate of cookies and the napkins and me with the coffee mugs. I set one in front of Miss Millicent, and hand the other mug to Mom. "I think I'd rather be here—keep an eye on things. Mila's on her way over, too."

"Suit yourself." Dad kisses me on the cheek, then gives Millicent a hug and Mom a kiss goodbye. "Millicent, please make sure she doesn't do any more ornament hanging, okay?"

Miss Millicent chuckles, pulling a deck of cards from her purse. "I'm going to keep her busy trying to beat me at cards. Don't you worry, Stark."

A moment later Dad's out the door.

"Anything else I can get for you?" I ask.

"I don't think so, Libby." Mom smiles my way, blowing on the top of her coffee to dissipate some of the heat.

"Maybe a time machine?" Miss Millicent suggests, one eyebrow raised comically high. "Then your mom could go back in time and

not stand up on that flimsy stool, in the dark, to hang that ornament, hmm?"

A joke, of course—she has no idea how close she is to the reality of what I've been going through. But unnerved, a high-pitched
laugh escapes me. It's a beat too late, and too loud for the room,
which causes both Mom and Miss Millicent to look my way in
confusion.

"A time machine! Good one," I reply. "If only, right? Right?"

"Indeed," Mom replies, sighing wistfully, her fingers tapping
restlessly against her mug. I know she's suffering with boredom.
The pain is well managed, but my mom is not great at resting or
staying still.

Miss Millicent bites into one of the cookies. "Delicious. Did
you make these, Libby?"

"Those cookies don't have burnt edges—my signature—so no,"
I say with a smile.

Mom chuckles kindly. She knows I'm not wrong, and that she's
only moderately more skilled than I am. Amelia's the best baker in
our family, though Dad is decent. "Evie dropped off a whole box of
Cookie Cottage treats earlier," she says.

"Ah, yes. I should have guessed." Miss Millicent looks at the
other half of the cookie, then points to its chewy interior. "They
use real candied ginger pieces. Divine."

I stand in the living room, unsure what to do with myself.
There are meals for the week, Dad's handling the clinic, Millicent's
going to keep Mom entertained and comfortable, and Amelia and
I cleaned the house top to bottom yesterday. Also, my family still
believes I'm heading back to the city tomorrow. On that note, so
does Austin.

"What time are you leaving?" He'd asked the night before when

I finally called. "You must be going stir-crazy. Any sign of the 'Harmony Hills rash' yet?"

Austin had laughed at his own joke, which, sure, was *my* joke. He once asked, very early in our relationship, if I ever imagined myself moving back here. I see now he was testing things, trying to decide if this was a relationship worth investing in. Like I've said, small towns held zero appeal for him. I'd replied, "Doubtful. I'm a city girl. Probably allergic to small-town life now—a few days too long might bring out the hives."

"No, no rash," I'd replied last night, irked but trying to conceal it. "Sorry, what was the question?"

I knew it was what time I expected to leave Harmony Hills, but I was stalling. Unable to say what I needed to, which was . . . *Austin, I'm not coming with you to L.A. It's over. I'm sorry to do this over the phone, but I need to let you know.*

A barely audible sigh. "When do you hope to get away?"

"Um . . . first thing, I hope." Another lie. I bit my lip, guilt blooming. "But things are up in the air right now."

"Oh? How come?" Austin asked.

"Well . . ." I started. "It's complicated." *Understatement.* "But I'm not sure I can get away, Austin."

"What does *that* mean?" Now he was irked, his words clipped. "We have a flight in less than forty-eight hours, Elizabeth. The tickets are nonrefundable, too."

Hearing him call me Elizabeth, after a week of everyone referring to me as Libby, was off-putting. Yes, I knew the tickets were nonrefundable (he had told me more than once) . . . but I also knew the trip wasn't about me. What did it matter if I was there or not?

"I know," I replied, giving in because I wasn't sure what else to do. Pushing the problem away for another day. "Don't worry. I'll be there. Leaving crack of dawn, day after tomorrow."

"Okay, that's good. We can order in before heading to the airport. Thai or Indian?" Austin sounded pleased the plan was shaping up as expected.

"You choose," I replied, my voice monotone. I hated being this person—the sort who swallowed what needed to be said.

"Thai, then."

I rolled my eyes. He always ordered Thai—the same exact dish, green curry chicken—though, I had no right to be annoyed. He had asked me my preference, after all, and I had volleyed it back to him.

"Did the flowers arrive? How's your mom doing?"

Austin had a gorgeous bouquet of flowers delivered the day after my mom's fall. It was thoughtful, and yet it also reminded me of what Helly said. How Austin didn't show up for me in the way I needed him to. Like offering to drop everything and drive to Harmony Hills as a gesture of support.

I would have told him "Thank you, I know that isn't possible, but I appreciate it" because said gesture would have wreaked havoc with his surgical schedule. Plus, it would have been over-kill for the situation. Mom was okay, Dad and I could handle the medical side of things easily, and Austin would merely be another person in the house to keep Mom company. To fluff pillows, or get her a glass of water when it was time for her pain medications. But I knew that wasn't what Helena had been getting at—Austin was great with the thoughtful deliveries, and words of support, but he wasn't *here* with me, or for me, in the ways that mattered.

Mom insists Amelia and I get out of the house. "I can handle only so much hovering," she says pointedly.

"Maybe we should get the tree for the clinic? At Liam's farm?" Amelia suggests, when it's clear Mom won't take no for an answer. "Didn't you say he offered, Libby? I know Miss Betty would appreciate not having to pick one up herself."

"He did offer," I reply.

A tingle of excitement courses through me at the thought of seeing Liam again—it has been days. He texted immediately once he heard about Mom's ankle, and then made a fresh bread delivery—including three loaves of cinnamon bread. But unfortunately, I missed him because I was with Mom at the fracture clinic in Westhaven.

"Becks is at the farm, too," Amelia says. "She's doing a checkup on the goats, I think."

"Sounds like a plan," Mom says. "Enjoy the day! It's too beautiful outside to waste."

"I'll text Liam to make sure it's okay from his end." I reach for my phone, but Amelia's already typing out a message.

"On it," she says. "I let Becks know we're on our way."

A text comes in from Liam, and I smile. "How's the sawing arm?"

"Is that Austin?" Amelia asks. It's fair to assume—in Christmas past—that receiving a text from my then boyfriend would make me smile.

"Yep." I swipe up to get rid of the text screen. "He's hoping Mom's doing better today."

"That's sweet of him," Mom replies. "Please thank him again for the flowers, Libby."

"I will." I'm flustered, hating my dishonesty. But how can I explain any of this, let alone the fact that Austin is actually my ex-boyfriend? "We'll be back for dinner. Can't miss that ham-and-pea casserole." Miss Millicent beams, pausing briefly as she deals the cards into neat piles on the coffee table.

"Oh God, is it the hot mayonnaise casserole?" Amelia whispers as we head out the front door.

"The very one," I reply. I shut the door behind us. "Maybe we should stop off at Season's Eatings?"

"Good idea," Amelia says, nodding. "But are we bad daughters if we leave Mom and Dad to suffer alone with that casserole?"

I shrug. "Dad said it's not bad. Apparently I used to like it, too?"

"Ha! You hated it." Amelia hits her key fob, unlocking the car doors. "You used to hide it in your napkin, then slide it under the table for the Muellers' dog."

She pauses, hand on the door. "What was that dog's name?"

"Rascal." I haven't thought about Rascal—the Muellers' three-legged rescue mutt—for years. I start laughing so hard I'm leaning on the open car door, trying to catch my breath. "He was so chubby, that poor dog."

"You certainly didn't help things," Amelia said, before getting into the car. She turns it on, and Christmas music streams from the radio. I buckle my seat belt, as my sister pulls away from our parents' place, heading towards Liam's farm.

31

Clover Hill—Liam's farm—is about fifteen minutes out of town, which gives me a perfect chance to talk with Amelia alone. She's been quiet, focusing on the drive. We've passed only one other car on the otherwise empty country road. I glance out the window, watching the snow-laden fields of Harmony Hills' farmlands pass by.

"So I was thinking . . ." I start, trying to harness my thoughts, which are a swirling mess.

"Hmm?" she says, eyes on the road.

"I was thinking I might stay longer," I say. "I have some extra vacation days to use up."

Then I think about the hospital, and my job. What happens if I never get back to the present? Do I simply return to the emergency room, as though this bizarre time-travel thing never happened?

"What about your holiday with Austin?" Amelia asks, eyes darting my way for a moment before going back on the road.

"I'm going to tell him to go ahead without me." I keep my tone neutral. "He's mostly going for work, so it's not really a proper vacation anyway."

"Since when? I thought it was your Christmas present? Aren't the tickets nonrefundable?"

I narrow my eyes. "How do you know that?"

Amelia shrugs, then shoots me a guilty look. "I heard you two on the phone last night. Sorry—I wasn't eavesdropping. You were on speaker."

"Yes, the tickets are nonrefundable." That's all I say, because I don't want to discuss my ex-boyfriend, who everyone thinks is my current boyfriend, right now.

"Speaking of Austin . . ." My sister turns down the radio. The joyful Christmas music fades, and my shoulders tense up.

"So don't get worked up, okay?" she starts. The tension spreads into my neck. "Don't get worked up" pretty much guarantees I'm about to get *worked up*.

"Becks told me that Liam thinks you and Austin broke up. That you're single." Amelia keeps her gaze straight ahead, and I hope she doesn't see my shocked—and guilty—expression.

"Oh . . . he does?"

"Can you tell me why he might think that, Libby?" she adds, her tone measured.

This complicates things, no question. I'm both alarmed and elated this part of our conversation didn't stay with Liam, because it means Liam has been talking with Beckett, his best friend, about me. About my relationship status. *This isn't good. (This is good.)*

"I'm not sure," I reply, despite being quite sure why he thinks this. Because I told him—flat out—that Austin and I were over.

"Hmm, well that's strange then." I see Amelia sneak a glance my way in my peripheral vision.

I don't turn to face her, and nod instead. "Definitely strange."

"Related . . . what's really going on with you and Austin?" Amelia asks. "I'm not prying, honestly. I'm just worried about you."

This is your chance. But, what do I say? *Austin and I broke up. Except it happens about nine months from now. Yes, I know I'm mak-*

ing zero sense, but ... hey, so do you believe in time travel? Because I have a story for you, Sissy ...

Right—that should go over as well as an empty stocking on Christmas morning.

"You can tell me. Whatever's going on, it's okay."

I force a weak smile. "Just regular relationship stuff. You know, busy schedules, hard to find time to spend together, feeling like ships passing in the night, blah-blah-blah."

"Isn't that all the more reason to get on the plane to California?"

My fingernails dig into my palms, and I fail to keep the frustration from my voice. "I want to be here right now, not getting on a plane to L.A. With Mom's ankle, and Dad running the clinic alone." I pause, taking a breath. "I could help out, at the clinic. At least for a couple of weeks, until Mom's able to get around better."

Amelia sighs. "Look, Libby, that's a nice idea, and I know Mom and Dad—and me, too—we'd all be happy for you to stick around, and be here over Christmas. But I worry about what happens next."

"What do you mean, 'what happens next'?"

She fiddles with the radio again, first turning it up, then turning it back down. I wish she would just turn it off and answer the question. "After you leave and go back to Toronto, I mean."

I twist in my seat to look at my sister, but a wave of nausea comes over me, and I quickly face forward again. "Just say what you're thinking, please."

"Fine. But you aren't going to like it." I note Amelia's hands grip the steering wheel more tightly. "The clinic has been struggling, Libby. Things have been tight. More than tight, actually," Amelia says.

"How tight, Mila?" My stomach continues to bubble with nausea, which has less to do with the car ride and more to do with finally learning the truth.

"*Tight*, Libby. Everyone's having a harder time making ends meet in this economy, including Mom and Dad."

She puts on her flicker, slowing the car to make a left turn. The tires crunch on the gravel. "Rent's increased, a lot, and billable hours have been down with people leaving Harmony Hills for bigger towns and more work opportunities elsewhere. It's been a whole lot of little things, but they all add up."

For a moment I say nothing, trying to absorb what she's saying.

"It's been tough on them," Amelia continues. "The clinic is their life's work, obviously, and more than that, Harmony Hills needs them. So they've taken on extra debt—remortgaged the house—to keep the doors open. I offered to help them, but I don't have much extra. Teachers don't exactly rake it in."

My stomach lurches properly now, and I worry I might throw up right there in the car. So this is how Claire and Kirby came to consider buying Munro Medical. This is why everyone looked uncomfortable when I talked about how nicely bronze ages. The clinic is floundering, and Mom and Dad are barely keeping it afloat.

"Why didn't they tell me? Maybe I could have helped out?" My voice is thin and weak. Even as I say it, I know it's too little, too late.

Amelia shoots me a look. "Really, Libby? When would they have told you? You never listen to your voicemails, and you barely respond to text messages these days. Plus, you haven't been home in over a year."

Over a year? That can't be right. But then I do the math. While I came home pre-Christmas last year, it was brief and because of Mom's ankle. The Christmas before that I was working, and then going out on my first date with Austin. I didn't make it back that holiday season, even though I promised to try. So technically, at least from Amelia's perspective in Christmas past, it *has been* a long time since I visited Harmony Hills.

"Still . . . *you* should have told me, Amelia." I know blaming my sister is a low blow, and not fair. She's been here while I haven't. She's kind enough not to toss that back at me.

"I was planning to talk to you about it when you came home for the party," she says. "And here we are, talking about it—so now you know."

"Mom's ankle isn't going to help things," I say, realization dawning. Last year, Mom ended up being off her feet for weeks. I drove back to the city after a mere two days, my focus on enjoying my Christmas vacation with Austin. I should have stayed in Harmony Hills. I should have asked more questions. I should have paid closer attention to what was going on.

"It sure isn't. They'll probably have to hire a doctor to come and cover for Mom, until she's on her feet again," Amelia mutters. My stomach churns.

"I love you, and I know you want to help, Libby. But staying a few days, a couple of weeks . . . it isn't going to be enough. I'm not sure how much longer they can keep this up. And I have no idea what that will mean, for them or for Harmony Hills."

Munro Medical has been a part of the community, and our family, for twenty-five years—my memories before the clinic are spotty, as I was a child when it opened. Mom and Dad are nearing retirement, but if they can't afford to keep the clinic running and they can't sell it, then what?

The rest of the car ride is mostly quiet, except for the holiday music Amelia has turned back up, probably to give us both a reprieve. There isn't much else to say. I stew in the guilt and worry, circling around and around, looking for solutions that don't present themselves. About five minutes later we turn onto a long,

gravel driveway that leads to Liam's farmhouse, and Clover Hill
Farm.

It's a winter wonderland out here, the surrounding fields and
rolling hills are blanketed in snow, as is the rooftop of the main
barn, the rustic wood beams painted a cheerful red with white
trim. The barn's roofline and large doors, which are painted black,
are adorned with twinkling lights. As we slow down for a narrow
bridge, I notice a babbling brook, its edges sparkling with delicate
ice crystals, winding itself along the driveway.

The sign that hangs from two white pickets near the main
house reads: WELCOME TO CLOVER HILL FARM: COME FOR THE ANI-
MALS, STAY FOR THE SNOWBALL FIGHTS!

"That's cute," I say.

"He has signs for every season," Amelia replies. "My favourite
is the Halloween one—they do hayrides and he has a corn maze.
It's pretty impressive."

"What does the sign say?"

"SPOOKY GREETINGS FROM CLOVER HILL FARM! THE PUMPKINS ARE
RIPE, AND THE FRIGHTS ARE JUST RIGHT."

I smile, imagining Liam coming up with these signs. Appreci-
ating the care he's put into making this farm a part of the larger
community—the work he's done to give back to Harmony Hills.
The guilt threatens again, but I tamp it down. I need a break from
the drama, and Clover Hill Farm—and Liam—seem the perfect
antidote.

Amelia turns off the car as the farmhouse's front door, a purple
colour that reminds me of fields of lavender, opens. Liam steps out
onto the impressive wraparound porch in a grey chunky-knit wool
sweater, distressed jeans, and brown leather work boots.

"Well, if that isn't a catalogue-ready photo. Not my type, of
course, but he really is sans défaut," Amelia says.

I keep my eyes on Liam. "What does that mean?"

"Flawless," she explains.

"Hmm. No one's actually flawless though, right?" I reply, though if Liam has any real flaws, I have yet to find them.

Amelia shrugs. "According to Becks, he's pretty darn close. I mean, hey, if the sweater fits . . ."

We look at each other, then start laughing. The final bit of tension inside the car dissipates.

Beckett comes out the house and stands beside Liam. They both wave—equally wide smiles on their faces, and I note Beckett has eyes only for Amelia. Despite everything going on, the fact that I get to see the start of what becomes the greatest love of my sister's life . . . I well up.

"You okay?" Amelia asks, pausing when she sees me wiping my eyes.

"Allergies," I reply, clearing my throat.

"In December?"

"It's a thing!" I'm indignant as I open my car door. "Let's go and have some fun, okay?"

"You said the magic word," Amelia replies, opening her own door.

"Which is?" We're now walking towards the porch, as Liam and Beckett come down the stairs to meet us. A slurry of excitement mixed with a hint of angst fills me when Liam smiles, eyes on mine.

"Fun," Amelia replies. "We've had enough drama for one holiday season, don't you agree?"

32

"It's really nice of you, to give away trees every Christmas." I touch the snow-heavy branches of an evergreen as we walk the forested trail, heading to the tree farm area. The other two stayed behind, as Beckett still had a couple of goats needing their hooves and nails trimmed. Amelia offered to assist—which both surprised me and didn't surprise me at all, knowing what I know—and so Liam and I headed out to find the perfect tree for the clinic.

"I imagine it's a ton of work—the farm, the animals, your bakery. Not to mention the resources," I add.

"I have plenty to go around," Liam says, not in a bragging way but matter-of-fact. His breath is visible in the wintry air, and he tugs his toque lower. Despite the cold temperature, it's beautiful out—the sky a cloudless robin's-egg blue. "I never expected the app to have the trajectory it did, but I'm glad I can make the most of it."

"I've been meaning to ask about this app. You mentioned it was health care–related. Would I know it?"

"It's called PILLS: Patient Interaction Life-Saving Log System," Liam says. "It tracks medications and drug interactions, but in a highly personalized way."

I stop in my tracks. "Of course I know it! It's a mainstay in the emergency room. I can't believe you created PILLS." I've used it many times when prescribing medications and have suggested most patients sign up for the service. It's free, user-friendly, and adds an extra layer of safety for both patients and medical teams.

"I did," he says, again with zero ego. "I have Jaclyn to thank for the idea, actually. Her brother almost died from a drug interaction that was avoidable—human error."

"That app has changed a lot of people's lives, Liam," I reply. "You must be really proud to have created something like that."

"I am proud of it. It changed my life, too, in a lot of ways," Liam says. "Some people, Jaclyn included, at least at first, couldn't understand when I opted out of development after PILLS. I did a complete one-eighty, coming here and starting the rescue and the bakery."

Our boots crunch through the crystallized layer of ice covering the snow. Otherwise, it's a serene walk, only the occasional chirp of a songbird breaking the quiet. "I never wanted to chase more in that space, because it already felt like I had enough."

"Success, you mean?"

Liam nods. "Money, too. I'm not all that motivated by a flush bank account, to be honest. Though I know it's probably easy to say it doesn't motivate you when you have enough of it."

He steps slightly ahead of me and, with the hand not carrying the saw, holds back one of the branches so it doesn't hit me.

"Thanks," I reply, thinking again of Amelia's term *sans défaut*. Liam Young certainly seems without flaw, which both awes me and gives me pause. I have plenty of quirks—okay, flaws—and I'm unsure if Liam's the real deal or simply too good to be true.

"I learned from my parents the value of giving back, especially into a community you've made your home. Like Harmony Hills, for me."

My throat catches. I think about the differences between Liam and Austin—it's becoming impossible not to. Austin, who always wanted more, who was restless in ways I didn't understand at first. Liam, on the other hand, craves stability, a home, a family. And then there's me. Someone who's lived stability but never fully appreciated it; someone who longed for the energy of somewhere "bigger." I realize I've been chasing more, too, without understanding what I already have.

"I know you get it," Liam adds. "Growing up here, with your parents running the clinic. You've seen that firsthand."

I nod, swallowing the lump in my throat. Everything feels so raw—so close to the surface. I used to pride myself on my steadiness, thinking it was a superpower, especially because of the work I do. Now I'm not so sure.

"Welcome to the land of Christmas trees," Liam says as we step into a small clearing. In front of us are rows of evergreens, in various stages of growth. Some short and round, not yet ready to grace living rooms with holiday cheer; others tall and majestic, with plenty of strong branches to string lights or hang ornaments from.

"This is incredible, Liam. Did you plant all these?"

"Not quite," he says, smiling in a kind but amused way that reminds me I know nothing about keeping a Christmas tree farm.

"The property already had a tree farm when I bought it. But it was about half this. So yeah, I did a lot of planting." He points to rows of puny, stubby evergreens. "See all those little trees over there?"

I nod.

"Those I planted. But the rest have been growing for quite a while. It takes about eight years for a tree to grow to six or seven feet, from a sapling," he says.

"Really? I had no idea." I point to the taller trees, some which are well above Liam's head—and he's over six feet. "How old are those ones, do you think?"

"I'd say at least ten years."

My expression shifts to one that is overly dramatic and pained. "Is it weird that I feel bad cutting down a tree that has spent ten years growing? Just to throw some ornaments and tinsel onto it, then send it to the curb for chipping?"

"Not weird at all—that's just a healthy respect for nature," Liam replies. "But does it help to think of it as the tree's purpose? These were all grown to become Christmas trees. To bring happiness to whoever chooses, decorates, and enjoys them for the season."

"Yeah, that helps. A bit," I reply, smiling.

Liam smiles, too, his cheeks and nose reddened from the cold. His green eyes are so vibrant, matching the colour of the evergreen boughs, and I'm soon upended by our closeness. By the intoxicating scent of cedar and cloves that I've come to associate with Liam. My heart races, heat rising in my centre. I'm only an arm's length away from him, and then, without planning it, move closer. I inhale deeply, gathering courage . . .

My phone rings. It's loud, and both Liam and I glance at my coat pocket, where the incessant ringing comes from. "Sorry about this." I fumble with the phone, hitting the side button to stop the ringing.

"Not at all. Do you need to take it?"

"Let me just check. In case it's about Mom." With a quick glance at the screen, my stomach drops. It's not my parents, it's Austin, and he's leaving a voicemail. *Thanks, Universe—message received*, I think. Followed by, *Seriously, Libby, what are you doing?*

"Everything okay?" Liam asks. I'm still looking at my screen, frowning.

Shoving the phone back into my pocket, I say, "Everything's fine."

"So . . . ready to choose a tree?" He turns away from me and back towards the rows of trees. "Thinking a seven-footer, maybe?"

"Sounds good," I reply, still lost in the whiplash of the preceding moments.

"Follow me," he says with a wave of his hand. "I think I know the perfect tree."

Liam stops in front of a tall, cone-shaped blue spruce. He grabs hold of one of the hardy boughs and gives it a shake; snow tumbles from the branches. "What do you think?"

"Sans défaut," I say, in a quite terrible French accent. "It's flawless."

"My feelings exactly." He crouches, resting his elbows on his knees as he looks up at me—his expression is hard to read. I wonder if, like me, he's thinking about more than the evergreen.

"Are you ready to fulfill your Christmas tree destiny?" Liam asks the tree, before looking my way again, dimples fully engaged with his grin. My knees wobble, and I almost have to sit down right there in the snow.

"The tree says it's ready. How about you?" Liam hands me the saw, and I take it, nodding. "Ready," I reply.

We position it against the trunk, him taking one side of the saw with his good hand, me the other. We're both crouched now at the base of the tree, and the spruce needles tickle my face as we take turns pushing and pulling the saw. The teeth bite into the bark, then the pulp of the tree. Soon I'm sweating, and have to take off my coat.

"I forgot how much work this is!" It has been years since I

felled a Christmas tree. The last time I remember joining my parents was when I was thirteen or so. After that, I always seemed to have something better to do. Studying. Hanging with Claire. I wish I'd continued the tradition, and I decide from now on I'll cut down my own tree—no matter where I live or what I'm doing.

We're making good progress until the saw gets stuck midway through the trunk. It won't budge. "It's really jammed," I say. Liam pushes, then pulls, but the saw remains embedded.

"Sure is," he replies, strain in his voice as he tries to free it. I hold the saw tightly, and tug on it with everything I have.

"Any give at all?" I ask, grunting with the effort. I'm also sweating profusely now, but it feels good using my muscles like this.

"Let's get on the same side, see if we can't pull it out." Liam and I each grab hold of the long end of the saw, the blade facing away from us. "On three, okay? One, two, three!"

There's resistance and then suddenly, the two of us tumble backwards into the snow.

"You okay?" Liam asks, sitting beside me, still holding the saw. I nod. "You?"

He nods before carefully setting the saw to the side. Then he starts laughing. "I saw this going much differently in my head."

"Same," I reply, laughing as well. "Personally, I imagined less sweat. Definitely less sweat."

Liam's hand reaches out, and I'm nearly breathless when his fingers touch my cheek. "You've got something . . . here."

He gently removes a spruce twig from my hair, and I mumble "thanks," because it's the best I can do, with him this close, and the feel of his fingers against my skin. My eyes meet his, and my mind empties. Then he leans towards me, hand on the side of my face, and—

"Liam, I can't do this." It comes out quickly, in one strangled breath.

For a moment neither of us moves, then Liam drops his hand to his side. "I'm sorry."

"No, don't be. It's just . . . it's complicated." I stand quickly and start brushing snow from my jeans. "I don't know what I was thinking. Clearly, I'm *not* thinking. Or thinking too much." I say this last part more quietly, mostly to myself.

Liam stands as well. "Libby, it was presumptuous of me . . ." He frowns. Seems frustrated, though I understand it's not with me. "*I'm* sorry I made you uncomfortable."

"Liam, it's not you." I take a deep breath, steeling myself. "I think I misled you, before, even though I didn't mean to. Austin—my, uh, well, to be honest, he's pretty much my *ex*-boyfriend—we're not technically broken up, but we're also not together right now."

"I thought you said you broke up," he says, tilting his head slightly.

"I did say that," I reply, swallowing hard. "It's more like we're on a break."

"A break?" Liam's brow furrows.

"Things have been fairly confusing lately." *To put it mildly.* "It's over, at least for me. I just haven't had the chance to talk to him about it. With the holidays and everything."

I'm finding it hard to get a full breath in, the relentless panicky feeling settling across my chest. What a mess I've made of this. "I should have been more up-front with you. If only you knew how"—*If you only knew how badly I want to kiss you*—"how very sorry I am."

"Hey, it's okay, Libby. You don't owe me an explanation." Liam sets a hand on my arm, gives it a gentle squeeze. But now there's an aloof vibe coming off of him, and he doesn't let his hand linger. "Besides, you have to go back home soon."

"Yeah . . . home." I could cry, because I'm as confused as ever. I'm no longer sure where home is.

Liam gestures to our half-cut-down tree. "We should probably get back to it, eh? Before Becks and Amelia drink all the hot chocolate without us."

His words hang in the air like a lifeline, diffusing the tension. I smile back, somewhat shakily, and nod. "Wouldn't want to miss out."

The saw glides smoothly this time. Liam gives it one final push, and the evergreen tilts, teetering for a moment before it falls gracefully into the snow. We both stand, admiring our work.

"You're welcome to submit a résumé anytime," Liam says, seeming more like himself now. "We can always use a Christmas tree lumberjack at Clover Hill Farm."

"Hmm. I'll keep that in mind," I reply, imagining what it would be like to stay put—to call Harmony Hills home once more. *If only it could be that simple.*

By the time we reach the farmhouse, Beckett and Amelia are on the porch, steaming mugs of hot chocolate in hand.

"Nice tree," Beckett says, and then Amelia adds, "Was beginning to wonder if we needed to send out a search party," with a subtle rise of her eyebrow that I know is meant for me.

"The tree took some coaxing," Liam replies, brushing snow from his gloves. "But it was well worth it—it's flawless."

"Sans défaut," I say, but I don't think he hears it.

33

"Do you know what you're doing, Libby?" Amelia asks, as we're double-checking the ropes we used to secure the tree on top of the car.

I know precisely to what she's referring—Liam. She sees right through the facade I've put on since we got back from cutting down the tree. The charged energy between Liam and me was surely palpable, especially to my little sister.

After we returned from getting the tree, Liam showed Amelia and me around the rescue. I fed the goats and the alpaca; Amelia learned how to remove eggs from under a nesting chicken without getting her hand pecked; and then Liam's dog George—the sweetest mutt—snuggled into me on the porch's sofa while we warmed up with hot chocolate.

We kept the conversation light and breezy, the reality of what had *almost* happened sitting right underneath the surface in my mind. It was agreed the four of us would meet up later, at the Sip and Glide ice-skating event—though I made it very clear, and Amelia backed me up, that I would not be donning ice skates.

"Trust me, you don't want her to put on anything with sharp blades," Amelia said, which made everyone laugh.

"Yes, I know what I'm doing, Mila," I reply now, hoping it's the truth.

She shifts the car into drive to head back down the laneway. I get a last glimpse at Liam, who's on the porch, hands in his pockets. He pulls one out to wave goodbye, and I raise a hand in similar fashion out the open car window.

"I sure hope so," she replies, glancing left and right before pulling out onto the main road. We drive more slowly with the tree on the top of the car. "He's a good guy, Libby. He's been through a lot, too."

"I know," I say, but slightly more forcefully than I intended. "Like I said, I know what I'm doing."

But . . . *what am I doing, exactly?* Blowing up the life I currently have—the one whose timeline I've been ripped out of—and assuming, like I did with Mom's ankle, that I can change anything that's happened? I met Liam mere days ago. Spending all this time with him in Christmas past is giving me too much bravado. There's definitely a spark there—he almost kissed me, between the evergreens. *Would have* kissed me if I hadn't stopped him.

"The two of you had some funny energy when you got back. Did anything happen out there?"

"No—we cut down the tree, had a nice walk in the snow." Neutral tone, nothing to hide.

"Okay then," she says, but I know I haven't convinced her.

"Fine. I haven't been totally honest," I say. "About Austin."

"I figured as much," Amelia replies, her tone softening.

"Things have been . . . not the best." I sigh, wondering how much I can get away with saying. "It's like I've had a glimpse of the future, and it's not what I thought it was going to be. I'm not sure it's what I want anymore."

"That's a hard thing to notice, especially when you're so close to something," Amelia replies.

"It really is."

"Well, you're brilliant and capable and wise, and I have no doubt you will figure this out. But I'm here if you want to talk about it. No judgement."

Reaching out, I squeeze her shoulder. "I know. And thank you. Also? Same goes."

Now Amelia smiles and gives me a quick, almost nervous glance. "Can I tell *you* something?"

"Yes, please," I reply.

She laughs to herself, shaking her head. "I can't believe it, and never expected it, but . . ."

"But . . . what?" I already know where this is going, but I wait for her to tell me.

"Let's just say I have a date for Sip and Glide." She glances over at me again, and she can barely contain her excitement. Her eyes are wide, her smile wider, and she lets out a tiny squeal that makes me laugh.

"Oh, reeeeally . . ." I set a finger to my lips. "With whom?"

"Nice," Amelia says, at my use of "whom." "Becks asked me out, and I said yes."

"Sissy, this is officially the best news I've heard all week. I'm really happy for you."

"Thanks, Libby—I'm happy for me, too." We laugh again, and then, emboldened by Amelia's good news, I pull out my phone. I know what I have to do. After only a second's hesitation, I type out a message to Austin. "Need to talk. Call you soon."

Then I put my phone on Do Not Disturb and turn up the radio, as Amelia and I sing along to the cheery holiday music.

❄

It's late afternoon by the time Amelia drops me off at our parents' place. We've taken the tree to the clinic, and Miss Betty is planning to decorate it tomorrow after the boughs have had a chance to fall. Amelia and I make plans for dinner—she's going to pick up a family-sized portion of lasagna from the diner.

"Mom and Dad can freeze that mayo-and-ham casserole," she says, with a slight shudder. "I'm sure it will keep . . . forever."

We chuckle, while also acknowledging the kindness of Millicent Mueller, along with the other neighbours and friends who have shown up for Mom and Dad in the past couple of days.

"I'll be back by six," Amelia says through the open car window.

"Sounds good," I reply. "Also, today was fun."

"It was," she says with a grin. After she pulls away, I head up the stone path towards the front door. I'm distracted, my thoughts swirling: *Liam . . . Amelia and Beckett . . . my mom's ankle and the clinic . . . the conversation I need to have with Austin.* Definitely not looking forward to that one, and I feel crappy to be doing it over the phone. However, I can't put it off any longer.

"I'm home," I call out, shutting the front door behind me. Holiday music mingles with voices—Mom's, Millicent's, and a male voice that at first I don't recognize. Dad is out on house calls, so it isn't him.

"Hello?" I take off my boots and hang my coat, then walk into the living room. "I'm back, and the tree—"

The words stick in my throat. *What in the world . . . ?*

"Libby! Darling, look who's here," Mom says from the couch, where she rests with her casted leg on the pillow.

"Austin," I say, my voice strangled. My ex is in my parents' living room. Wearing jeans and a navy-blue sweater over a blue-and-white-checkered button-up shirt that I gave him for his birthday—*last year*. His blue eyes a near-perfect match to the colour of the shirt, which is why I bought it for him. His short blond hair as perfectly coiffed as ever . . . as is the wink he gives me now, which makes my stomach do a flip-flop, but in a not-pleasant way.

"Hey, babe," he says, striding over and hugging me. I smell his soap, which he has imported from France but is indiscernible from local grocery-store soap, followed by his cologne, a musk and to-bacco scent that I used to find intoxicating but which now feels overpowering.

Austin pulls back to kiss me, but I turn my head slightly at the last moment and his lips land near the corner of my mouth. He gives me an odd look—my lukewarm greeting certainly not what he anticipated—but recovers quickly, smile intact.

"Wow . . . how . . . why are you here?" I cross my arms over my chest. I can't catch my breath, and I'm lightheaded. With one hand I reach into my back pocket, my shaking fingers finding my cell phone. "Didn't you get my message?"

"I just did, actually," Austin replies. "We were stringing popcorn for the tree, and then these two card sharks took advantage of my less-than-stellar bridge skills."

A charming smile delivered effortlessly to Millicent and Mom. The popcorn garland is around the tree, the bowls with a few ker-nels left in them still on the coffee table.

"What do you want to talk about?" His expression is open, mildly questioning. Mom and Millicent are watching me as well, though Millicent's eyes keep shifting back to Austin. He's undeni-ably good-looking and charming. But in a less genuine way than Liam is, I'm realizing now.

"Uh . . . maybe we could go upstairs?"

"Sure thing," he says, before turning towards Millicent. "It was nice meeting you, Millicent. Hope to see you again soon?"

Millicent nods. "Lovely to meet you, Austin. Libby's a lucky woman."

She gives me a smile, as Austin says, "Oh, I'm the lucky one."

It's bizarre, having Austin in my childhood bedroom. We sit on the bed, and he looks around. "Wow—your parents haven't changed much, huh?"

"They've changed nothing," I reply. "Same with Amelia's room. Though she's home more often than I am."

"Home?" Austin turns my way.

"I mean at my parents' home, obviously," I reply. But in truth, this *does* feel like my home—not only the house, but Harmony Hills, too.

"My parents turned my bedroom into a gym the week I moved out," Austin says, in a tone that implies that's a more appropriate choice. "You weren't kidding about the Christmas stuff. It's everywhere."

I consider what the house looks like through Austin's eyes. The festive decor, the holiday knickknacks, like the Christmas lantern lamp and Polar Express train in the living room, the twinkle lights strung around all the doorways, the scent of cinnamon and pine diffusing from my bedside table.

"My parents enjoy Christmas." I'm defensive, and I think about his whole kids-shouldn't-be-lied-to-about-Santa-Claus position. "There are worse things than having a house full of holiday cheer."

I sound petulant, irritated. I don't want to be reacting this way, but his unexpected arrival has set me off. Particularly because I never expected to see him again, least of all in my childhood home . . . the same afternoon that I almost kissed Liam. Now I feel guilty, though I remind myself that technically—at least in my reality—Austin and I are no longer together.

"Hey, I didn't mean anything. I'm impressed, actually," Austin says, shifting closer to me to hold my hands. "Don't be like this, okay?"

Like what? I think. But I ignore this, and plough ahead. "Why did you come here, Austin?"

Now he frowns. "That doesn't sound like someone who is happy her boyfriend dropped everything and drove five hours to make sure she's okay."

"I told you I was fine," I reply, evenly. "We agreed I'd come back to the city tomorrow."

"Come back 'home,' you mean, right?"

I give him an exasperated look, and he changes tack.

"I was worried about you. Helena said you weren't ... yourself." Austin reaches out to brush his fingers on the side of my face, where Liam's fingers lingered not long ago. But while the feel of Liam's hand on my skin electrified me, I have a sense of dread when Austin does it.

"Helly overreacted." I shift on the bed so I'm out of his reach. "I had food poisoning, got dehydrated and a bit loopy, imagined a few things that didn't happen, and then got some electrolytes in me and was better in no time."

Austin keeps his eyes on me but doesn't say anything.

"As you can see, I'm perfectly coherent and lucid." I'm nervous, though, and my palms are sweating. I press my hands into my quilt and am about to issue another round of reassurances when suddenly Austin's lips are on mine. I'm so taken by surprise I don't have time to pull away.

After the kiss, Austin holds my head to his, our foreheads pressed together. My body is rigid, but he doesn't seem to notice. "I've missed you," he whispers.

My eyes are on the quilt, regretting everything that has led to this moment. Then Austin's body shifts, putting some blessed distance between us. "What's that?" he asks, his voice strained. He sounds nervous.

Following his gaze, I see my duffel bag—his sweatshirt resting on top. My stomach twists. "Oh, that's my overnight bag."

He's off the bed in a flash, pulling the sweatshirt from my bag. I hold my breath while he runs his hands across the fabric. His fingers pause on the sleeve, which is folded on top of the sweatshirt. "How did this get here?"

My thoughts ricochet between answering "I don't know" and "You tell me!" But then I say, "I borrowed it. I found it in the back of the closet and didn't think you'd mind."

"I don't mind," he replies, facing me again. I think of the ring box, no longer in the sleeve of that sweatshirt but tucked inside the duffel bag. "What's mine is yours."

Our eyes lock, and for a moment I have this crazy thought he knows that I know. That maybe he's about to propose, even without the ring.

It's a ludicrous thought, because why would he choose this moment, over so many others we've had recently? Birthday dinners, quiet nights at home with Thai takeout, a good movie, and some heart-pounding sex. Even Valentine's Day, however clichéd, could have been a reasonable option.

"I should head downstairs," I say, sliding off the bed as well. Wanting to stop whatever momentum might be building. "Amelia's coming back with dinner soon. I need to set the table."

"Sure, sure," Austin says. I go to step past him, to open the bedroom door, when he adds, "Wait. What did you want to talk about?"

I pause for a beat. Then take a breath and smile. "Nothing that can't wait until after dinner."

34

"I assume you'll be spending the night?" Mom says to Austin, from the end of the table. Her leg is on a cushion, propped up on a chair. She's eating well—her lasagna nearly gone—which I'm glad to see. I've barely made a dent in my own dinner, my stomach too unsettled to eat.

"I booked a room at the bed-and-breakfast," Austin says. "I didn't want to put you out, with everything you have going on."

"Nonsense," Dad says, taking a forkful of saucy noodle and cheese. "We're thrilled to have you."

"The bed-and-breakfast might work better," I say. "My bed is only a double. We'll be a bit squished. We're used to a king, right?"

"I don't mind if you don't mind," Austin replies, winking at me. *Ugh.* I used to love that wink.

"It's settled then," Mom says, picking up her knife and fork again.

Amelia catches my eye with a *You okay?* look. I give my head the smallest of shakes, and she nods, a determined set to her mouth.

"I don't want to put a wrinkle in things, but Libby promised she'd stay over at my place . . . to, um . . ."

"To have a girls' night." I smile brightly at Amelia, then at Austin. "We need to . . . tag the candy canes. For the tree lighting. It's a lot of work for one person."

Amelia nods. "It is. So much work."

Dad looks between us, sensing there's more to this exchange. Then Austin chimes in. "I'm happy to help. If I can sculpt faces with these, I can tie tags onto candy canes." He holds up his hands, and Mom laughs.

"The more the merrier, right, girls?" Dad says, crumpling his napkin. "I have some paperwork to finish up, but I'll see you before you head out in the morning."

"Head out?" I ask, though I know exactly where I'm supposed to be heading out. "Right, back to the city." I set my fork down. There's no point in pretending I'm able to eat.

"Back *home*," Austin clarifies, obviously to make his point from earlier. "As much as I'd love to stick around Harmony Hills for Christmas . . . It's my favourite season," he adds, making Mom and Dad smile, and me frown. "Elizabeth and I have a plane to catch."

Back home.

There's a plaque that has hung in the Munro dining room for as long as I can remember. It never comes down, even at Christmastime, when Mom needs every inch of space she can get for the holiday decorations. I painted it when I was six years old, carefully following the stenciled letters on the heart-shaped wooden plaque. It's crudely done, the paint outside of the lines in more than one spot.

It was a Christmas present for my parents, and Millicent Mueller helped me—ever patient as I sat at her kitchen table, my paints and brushes strewn across the plastic tablecloth she always set down for crafts. The plaque reads HOME IS WHERE THE HEART IS.

The city is not home. *This is home*—Harmony Hills, where my family, friends, neighbours, and, most unexpectedly, a kindhearted man with gorgeous green eyes and sexy-as-heck dimples live.

"Excuse me," I mumble, pushing my chair back quickly. "I just remembered a call I have to make."

"You okay, Sissy?" Amelia asks quietly as I brush past her. I nod, but she catches the stricken look on my face. Then I hear her getting up from the table to come after me, followed by Austin saying, "I'll go," right before I open the front door and step outside.

It's dark, the moon lighting a path through the snow, which glitters under the streetlamps. The snap of cold brings goose bumps to my exposed skin, and I shiver as I gulp in a few shallow breaths. Everything's a mess, and I am not coping well.

Austin opens the front door moments later. He's wearing his coat, and he turns up the collar against the cold. It occurs to me he has not brought me *my* coat, nor is he offering me his, even though I'm clearly shivering.

"Are you all right?" he asks. There's sincerity and genuine concern in his voice, and I feel a moment of regret for what I need to do.

I sigh, my teeth chattering. "Not really."

"What's going on?" Austin gently takes my arm, turning me towards him. "Elizabeth, tell me."

"You wouldn't believe me, even if I could figure out how to explain it," I say quietly, with a mirthless laugh.

"Try me."

Try me. Austin is science-minded and pragmatic, so a time-travelling narrative is going to be a nonstarter. But what do I have to lose? There is no relationship to salvage. Plus, I'm tired of hiding from everyone the truth about what's really going on with me.

"Fine," I say, after a beat. "I've come back here from the future. From next Christmas, specifically. And we're not together anymore, Austin. We break up in September. There's a toilet-paper-roll situation and we fight about it, and then it's *over*, just like that."

Austin looks amused, his lips turning up into a smile. "Toilet-paper-roll situation?"

"I'm serious, Austin. Amelia gets married next Christmas; oh, and she's pregnant—yes, my baby sister is having a baby," I say, when Austin raises an eyebrow.

"And I was supposed to go to Mexico to drink margaritas for Christmas, but Helly couldn't go with me, and then Amelia called to ask me to be her maid of honour, and then a pig named Mary Piggins knocked me out cold at the ceremony, and when I woke up I was *here*." I take in a big breath. "Except *here* is actually *last* Christmas."

Austin watches me, his expression difficult to read. For a second, I wonder if I've misjudged him, but then he laughs. "Were you and Amelia day drinking?"

I shake my head. *What did you expect, Libby?* "I understand this is . . . impossible to comprehend. But I assure you—it's last Christmas, and I'm reliving everything. Except . . . everything is also different? I don't understand it either, like, at all. But it's happening."

His smile fades. "Oh, you're not joking."

I shake my head.

"Are you concussed? Did you pass out when you were sick, knock yourself out?" Austin frowns, raises his hands to my head to feel around for a bump. I duck out of the way.

"Stop, please. I told you I'm fine," I say.

"This doesn't seem like 'fine' to me," he replies. "I know we're supposed to be getting on a flight soon, but I don't think that's a good idea."

I let out a long breath. "Exactly, that's what I've been trying to say. You and I, we aren't—"

"Where's the nearest ER?" Austin pulls his phone from his back pocket, starts typing something into the search bar. "Does your mom have privileges?"

"What? No, I'm not going to the hospital, Austin."

"The hell you're not. You need a CT," Austin says, reading his phone screen. "Westhaven . . . How far away is that?"

I've seen this side of Austin before, and I used to love his take-charge, confidence-for-days self. Tonight, however, it's problematic. *Big mistake, Libby.* I needed to be honest, but about our relationship status . . . not offering some far-fetched tale. I know he isn't going to let it go, which means I'm going to have to be explicit: Things are over between us. Otherwise, he'll toss me over his shoulder and get me into a CT scanner by the end of the night, regardless of how much I protest.

"I don't need a hospital," I say firmly, and then add before he disagrees, "Give me a second to explain, okay?"

He nods.

"Yes, I did pass out the night I was sick—it was seconds, literally," I say, noting how his frown deepens. I'm scrambling, looking for a way to explain my unbelievable story and diffuse the situation. "I didn't hit my head, but I've been having . . . strange dreams ever since."

"Have you had headaches?"

I shake my head. "I told you, I'm not concussed."

"Nausea or vomiting?" he asks, ignoring me.

"Nope. No headaches, no dizziness, no nausea or vomiting. Just odd dreams," I say, adding, "Very realistic, though."

It's a weak explanation, but surely he'll want to believe this is nothing more than the aftereffects of a bad case of food poisoning. Who wouldn't?

Austin presses his lips together, his blue eyes scanning my face. "So what was all that stuff before. About Christmas past? About your sister?"

"Like I said, very, very weird dreams. That's it." I keep my voice even, hold eye contact. I'm about to say, "Hey, also? I think we need to talk about us . . ." but before I get the words out, Austin pulls me against him, wrapping his arms around me. I know I've missed my moment.

"I'm glad it's nothing more," he says, leaning back to look me in the eyes. "But I'm sorry I wasn't here to take care of you, babe."

"It's okay. I know you don't do sickness." I smile as brightly as I can, then gently extricate myself with an exaggerated shiver. "Hey, let's go back inside. I'm freezing."

"Sure. Your parents mentioned an ice-skating thing tonight?" Austin says, opening the front door. "You up for it? I'd love to see more of this town, though I'm sure that won't take long."

He laughs at his own joke, but I don't join him.

"Aren't you tired after that long drive?" I ask, my tone mild. "We can skip it."

I don't want to go ice-skating with Austin. First of all, I want to get Austin out of this house and back to the city. Without me, though I haven't yet sorted that one out yet. I know I need to break up with him—again, in *this* timeline—but I'd prefer to do it when I'm steadier. Most definitely not in my childhood home, with my family underfoot. Truthfully, I'd prefer not to do it at all. Maybe I won't have to, if time somehow resets itself.

More than all of this, however, it's about Liam. He's going to be at the rink tonight, and I'm not at all prepared for my two worlds to collide. I was sort of hoping to put that awkwardness off, say, forever.

"I'm not tired. You know I can pull an all-nighter and then do surgery the next day." Austin hangs up his coat, giving me another practiced wink. "I won't take no for an answer."

35

The Sip and Glide ice-skating event begins late, at eleven p.m. It's adults-only, with a bar set up at one end of the rink serving holiday-themed drinks, like spiked eggnog, hot buttered rum, and Irish cream hot chocolate.

I've only ever attended twice before, when I came home from medical school over Christmas. It's fun and festive, even if you're not an eggnog connoisseur or ice-skating fan. Which I am not. However, tonight I have a pair of skates over my shoulder because someone (my mother) didn't think I should make Austin skate alone.

The rink glows against the nighttime sky backdrop. Candy-cane poles, set every few feet, are wrapped in twinkle lights, with old-fashioned outdoor bulbs hanging in lines between them. There's music playing from speakers at each side of the rink—Christmas carols, of course.

Amelia, Austin, and I have come over directly from Amelia's place. We spent the last two hours tagging candy canes for tomorrow's tree lighting. It wasn't lost on me that last year's Elizabeth would have loved Austin showing up the way he did in Harmony Hills. Appreciated how my boyfriend and sister had a chance to spend some time together. But this version of me—Libby, stuck in the past with a clear view of the future—is melancholy at best, and panicked at worst, by what's transpired over the past few hours.

I'm dreading the evening and have already tried to convince Austin, more than once, unsuccessfully, to make it an early night and skip ice-skating. I considered claiming illness, but I'd only narrowly avoided a trip to Westhaven and its CT scanner, so I know it's not an option. Austin also used to play hockey, so skating is definitely in his wheelhouse. He's borrowed Dad's skates because the two of them share the same size feet.

I'm nervous when we arrive at the rink, a couple of minutes early. A fluttering in my belly, a slight quiver of my hands noticeable only as I lace up the first skate. Amelia and Austin are getting us drinks at the pop-up bar on the other side of the rink, and I hope—foolishly, for Harmony Hills is too small for anonymity—they don't run into anyone. And by anyone, I mean Liam.

I haven't seen him yet, but with every passing moment I grow more anxious. I don't know how to explain Austin's sudden arrival to Liam. Especially after what happened earlier, when I told him we were on a break and made it sound like I wanted it to be permanent.

"Hold it together, Libby," I whisper to myself. My eyes are on the laces as I tie a bow, but when there's give on the bench, I glance over to find Liam beside me. He's wearing a red-and-black-plaid flannel jacket, unzipped, over a black wool sweater, jeans, and the same boots he had on earlier today. He hands me a hot chocolate with a smile, and the Irish cream scent wafts up with the steam.

"I took a guess," he says. "Couldn't decide if eggnog or grown-up hot chocolate was more your thing."

"Nailed it," I reply, smiling back. Despite how stressed I am, the sight of him buoys my mood and a warm flush of happiness fills me. "I have a tenuous relationship with eggnog. I used to like it, before I overdid it at a work Christmas party." I wrinkle my nose, grimacing.

"Been there," Liam says, chuckling and gently tapping his take-out cup to mine in a "cheers" gesture. He points at my skates. "Thought you said you were more of a bench warmer?"

His eyes crinkle, and the dimples shine through, despite his five o'clock shadow. Seeing those smile-induced lines around his mesmerizing green eyes reinforces that Austin's face doesn't have character like this. He's too focused on creating a wrinkle-free canvas, and his smile never fully reaches his eyes as a result.

Austin. *Jingle hell* . . . I see him now, coming towards me. Towards us. Amelia's found Beckett over by the bar, and the two are sharing a hug. I have to get off this bench, now, and away from Liam—for everyone's sake.

"Uh, thanks for the hot chocolate. I'm going to . . . I need to find Amelia." Then to myself I quietly add, "*This is not a drill.*"

I'm in such haste to get out of there that I forget I'm wearing ice skates—and that I've finished doing up the laces on only one skate. Which proves to be an unfortunate oversight a moment later when I trip over the untied lace and stumble forward right onto the ice rink.

I manage to stay upright, my arms windmilling, my hot chocolate flying through the air behind me, for a few torturous seconds until my skates slip out from under me.

I hear "Libby!" and "Elizabeth!" shouted simultaneously, from Liam and Austin respectively. I see stars, and they aren't the ones in the sky above me—definitely bumped my head this time. I close my eyes and groan.

"Ouch," I mumble, wondering what I was thinking when I put

these skates on in the first place. The voices get closer, and it's Liam who's by my side first.

"Libby, are you okay?" He slips a little on the ice—he's wearing boots, not skates—and then crouches beside me. His smile has been replaced by a frown, the lines deepening between his furrowed brow. He helps me sit up, his arm strong behind my back.

"I'm okay," I say, my voice weak, for I know what's coming next. My two worlds are about to collide.

Liam murmurs "That's good," then chuckles as he laces up the other skate for me. "There . . . problem solved," he says, flashing me that smile (*all* the dimples) I've come to adore.

Problem definitely not solved, I think.

Austin is there a split second later, but he stops just short of the ice and stands on the rink's wooden ledge. Then he carefully steps onto the ice, making sure he doesn't wipe out as he takes the couple of steps to where I'm sitting. With a quick glance at Liam, Austin then stands over me with his hands on his hips, a furrowed expression on his face. "Elizabeth, Jesus! What happened?"

Liam looks at me, then at Austin, then back to me. *Well, here we go*, I think, standing up with some difficulty due to the awkwardness of the skates. But Liam's right there, holding my elbow and making sure I'm steady.

"Austin, this is Liam Young. Liam, this is . . . Austin Whitmore," I say. My entire body quivers from adrenaline and nerves.

Austin reaches a hand out to shake Liam's. "I'm Elizabeth's boyfriend. Nice to meet you."

Then he crosses his arms over his chest, glancing between us. A relaxed smile comes across his face, but I recognize a hint of displeasure underneath it. "So how do you two know each other?"

"Funny story," I start, letting out a quick laugh. "Liam has a rescue farm—and a boulangerie, which is a fancy French name for a bread bakery."

"I know what a boulangerie is," Austin replies, nodding. He smiles again, but it's more strained.

"Of course you do," I say, and it comes out tinged with sarcasm. Liam raises an eyebrow, but Austin doesn't seem to notice. "Anyway, he was walking his potbellied pig—sorry, Miss Elsie's pig, Mary Piggins—and I was . . . getting some fresh air . . ." *Libby, you are making this much, much worse.*

"And Mary Piggins startled me, and I fell into the snow. Then she bought me a hot chocolate as an apology—well, Liam paid for it, obviously." I laugh again, but neither Austin nor Liam join me.

There's a pain in my chest, and it nearly takes my breath away. Liam won't meet my eyes, and his hands are stuffed deep into his pockets as he shifts from one foot to the other. One could assume it's from the cold, but I know that has nothing to do with it. I've hurt him, even if I didn't mean to, and certainly didn't want to.

An awkward moment of silence settles between the three of us, then I hear Beckett calling Liam's name. She holds up a pair of black hockey skates with one hand, another pair slung over her shoulder by the tied laces. I notice she's also holding Amelia's hand. My sister catches my eye, and her grin fades when she sees me standing with Liam and Austin.

"Well, looks like my skates are ready," Liam says. He still doesn't look my way, and I want to reach out and grab his arm to keep him here. So I can apologize for . . . everything, I guess. To reiterate that it's truly over with Austin, despite how this looks.

Also? I want him to know I'm falling for him—*have* fallen for him—and that I've never felt more like myself than I do when we're together. However, instead of saying these things, I stand still as a statue and dumbly watch him walk away.

"I got you an eggnog," Austin says, gesturing towards the bench where two red Solo cups rest.

"I don't like eggnog."

"Since when?" Austin asks, which is fair enough. Last holiday season—so only two weeks ago in this timeline—I drank far too many glasses of eggnog at the hospital's Christmas party, to the point where Austin said, with a laugh, "How about you save some for the rest of us?"

Again, I'm amazed I didn't see it before now. How Austin could be casually unkind, but in a way that made it hard to recognize in the moment. "Since . . . it doesn't matter. I don't want eggnog."

"Fine—we can get you something else." Austin lets out an irritable sigh. "But maybe take off the skates first? I don't want to have to call you 'Clutzabeth' instead of Elizabeth."

He smirks at his own joke, and then he offers his hand to help me off the ice.

"Actually, I prefer Libby now." I ignore his outstretched hand and, inch by inch, feet turned out penguin-style, make my own way off the rink.

36

December 22

It's early the next morning, the day of the tree-lighting ceremony. I'm lying on the floor of my bedroom, on an old yoga mat with a decades-old afghan my nana knitted covering most of me, except for my socked feet. Austin snores lightly, still asleep in my bed, snuggled under the much-warmer quilt. I've swapped my pillow for a sweater under my head, because I hate the slippery feel of a silk pillowcase, and Austin brought one for each of us. Insisting we put them over the cotton pillowcases I prefer, because: *wrinkles*.

We didn't stay long at the ice-skating event. Shortly after the kerfuffle with my skates, and Liam, I told Austin I wasn't feeling well—blaming it on the eggnog I ended up drinking. At least it was heavily spiked, I reasoned, longing to anesthetize myself after the jarring, awful moment on the rink.

Then once we got back to my parents' place it took me hours to fall asleep, the tree farm and ice rink events running on a continuous, torturous loop in my brain. *Liam and me, about to kiss … Austin in my parents' living room, joking with Mom and Millicent … Falling on the ice … Liam's face when I introduced him to Austin …* Repeat. I'm shaky with exhaustion after only a couple hours of restless sleep.

I'm also highly disappointed to hear Austin's snoring, because I had half hoped when I opened my eyes this morning, everything would be reset. I would have returned to the present—Austin would not be in my bed, last night would never have happened, and Liam would be the gorgeous, sweet guy I only just met and would like to get to know better.

No such luck. I'm still in Christmas past, and last night wasn't the bad dream I longed for it to be. I sit up, wincing with the aches and pains in my back, neck, and hips. Probably from my ice-rink tumble, made worse by sleeping on the floor on a thin yoga mat. But Austin was spread-eagled on my small bed, and there simply wasn't enough room for the both of us.

Austin and I are supposed to be hitting the road by nine, in our respective cars, which would get us back to Toronto midafternoon. We're cutting it close; our flight to L.A. leaves later this evening. The thing is, I can't get on that flight. It's past time to tell Austin the truth—that this isn't going to work out between us. He may not be the guy for me, but he deserves my honesty. However, I can't do it without a cup of coffee, so being as quiet as I can, I slip on my robe and tiptoe out of the room. I'm surprised to find Mom and Dad already up, still in matching Christmas pjs with half-empty mugs of coffee.

"Morning, Libby," Mom says. "How did you sleep?" She's reading, the book open on her lap, leg propped up on the Santa Claus pillow and crutches resting beside her.

I kiss her cheek, and say, "Fine." My subdued tone tells a different story, but I leave it at that. "How's the ankle today?"

"Fine," Mom replies, in a similar tone.

"Coffee's hot," Dad says, eyes on his newspaper crossword puzzle. The clinic is closed until after Boxing Day, and I'm glad he's getting a much-needed rest. Though if there's an emergency, or someone requires medical care, he's only a phone call away. There's no such thing as a day off in small-town medicine.

I pour myself a mug of the steaming, fragrant coffee—adding a generous pour of creamer until it's the right shade of beige—then sit on the chair opposite my dad, tucking my legs up underneath me.

"I'm going to stay." I sip my coffee and watch my parents' reaction over the rim of my mug.

"Stay where?" Dad asks, followed by, "What's an eleven-letter word for a 'flourless chocolate cake' typically served at Christmastime?"

"Bûche de Noël," I reply after a beat. Dad's impressed, whistles softly. "Nicely done, Libby."

"Anyway, as I was saying . . . I'm going to stay here. In Harmony Hills. At least until you're back on your feet, Mom. I'm licensed in family medicine, so that's not an issue—I can step right in with your patients."

"But what about the hospital? Your trip with Austin?" Mom asks. I have their full attention now. The book has been closed, the crossword set down on the coffee table, pencil resting on top. "What's going on, Libby?"

I sigh, take a fortifying sip of my coffee before launching into the whole sordid tale, minus the time-travel bit. I've learned that sharing that piece of the story doesn't lead to anything except threats of hospital visits and time spent in CT scanners.

However, I do share my dream of one day joining Doctors Without Borders, and how I've realized Austin and I want different things for our futures. I tell them how much I've loved being home this past week, and how much I've missed everyone, and Harmony Hills. I explain that I have a plan, and I hope they'll support me because I'm going to do it anyway.

Mom chuckles at that. "As expected," she says.

My parents listen until I'm finished. Then they exchange a look, before Dad says, "Having you here would be a huge help, especially with your mom's ankle. But we don't want to get in the way of your plans. And definitely not the career you've worked so hard for."

"I have so much vacation time banked. It will be fine." I think about how, a year from now, my career will be a question mark. At least my career as an attending emergency room physician in a major Toronto hospital. Truthfully, I'm not sure I'll go back to the city. Only time will tell, and I'm growing more comfortable with the uncertainty.

"What about L.A.?" Mom's eyes shift towards the stairs, and I know she means more than just the plane ride and vacation.

Sighing, I unfurl my legs and hold up my coffee mug. "I'm going to need another one of these before I deal with L.A."

"What the hell happened this week?" Austin asks, his voice too loud for the space. He's angry, pacing my small bedroom, back and forth in front of the closed door. I sit on the bed, watching him.

"Will you stop doing that?" I ask. "Please just sit here with me."

But he ignores the request, continues his pacing. "This isn't you, Elizabeth. This isn't you."

I understand why he believes this. For the entirety of our relationship, I've happily let him take the lead. I've acquiesced on things like what takeout we order, whose condo we sleep at, which shows we watch, because I told myself I didn't really care, and Austin is someone with more . . . *preferences*.

Up until the which-way-does-the-toilet-paper-go-on-the-toilet-paper-holder thing, I'm not sure I made it clear that I, too, had preferences. Which is on me, and while it's easy to paint Austin as the bad guy here, it's not fair, or accurate. It takes two to make or break a relationship.

"Austin, I understand that this probably doesn't make sense to you right now. I haven't been happy, for a while . . ." Though in truth I've actually been quite happy recently, thanks to Liam, and Harmony Hills.

"I don't think we bring out the best in each other," I add, my tone softening. "Do you, honestly?"

He stops pacing then and stares at me. His blue eyes are blazing, his cheeks reddened from his pent-up frustration. He runs a hand through his blond hair, but it's short so the strands stay put, and lets out a long sigh.

"I do. Or I did." He seems about to say something more, but then closes his mouth in a tight line. "But I'm not going to talk you into something you don't want. Even if I think you're making the biggest mistake of your life."

"I'm sorry," I reply. I know this is far from the biggest mistake of my life, but there's no reason to say that now. Austin nods, then pivots, bending to grab his leather overnight bag. He sets it on the bed and packs the couple of shirts and toiletries he's set on my desk, shoving them in with more force than is necessary.

"Austin." He pauses when I say his name, before turning to look at me. It's then I see he's not angry—he's hurt. The confident smile, the effortless wink . . . replaced by a heaviness that weighs down his eyes, the corners of his mouth. Like he's just had a surgery go wrong, or lost something that mattered greatly to him.

"You're an amazing guy," I say, my voice steady but kind. He drops his eyes, fidgets with the bottle of cologne in his hand. "Really. You're driven, talented, and passionate about the things you love. I'm sorry things can't be different with us."

He exhales, his features softening, though there's still tension in his jaw. Then he zips up the bag and opens the bedroom door. "I'm going to head out."

"Drive safely," I say. "It snowed last night. The roads might be slick."

Austin stands in the doorway, opening and then closing his mouth, leaving whatever he wants to tell me unsaid. Finally, he says, "Merry Christmas, Elizabeth."

"Merry Christmas, Austin," I whisper, but he's already gone.

After he leaves, I sit in the silence of my bedroom, the faint scent of his cologne lingering in the air. I pull the afghan around me, eyes drawn to the frosted window. The world outside is quiet, the snow blanketing everything like a layer of soft, fluffy cotton.

For years, I believed happiness was something I had to chase— measured by career milestones, strategic plans, the right relationships. But sitting here, in my childhood home with memories rooted in every corner, I finally see it: happiness isn't about what's next, it's about cherishing the life unfolding right in front of me. This time swap, as bizarre and disorienting as it has been, has given me the greatest gift you won't find under the tree: the realization that what I was searching for wasn't missing—it was here all along, waiting to be unwrapped.

37

"Have you seen Liam?" I ask Beckett. We're standing towards the back of the crowd gathered for the tree-lighting ceremony. The sky is black, dotted with stars, and there's the smell of snow in the air. There's already plenty of it on the ground, and the weather forecast suggests we're getting another dump this evening—maybe not in time for the tree lighting, but certainly ensuring a white Christmas.

Amelia and I have just finished hanging candy canes with the rest of the holiday squad volunteers, tagged with the notes we attached the evening before. After the ceremony, everyone's invited up to pick a candy cane off the tree, as a fun and sweet keepsake from the event. The wish notes say things like "You're on the 'nice' list!" and "Unwrap your best year yet!" for the adults, and have holiday-themed jokes like "What kind of photos do elves take? Elfies!" for the younger set.

"I haven't." Beckett cranes her head, looking around as people mill about, waiting for the ceremony to begin. "He was walking Mary. I've been looking for him, too, but he said he . . . wasn't sure he was going to come."

Beckett gives me a sad smile, and I'm equal parts mortified,

embarrassed, and despondent. I want to ask if it has anything
to do with me, or with the Sip and Glide fiasco, but I also don't
want to appear self-centred or presumptuous. *Maybe Liam, whose
self-professed favourite holiday is Christmas, has other plans? Like
walking a potbellied pig instead of showing up at what is arguably
the biggest event of the season?*

Right, Libby. You don't live in Harmony Hills and "make other
plans" on the tree-lighting night. No chance.

"I'm sure he'll be here," Amelia says, reaching for my hand and
giving it a squeeze. This is her second date with Beckett, and it
suddenly occurs to me that exactly a year from now we'll be gathering for the tree lighting again, but this time there will also be a
wedding. Beckett and Amelia's.

Now that I've broken up with Austin, nearly a year earlier than
before, I wonder what this means for the following Christmas.
Where I'll be living, what I'll be doing . . . and who (if anyone) I'll
be doing it all with.

Amelia told me she explained things to Beckett, about how
Austin showed up unannounced and uninvited, and most importantly, that I ended things for good this morning. I was desperate
to ask if Beckett had spoken to Liam about it but couldn't find a
way to bring it up without looking, well, desperate.

I tried calling Liam shortly after Austin left, hoping to better
explain things, but he didn't pick up, and so I left a message. And
two texts. Then I called Helena and unloaded all my misery onto
her, and she (thankfully) talked me out of leaving a second message, and a third text.

"He'll be in touch if he wants to, Elizabeth. I know this isn't
your strong suit, but you're going to have to be patient."

A series of Christmas bells pierce the air, indicating it's almost
time for the tree lighting to begin. We move closer to the large

evergreen, which is brimming with decorations but not yet illuminated. Just then Beckett says, "Oh, there he is." To Amelia she adds, "I'll be right back—save me a spot, okay?"

My head whips around, searching for Liam's tall figure, his wavy dark hair, those green eyes I am easily lost in . . .

"Oh . . . my . . . um, Libby?" Amelia says, but I'm still looking around for Liam, having now lost Beckett in the crowd with no clue which direction she was headed. "*Elizabeth Mae Munro, this is not a drill.*"

There's an urgent tug on my coat sleeve as she says my full name, which immediately makes me look her way.

"What? What is it?" I'm only half paying attention, because I don't want to miss a chance to talk to Liam. She doesn't say anything, just points. It's then I see why she sounded so urgent.

Austin. At the entrance to the town square, walking towards us with a big smile and a purposeful stride.

"What the heck is he doing here?" Amelia whispers. "Shouldn't he be on a plane right now?"

But there isn't time to formulate an answer, even if I had one, because a moment later Austin stands in front of us.

"Hey, Amelia," he says, giving her the Austin smile that could likely charm even the Grinch. It doesn't have any effect on my little sister, however, and she just stares at him and gives a bland half smile. "Anyway, I'm glad you're here. What about your parents? Where are they?"

He glances around, before saying, "Wow, you weren't kidding about how seriously this town takes Christmas, Elizabeth."

But in his voice I don't detect awe or a sense he's impressed—it comes out more like he finds the entire scene, and therefore my one-of-a-kind hometown, trite.

"What are you doing here, Austin?" I finally manage to sputter.

He turns his attention back my way, and there's a glimmer of nervousness in his expression. His blue eyes won't stay on mine, and he's wringing his hands. Very odd for Dr. Austin Whitmore, aka Mr. Confidence. "I was halfway home, and all of a sudden it hit me. What you need from me, to make this all okay."

He reaches for my hands right as the tree-lighting countdown begins.

"Twelve! Eleven! Ten! . . ."

"Elizabeth, babe, in you I think I've found my match," Austin starts.

"What?" I'm confused, though part of my brain understands what's happening before the rest catches up. I'm distracted by the tree-lighting countdown, by Amelia still standing right beside me, by the tugs she is once again making on my coat sleeve.

"Austin, now isn't really a good time—" I start, raising my voice to be heard over the choir of the countdown.

"Six! Five! . . ."

"Libby . . . Mon Dieu! Libby, he's—" Amelia's voice is strained, cut off by what Austin says next.

"I love you and can't imagine life with anyone else," Austin says to me, before dropping to one knee. He releases my hand and reaches into the pocket of his navy pea coat.

"No, no, no . . . Austin, stop," I whisper.

He opens the small velvet box—the one I found in the arm of his sweatshirt but then tucked into my duffel bag (When did he get it? How did he find it?)—and plucks out the diamond ring inside, extending it towards me. "Will you marry me?"

"Two . . . One!" The crowd finishes the countdown with a cheer, and in a flash the tree is illuminated—hundreds of lights twinkling against the night sky. There are so many voices around us, the sounds of celebration deafening, and I can't catch my breath.

I'm numb, standing there gawking at Austin with my mouth hanging open. Unable to reconcile that my ex-boyfriend has just proposed to me at the tree-lighting ceremony, only hours after we broke up and he left town. A strangled gasping sound leaves me, as I can't believe what's happening. Unfortunately, Austin deciphers that sound as my answer, and shouts, "She said yes!"

Then he slides the ring on my finger before I can correct him. Jumping to his feet, he hugs me tightly. "I'm so happy, Elizabeth," he says, his voice muffled by the toque I'm wearing.

"I didn't . . . No, it's . . ." I wriggle out of his embrace and stare at my finger, where the impressive diamond ring rests. For one moment I imagine what it would have been like to have received this ring and a proposal from Austin in the *other* timeline. It's unsettling to know I likely would have said yes if this had all gone down differently. But now I understand what I truly want.

It isn't *this*.

It isn't the life I had—could have, maybe, if I say yes right now—with Austin in Toronto, or in L.A. Rather, it's a life in my quaint hometown of Harmony Hills, and if Liam could be a part of it, even better.

"Liam," I say, my voice catching. He's standing slightly behind Amelia, whose hand covers her mouth in shock, as she stares at my ring, then at my face, then over at Liam.

Liam glances first at Austin, who is being congratulated by a few people standing near us, before his eyes shift to mine. I take a step towards him, tentatively at first. But then I'm impatient to get to him, so I take a couple more steps in quick succession. I need to tell him none of this matters and I most certainly am *not* engaged to Austin, regardless of how this looks.

"Liam, please, hear me out. This is not what it—"

However, I don't see Mary's leash, which has stretched taut

between where Liam stands and where she's snuffling around, looking for a tasty morsel of something dropped in the snow—probably a candy cane.

I don't get another word out, because a second later I'm tripping over the leash in a quite dramatic fashion. "Ass over tea kettle—good job!" as my granddad used to say whenever Amelia or I would fall down, which always made us laugh, despite scraped knees and tears.

It happens so fast, and a second later, the lights go out in a flash.

Something's pushing against my side. It's incessant and gets more so by the second.

"What's going on?" I say, blinking my eyes. They feel heavy, like I've been asleep for hours. I'm trying to figure out where I am. It's dark, obviously nighttime, the only light a soft glow coming off the massive evergreen to my right. My face is chilled and damp, and I realize it's snowing when I feel the icy pinpricks from snowflakes landing on my cheeks, the tip of my nose, my lips.

My mind takes a moment to catch up, but then, in a rush, I remember everything. The tree lighting. Austin . . . proposing! Me trying to get to Liam to explain, then tripping over—"Mary, sit. Sit!" That voice I know. Liam, sounding stern but also slightly panicked.

"Liam?" My throat is dry, and I wonder how long I've been lying on the ground.

"Libby? Honey?" Dad says, crouched beside me. I look his way and see he's wearing a suit under his long wool coat. *Why is he wearing a suit?* And next to him is Mom, but she's on her knees, in a burgundy velvet dress with a high neck and a crystal-encrusted wreath pin to the side.

"Your ankle! You shouldn't be on the ground. Wait, did you fall? Are you okay?" I try to sit up, because I'm worried about my mom, but there are a half-dozen hands holding me in place. A cacophony of "Shhhh, Libby, lie still. Stay down."

Then I see Amelia—*Why is Amelia crying?* She's in a long white dress and looks panicked through her tears. Liam stands beside her, those gorgeous green eyes filled with concern. He looks different, too, though it's subtle, and I can't quite put my finger on it.

"Where's Austin?" I ask, for I don't see him anywhere. I lift my hand to my face, but I'm wearing gloves so can't see the engagement ring my ex-boyfriend just put on my finger. I feel a rush of panic and despair.

"I can't believe I'm engaged without agreeing to be engaged," I mutter, before groaning and closing my eyes again. *Another day, another mess, Libby.*

Now my parents are speaking to each other in hushed but urgent tones. I open my eyes and see Amelia wringing her hands. She glances over at Liam with poorly concealed panic. I watch his handsome face drain of colour, and I remember I haven't yet had the chance to tell him none of this with Austin is real. I desperately want to be alone with him, to explain everything, but my parents won't stop fussing over me.

"It's okay, honey," Dad says. "Don't worry about any of that. Just lie still so Mom can check your head. Any pain?"

"No, no, I'm okay." Mom's hands expertly feel around my head, looking for signs of trauma.

"Want me to call an ambulance?" Beckett asks, her arm now around Amelia's shoulders. Everyone looks freaked out, and it's starting to freak me out.

"I don't need an ambulance. You guys, it's okay, I think I just—Hey, Mary, what are you doing?"

Mary's back to snuffling at my coat pocket, her snout pressing hard into me. I nudge her snout away, then dip my hand into my pocket and pull out a candy cane. I see the tag and am instantly confused. It's not one that Amelia and I tied onto the candy canes the night before, with the jokes and the Christmastime well-wishes.

I stare at the tag, blinking to make sure I'm seeing what I think I'm seeing.

'Tis the Season to Be Married!

Suddenly, I know exactly where I am. Then I look at my sister, and another piece of the puzzle falls into place. Amelia's white dress is her *wedding* dress—I recognize it now. Tonight is the tree-lighting event, as well as the night Amelia and Beckett got married.

It's the same night Mary Piggins knocked me over for the first, though far from the last, time.

This is the night I made a wish on the magical snowfall and next opened my eyes to find myself in Christmas past, the year before.

It's *this* Christmas, again.

I'm back.

38

December 22, Present Day

I'm back, which means the whole fiasco with Austin and the tree-lighting proposal never happened. This Christmas, I'm single, and therefore there's no need to explain anything to Liam—he's never met Austin, and I'm not engaged to be married to my ex-boyfriend. We've been broken up for months in this timeline.

But . . . *wait . . . wait a gosh-darn minute . . .*

I rip my glove off, see the ring. Sparkling its fractals in the twinkling evergreen lights. Any relief I felt a moment earlier melts away, like a snowman in the late-winter sunshine.

How is this happening? I'm sure it's Christmas present, right? Amelia's in her wedding dress, about to marry Beckett; Mom's ankle is clearly fine. I glance down at my legs, expecting to see my beloved suede boots. Instead, I'm wearing practical winter boots with a rim of fluffy faux fur around the top. But these aren't Mom's Sorel boots.

What's going on?

"I need to get this off . . ." I sit up quickly, ignoring the stars that cloud my vision. Then I twist at the ring. It's snug, and my fingers are cold and slow to work, which makes the task much harder than it should be.

"Why can't I get this off?" I mutter, frustration seeping into my words.

"Libby, stop." Liam's crouched beside me. He gives Mary's leash to Beckett and sets his warm hands on mine. It feels wonderful, and I let out a small, contented sigh. "What are you doing?"

His voice is low, his tone underpinned with worry. His brow furrows as he watches me closely. Those emerald eyes . . . I almost forget where I am, and what's happened.

"Liam, I'm not sure exactly what's going on, but I need you to know it's over."

"What's over, hon?"

Something in me snaps to attention. *Hon?* But I keep going, wanting to get this explanation out and over with.

"With Austin. It's over. And I don't understand why I'm still wearing this . . ." I pause, for I don't know how to explain the ring and how a year has passed in the blink of an eye.

"I think you hit your head, Libby." Liam glances over at my parents, then back to me. "I'm going to drive you to the hospital, okay? Kirby's there, and Claire said he'll meet us in the ER."

"Claire?" I look at the small crowd around me, searching for my friend. I find her, and she gives me a little wave—then I see she's holding Lucy's hand, the toddler (no longer a baby) bundled up in an adorably puffy snowsuit. Further confirmation I'm back in the present.

"But I don't need the hospital. Like I said, I'm fine. I don't think I hit my head."

I take my hand out of Liam's. "Just let me get this off, and we can talk, okay?" *Twist, twist, twist* . . . I feel some release. Good. "I don't know where this came from, honestly, but it's almost off."

"Libby . . . *I gave you that ring*." Liam sets a hand to my face, forcing me to look into his eyes.

Waves of shock move through me as I stare at him. What does he mean, "I gave you that ring"?

But before I get the question out, Liam's lips are on mine, and he's kissing me. My eyes close, and I breathe him in. Scents of cloves, cedar, freshly baked bread . . . and I'm kissing him back, fiercely, because I've been waiting to do this almost since I first laid eyes on him.

I've imagined what it might be like to kiss Liam, and I'm delighted to learn the reality is even better than the fantasy. My heart races, my skin tingles, the rush of blood to my head makes me woozy—all the while his lips stay on mine—and then . . .

I am struck by an unshakable truth: I may have returned to the present, but the past year of my life has been irrevocably altered. Reshaped by the choices I made . . . in the past. Like an explosion of fireworks, the memories surge, flooding my mind in a dazzling cascade.

39

One particular memory, from four days earlier, rises to the top. It's late morning, and we're putting the final touches on the Christmas tree. The branches are draped in twinkle lights but are also somewhat sparse, as I haven't been able to find the packed box of ornaments. It's been only a week since I moved in, and we're still living amongst boxes. With the holiday season upon us, there's little time between the practice and the farm for unpacking.

I never ended up moving back to Toronto. Only a quick trip to the city in the middle of January to pack up my apartment. Then I drove back to Harmony Hills, with everything I owned in the rented U-Haul. I stayed with Amelia, in her sweet, two-bedroom cottage with gingerbread trim and a wraparound porch that quickly became my happy place. A few months later Amelia and Beckett decided to move in together, and I took over the lease on Amelia's cottage. It was bittersweet when I gave notice two months ago to Rosalie Everhart, the cottage's landlord, but I was ready and eager to take the next step with Liam.

"I made up the bed for Helly, and just need to finish Adelaide's," Liam says, coming into the kitchen. "What time do you think they're pulling in?"

"Not sure exactly, probably early afternoon?" Helena and Adelaide—who is Helly's mini me, both in terms of looks and personality—are staying with us for a couple of days before Christmas.

"Poor child, turning out exactly like her mother," Helly said, when we chatted on Adelaide's third birthday a couple of weeks ago.

"Poor you!" I replied, laughing, for I can only imagine what it's like to parent a child who knows exactly what your buttons are and how to push them.

"Okay, that's good," Liam says now, standing in the middle of the kitchen with his hands on his hips. He's lost in thought, glancing around and muttering to himself.

"What's up?" I ask, pouring coffees for us in the mugs we made at a Valentine's Day pottery class we took with Beckett and Amelia. They are mugs that only their creators could love, with mismatched handles, uneven rims, and lopsided hearts we painted on them. But I don't care—it's my favourite mug, and I use it every morning.

"Nothing's up. Just trying to remember where I put the screwdriver. I wanted to make sure the screws on Dell's toddler bed are super tight."

I reach behind him, tugging the tool out of his back pocket. "You mean this screwdriver?"

He sets a hand to his forehead and laughs. "Obviously, I need this," he says, taking the mug from me and then kissing me. "Thanks, Libs."

We sit at the kitchen table, the tree sparkling in the corner. "If only I could find that box of ornaments," I say, sighing. Sipping my coffee, with the peppermint-mocha creamer that Liam and I both like—his sweet tooth rivals mine, it turns out. "Maybe I left it at Amelia's? I'll double-check after I'm done at the clinic. Do you need a hand with the bread?"

When Liam doesn't answer, I duck so I'm directly in front of him. "Hey, Mr. Young. You okay?"

He shakes his head, smiles wide—damn, those dimples still get me. "Sorry, distracted. You know how chaotic chili night is for Pops and me," he replies.

"Put me to work, then." I take a last sip of my coffee before setting the mug into the sink. "I'll come over after my last patient."

I set my hands on either side of his face and kiss him before saying, "I don't know what I did to deserve you, Liam Young, but you're the best thing since sliced bread."

He smirks. "That's funny, because I was just thinking the same thing—except you're the whole loaf, Libs."

I groan, and he pulls me into a hug. "Come on, that was cute," he says, grinning. I kiss each of his dimples.

"Fine, it was cute," I murmur, with a lopsided smile.

Holding me tighter, he asks, "Are you sure you have to go?"

I glance at my phone, then press even closer to him, wrapping my arms around his neck. "I can probably spare a few more minutes. What did you have in mind?"

His hands rest on my waist, and his touch is both grounding and electric. "Was thinking about starting a new holiday tradition. Just for us."

I tilt my head. "What kind of tradition?"

He leans back slightly, but keeps his eyes on mine. "We could write down our favourite memory of the year together on note cards, and then tuck them into the tree. We can open them Christmas morning."

"I love it," I say, and I do. "Okay, Mr. Sentimental. Let's do it. Starting this year?"

"Starting this year." He leans in, brushing a soft kiss across my lips. "Merry early Christmas, Libs."

"Merry Christmas, Liam," I murmur, resting my forehead against his, the tree glowing behind us.

The clock ticks up on the stage, and the energy in the room, along with the volume, cranks up a notch. The young kids—including Adelaide, Jonah, and Jasmine—are making ornaments on the stage, supervised by Harmony Hills' kindergarten teacher, who was a new hire this fall and is already well loved by the students. The chili dinner is finished (the golden kidney bean trophy going to the Livery-Quinn family again, with Chase declaring a goal for a "three-peat" next season), and we've moved on to the other main event: gingerbread house decorating.

"Everyone dialed in? We've got this, you guys," I say to Liam, Beckett, and Amelia as soon as the bell rings. In front of us is our gingerbread house, and we're creating a replica of the rescue barn at Clover Hill Farm. Beckett is sculpting a decent goat out of marzipan, while Amelia and I carefully apply sections of sour cherry ribbon to the roof to look like shingles. Liam's focused on the icing patterns, currently creating the barn-door effect. But he seems off—his hands shaking as he applies, and then reapplies, a strip of the icing.

"You okay?" I ask him, raising a brow at the latest wiggly line. Amelia glances up from placing the candy shingles, tucking a strand of hair behind her ear as she and Beckett exchange a smile. I know I'm missing something, because I recognize their tells when they're hiding something—Amelia with the hair-tucking, and Beckett sporting a demure smile that isn't her usual wide, toothy grin.

When they came over to the cottage the week before I moved out, Amelia tucking and untucking her hair, Beckett smiling softly, neither of them getting to the point for the visit, I knew it was about the pregnancy. I had been anticipating it, invoking hard-fought patience to allow it to play out naturally. Amelia finally spilled the beans, and I burst into happy, genuine tears at the news, even though it wasn't a surprise.

"What? What's going on?" I ask now, looking from Amelia, to Beckett, and finally back to Liam.

"Could you hand me a couple of those gumdrops?" Liam asks, and his voice cracks. His eyes don't leave the gingerbread house, his hands squeezing out the icing in yet another not-straight line.

My eyes are on Liam, as I reach into the dish of gumdrops.

Then, my fingers touch the sugar-coated, jelly candy, and as I start to take one out, they connect with something solid. Something that is not a gumdrop.

"What the . . . ?" Hand still in the candy dish, I look to see something silver under the white and green gumdrops. "What is that?"

My heart is in my throat, and my eyes snap to Liam's.

He's grinning, the icing bag discarded on the table. Amelia's crying, though smiling, and Beckett—also smiling—has her hands so tightly clasped together her knuckles are whitening.

Next I see my parents, standing up from the table where they're competing with Miss Betty and Liam's granddad, who have been dating for about five months now. Helena, who arrived in town only a few hours earlier, Claire, Kirby, and Chase are also standing, at the decorating table next to ours. As expected, Helena and Claire hit it off within minutes of meeting each other, and are already vowing to do a weekend trip somewhere with a spa ("and no children") for the three of us in the new year. My two best friends—past and present—have their arms wrapped around one another, trying to contain their obvious excitement at what's happening.

Liam, now beside me, turns my chair to face him. My fingers are out of the gumdrop bowl, numb with anticipation. The room has gone silent, the sense that everyone is holding their collective breath. I hear the clock ticking, have the absurd thought that we will obviously not be winning the gingerbread house decorating this year. It feels like I'm in a dream, everything moving slowly.

Liam reaches into the candy dish, pulling something out. In his fingers is a sparkling ring. He drops to one knee.

"Libby, this has been the best year of my life," he starts.

"Yes! Liam, oh my goodness. Yes! My answer is yes!" I bend over and grab his face the way I did this morning and kiss him. The excitement and adrenaline thrums through me, and my entire body shakes.

Everyone starts clapping, and Liam, laughing, says, "You didn't even let me ask the question!"

"Liam Young, you are the most amazing man I have ever met. You're kind, sweet, strong, brilliant, patient, not to mention gorgeous . . ." Again, laughter rings out through the room. "I can't imagine my life without you in it. You're the marshmallow foam to my hot chocolate, and I am forever and ever yours."

"Mind if I have a turn now?" Liam asks softly, with an adorable smirk. I press my lips together and nod my head. *Don't cry, don't cry, don't cry . . .* I don't want to miss a single moment of this.

"Libby Munro, as I was saying . . ." He grins, more laughter around the room. "You are the love of my life. The cheese to my macaroni. The meatloaf to my mashed potatoes. The ornament to my Christmas tree. The icing to my gingerbread house."

I'm laughing through my tears, waiting to be asked the question that will change my life.

"Will you marry me, Libby?"

"Yes, yes, yes! You had me at 'hand me a couple of those gumdrops,'" I say, as Liam slides on the ring—a white gold, diamond-pavé band with a solitaire nestled into a beveled setting. "Yes, Liam. I can't wait to marry you."

He pulls me into a hug, right off my feet, and swings me around while our family and friends clap and cheer.

"I think I just had my favourite memory of the year," I whisper in his ear. "But pretend to be surprised when you open the card on Christmas morning, okay?"

"Deal," he whispers back, and then we kiss, and spin, and kiss some more until I'm dizzy and laughing. "I love you, Libby Munro."

"I love you, too, Liam Young," I say, breathless with the joyful surprise of it all.

40

I remember …

Tripping over Mary Piggins's leash in Christmas past, during the tree lighting. A moment of blackness before coming to, in Liam's arms, on the ground. Then, not long after, giving Austin back his ring and telling him that I was sorry, but I couldn't marry him—it was over, for good this time.

I dropped a gift off to Liam at the farm the next day, as a "Merry Christmas/I'm sorry I screwed up" present. It was a bold move, but I was done doubting myself, and I definitely didn't want to waste any more time. Along with the ceramic ornament—a mug of hot chocolate, with whipped cream and sprinkles on top—I wrote a card, which read: "You're the marshmallow foam to my cocoa. Merry Christmas! Libby xo."

It went over exceptionally well.

Then, it was New Year's Eve and our first official date. We watched fireworks in the main square, shared a first kiss at midnight that felt even more explosive than the fireworks, and I decided—as we rang in the New Year—that I was staying in Harmony Hills, indefinitely.

Next, packing up my Toronto apartment, moving into Amelia's

house, joining my parents at the practice, in which I gladly invested both my time and resources. Patients called me "Dr. Libby," and serving the community I called home again, alongside my mom and dad, fulfilled me in a way I never imagined.

The whole family took a late-summertime trip to Brazil to visit Liam's parents, who were currently stationed there. On most Sundays, I worked alongside Liam and his granddad at the bakery, and I discovered that if I ever left medicine, I might have a career in sourdough baking.

I was hand in hand with Liam at the various Harmony Hills holiday events throughout the year. St. Patrick's Day green beer at Beans & Brews. Cheering Amelia on at the pie-eating contest at the Harvest Festival. Tirelessly making the corn maze and creating a haunted barn at Clover Hill Farm during Halloween. Becoming an assistant tree feller during the Christmas tree harvesting season, helping feed and care for the animals at the rescue, which has grown to include a second barn—newly built. Helping plan Amelia and Beckett's wedding, as maid of honour and man of honour.

Most surprisingly, perhaps, is that Mary Piggins is now *my* pig. If I'm not walking her in town in one of her many sweaters, you'll often find me snuggling her on George's dog bed (who is a good sport and always shares) in front of the fireplace, or sneaking her bits of candy cane when Liam isn't looking.

Oh, and I've stayed true to my New Year's Resolution: no more bacon.

As I sit on the snowy cobblestone in front of the lit-up evergreen, Liam still crouched in front of me, the memories come fast and furious. I remember it all. The last year of my life—our lives—fills my mind like clips from a film, or camera snapshots, weaving the past and present into one. Timelines stitching back together, so that everything makes sense again.

"You gave this to me. On Christmas chili night. At the gingerbread house decorating," I whisper now to Liam, breathless as I stare at the beautiful ring. In the dark I hadn't noticed the differences between Austin's ring and the one Liam slid onto my finger mere days ago.

"You asked me to marry you. With gumdrops . . . and I said yes."

"You said yes." Liam smiles, tears in his eyes. "You're okay."

"I'm better than okay. This has been the best year of my life, Liam."

The snow is coming down heavily now, and then I remember the magical wish.

"Gather 'round, young and old, a wondrous sight, a tale to be told," I begin, my voice loud enough to reach those gathered around us. Liam helps me to my feet. "Come on, everyone—look at the snow! We need to make a wish!"

The group around us joins in, and soon everyone is reciting the poem, in unison.

"With sparkling lights and branches green,
A special wish for a festive scene.
As snowflakes fall on this glorious night,
Close your eyes; close them tight,
If you believe, just wait and see,
What magic comes from the Christmas tree!"

I glance at the evergreen—the boughs adorned with holiday decorations, including the *'Tis the Season to Be Married!* candy canes, and the twinkle lights creating a beautiful, soft glow across the snow sticking to the ground—and then watch as the towns-people of Harmony Hills close their eyes to make their wishes, Liam included. The snowflakes land on his eyelashes, and he smiles softly at whatever wish he's making.

My eyes stay open as I take it all in, for I don't need to make a wish tonight. I'm already living it, and I can't wait to see what magic *this* life has in store for me.

Acknowledgments

Much like the perfect Christmas cookie, this book took just the right mix of ingredients—and I couldn't have baked it without the many elves who sprinkled magic on its pages.

To my better-than-Rudolph-on-a-foggy-night agent, Carolyn Forde, and the entire Transatlantic Literary Agency team—may your stockings be stuffed with sparkling manuscripts.

To editor extraordinaire Brittany Lavery and editorial wizard Muna Hussein, who read more drafts than Santa reads wish lists—may your edits be as speedy and joyful as a perfectly greased toboggan run.

To marketing and promotion superstars Rebecca Snoddon and Natasha Kempnich—may your holidays sparkle like a flawlessly executed campaign.

To the powerhouse team at Simon & Schuster Canada, led by the North Star herself Nicole Winstanley—may your catalogue shine brighter than twinkle lights on Christmas Eve.

To Amy E. Reichert, Ashley Audrain, Carley Fortune, Colleen Oakley, Hannah Mary McKinnon, Jennifer Robson, Lisa Steinke, Mary Kubica, Nicole Blades, Roselle Lim, and Taylor Jenkins Reid—

thank you for being just a text or phone call away. May your deadlines melt like a snowman in a heat wave.

To my parents, the original makers of holiday magic; to Adam, my "home for the holidays" (every day of the year); and to Addie, the whole reason traditions matter—may your hot chocolate come with marshmallows, your shortbread be made with real butter, and your presents always be "batteries-included."

Finally, to you—the readers. Thank you for putting this book in your carts, and for turning the pages. May your reads never end on a cliff-hanger (unless that's your thing), and your season be as satisfying as the perfect holiday romance epilogue.